DISSONANCE

Volume Up: Rising

AARON RYAN

The Resistance Rises

Published in 2024, Edition 1.

Paperback ISBN # 9798990878990. Hardcover ISBN # 9798990878983. eBook ISBN # 9798990878976.

Cover creature art by Rodrigo Vivedes (https://www.artstation.com/rocoviart)

Edited by Denouement Editing & CM LLC. Published independently.

This is a work of fiction. Any similarities to persons living or dead, or actual events is purely coincidental.

For Sweeps, Bren & AJ:
my true loves.

You've helped me to survive.

I CHAPTERS

I NOTE ON AI

We live in an age of AI. Every day, more and more services spring up promising revolutionary and innovative results using artificial intelligence. The authoring industry is not immune to this.

I want every one of my readers to know that not once did I employ, nor will I *ever* employ, the use of AI to sculpt any part of any of my stories. Those who know me know that I am staunchly and adamantly opposed to such cheats.

I'm very proud to be a verified human. The ability to create is a gift that I was endowed by my Creator, and I will never forfeit that nor set it aside to propagate something synthetic and imitative.

Everything you've read by me in this saga, and in my other works, is 100% entirely created by me, the genuine article. I'm a verified human, and always will be.

To my fellow authors, I urge you to preserve the sacred gift of human creation and never stoop to such lows. Always cherish this gift you've been given. If you encounter writer's block, take a break. Don't cop out. Don't take the road more traveled by. Don't cheat. Toe the line for all of us, and keep creation – *true* unadulterated creation – alive.

Long live humanity.

Sincerely,

Aaron Ryan,
Verified Human

I PREFACE

Recap from Volume Zero:

The year is 2026. Andrew Shipley is just like the rest of humanity, going about his business and providing for his family as a firefighter. He and his wife Melissa attend Mount Pleasant Baptist Church in Blue Spring, Kentucky, with their young children Cameron, Adelynn, aka 'Sissy,' and Wyatt, aka 'Rutty.'

In early June 2026, cellular service begins to be disrupted. Lightning storms afflict the earth. Satellite communications are affected, and all oceanic satellites cease transmission. Shortly thereafter, their Jack Russell Terrier, Jack, exhibits strange behavior. His ears bleed, and he howls in pain. He, along with all the other canines and animals with sensitive hearing, are suddenly afflicted with high frequencies. Jack recovers, but the ominous development frightens the family.

The family enjoys a church picnic where they meet fellow parishioners, eat BBQ, and play frisbee, etc.. While there, Melissa meets Anya Mayfield, her husband, Justus, and their 2-year-old son, Liam.

The family then heads to Seattle to visit Andrew's mother and father. His father is in failing health with dementia. The visit is good and restorative, but Andrew's dad, Jim, has good and bad days. Following their return, the older kids head off to a weeklong camp.

On June 6th, 2026, while Andrew and family join best friend Mick and family on the lake, they see them. The aliens descend down from the sky, silently on June 6th 2026, hovering at a geostationary orbit over our planet, remaining there, virtually motionless, for three months. There are hundreds, and then thousands, and then hundreds of thousands of them, still coming down, falling ominously into position across the entire globe. No country is immune. No one knows what they want, nor why they are here. Some think they are angelic messengers. People fly drones up to them to investigate. They don't move or react. In the heat of summer, they sweat. On the backs of the necks of each hovering alien seems to be implanted some kind of small green gemlike device, like a chemotherapy port.

The stock market dives. Individuals take matters into their own hands and a few shoot at the aliens. When the aliens are struck, they rise back up in the sky, and three more take their place. Humanity realizes such action is futile. In an effort to quell the panic, the President holds a State of the Union address where he assures the American people that we have the best scientists and technologists developing a formidable defense, and construction companies have begun developing underground bunkers should the aliens' intentions prove hostile. These bunkers are known as 'Blockades.' They will be finished within a few months' time all over the globe, using underground automated drills and excavation teams. Blockades will be equipped with sanitary needs, food, hydroponics, heat, and walled in by massively tall gun towers: the only known defense against the aliens. In a thin attempt at humor, the President assures the American people that life will go on, despite our living like moles.

Three months later, on September 3rd 2026, as Andrew and his older children Cameron and Sissy participate in a fun church-sponsored marathon, the aliens suddenly activate and begin hunting down all of mankind. In the terror and pandemonium, Andrew witnesses the aliens' horrifying ability to paralyze humans where they stand, consuming them at their leisure. Andrew and his kids escape and take refuge in a small office on a nearby property. Meanwhile, Mick's entire family is killed, leaving him to attempt a desperate escape into that same small office. Despite his best friend's anguished pleading, Andrew refuses to let him in, terrified for his own children's safety, and hears Mick's final moments through the door. He texts a frantic message to Melissa to lock herself in the attic with their youngest, Rutty. He assures her that he'll come home with the older kids and fills her in on what happened during the race. Melissa shares what she's seen on the news.

After sunset, the aliens move on. A brave citizen drives through the macabre scene and searches for survivors after the aliens have moved on to kill others. The man's name is Hudson, and he is in a hybrid vehicle, and the silence provides them the ability to return home. Once home, they reunite with Melissa and Rutty. Aliens invade their home and attempt to access the attic ladder but become distracted by other noises and leave. Mercifully, Jack – who can barely hear anymore – doesn't bark, and the kids sleep through the ordeal.

They escape with the help of Hudson, in their own hybrid vehicle and his. Hudson and his wife, Andrea, equip them with armament and weapons, and they all head for a Blockade they hear has been constructed in Clarksville TN, south of them. Hudson and Andrea are behind the Shipley family and distract aliens who have set upon them, dying in the process. The Shipley family flees to the Blockade and begins their long, slow life of hiding.

By December 2026, eighty-five percent of humanity is dead. No one knows what to do, and no one can fight back. Soon, all of humanity learns the Number One Rule as it pertains to aliens: *You just... don't... look.* Mankind ends up calling them 'gorgons' due to their unique ability to, with just one look, paralyze us.

Andrew joins up as a soldier on recon missions for food, ammunition, and straggling survivors. The missions are physically and emotionally grueling with several team member casualties. Andrew blames himself but perseveres. Eventually, he is promoted up to First Lieutenant.

One day in 2034, Cameron and Rutty steal out to hunt a deer, thinking they could bring it back to the Blockade and be regarded as heroes for providing protein. In the process, they are pursued by teacher Christopher Jackson, who is killed by a gorgon while trying to shepherd them back to the Blockade. They are terrified. Andrew and his fellow soldier Ray rescue them, successfully bringing them back to the Blockade.

Melissa's smoking has had long-term effects, and she has developed lung cancer. On July 22nd, 2035, she succumbs to her cancer with Andrew, Cameron and Rutty by her side.

Cameron eventually enlists at age 18, and on October 20th, 2037, he heads out on his first mission. He and the team, along with Andrew Shipley, Captain Stone and two others, are sent on a recon mission for food, supplies, and survivors up to the old zinc plant nearby. While there, they are set upon by gorgons. Andrew throws himself in between a gorgon and Cameron, saving his son's life, and dying in the process.

The story continues in *Dissonance Volume Up: Rising...*

I FIRST PERSONS

It was *such* a pleasure to write four first-person perspectives in this latest installment of the Dissonance saga. I had never written even a *dual* first-person perspective novel before. To attempt to write one from *four* first-person perspectives was a true undertaking, but one that I was excited about.

I rose to the challenge, and I hope you enjoy it.

For clarification, in this last prequel bridging the gap between *Dissonance Volume Zero: Revelation* and *Dissonance Volume I: Reality*, you'll be reading from the perspectives of:

1. First Lieutenant Miguel Monzon, stationed in Nashville with President Graham
2. Pastor Rosie, living in Blockade DN436 in Clarksville TN

3. Sergeant Joseph Bassett, stationed at Blockade
    DN282 in Alpharetta
4. Private Allison Trudy, stationed at Blockade DN282
    in Alpharetta

Each chapter will have the name of each person from whose perspective that chapter is written. I promise there will also be an enjoyable surprise waiting for you in this as well.

Thank you so much for reading my books, and I welcome you to email me at me@authoraaronryan.com with any feedback or questions. I am so immeasurably grateful for all of my readers. Thank you for exploring post-apocalyptic Earth from 2026 to 2042 with me.

Oh! One more thing: if you see the word 'gorgon,' remember to look away! 😊

Sincerely,

Aaron Ryan,
Verified Human

1 | ROSIE

Tuesday, October 20th, 2037, 1137 hours

"Bring them in, bring them in!" I cried.

I paid no heed to the man who, perhaps, regarded my accent as strange. Obviously, he'd never been in church down here and gotten to know me. All things in due time.

They brought in the Lieutenant's body. He was bleeding badly, and his son, eighteen years old, was crying hysterically. He moved past me, and I noticed a strange odor about him…covered in blood – his father's, certainly – but there was something else.

His other son, fourteen, sprinted into the infirmary, eyes wide, and began to convulse with tears when he saw the Lieutenant. The younger brother stopped short, ran into his older brother's arms, and both racked with sadness.

Captain Stone had returned from the latest mission, along with Private Jet Shipley and Private Markus Jentzen. Corporal Ray Ferro had died on the way back, apparently holding them off. That was a sore loss; he was a good man with a great heart.

Ferro's daughter, Sarah, was the nurse here. She feverishly began to attend to the Lieutenant, but there was too much blood. His body was frozen solid, as if rigor mortis had already set in, and he had a bite out of his right clavicle and part of his neck. Ferro halted momentarily at the news of the loss of her father – we all did – but the Captain consoled her and urged her to attend to her duties and do what she could. She was as distraught as the rest of us, probably more so, but, slowly, she gathered herself together, set her jaw firmly, and resolved to try to save the Lieutenant's life.

I had never seen someone absorb such painful news and yet do what was required of them through such unspeakable trauma. Indeed, Sarah was made of stern stuff.

But now, working on the Lieutenant, I could read it on her face as she surveyed the dying man: she was staring at a medical impossibility.

Captain Stone ordered everyone out, and they hooked him up to an IV drip.

"What can I do, Captain?" I asked him.

"I don't know, Rosie, I don't think there's anything we can do. He's lost so much blood," he said regretfully, shaking his head.

Nurse Ferro had finished hooking Shipley up to the IV and ECG. "I've got a heartbeat!" she cried.

Out of the corner of my eye, I saw the boys pull away from each other and gasp, tears still pouring from their eyes. The younger of the two, 'Rutty,' as he was known, had his hands over his mouth. He looked a spitting image of his mother, who had passed away a few years ago from cancer. I knew Rutty well. We had prayed together often over his mother. Over our Blockade. Over the world.

His older brother, Cameron, or 'Jet' as they called him in here, looked more like the Lieutenant. I didn't know him quite as well.

The ECG grew softer and more erratic. *Beep... beep... beep...*

Reflexively, my hands went to my mouth and clasped in prayer. I watched the whole desperate scene, darted from the boys, and then back to their father. My vision swam with tears.

"Shipley," I breathed, looking at the Lieutenant's body. A gorgon had attacked them while they were out on patrol at the old Zinc Plant, or at least that's what I made out from the scattered murmurs and hysterical calls once they had opened the Launch doors and quickly ushered them all back in. I had been in the middle of a service in the Pavilion when I heard the commotion. We scattered and flooded the Launch foyer to receive them.

"Pressure! Put pressure on his wound!" Nurse Ferro cried through tears. The Lieutenant's sons came over and tried to help, but Sarah was having none of it. "Get out of the way!" she yelled. "Captain, elevate his feet with this!" She tossed a crude pillow to the Captain who was at the foot of the stretcher, and he quickly inserted it under the Lieutenant's cold legs. The ECG beeped faintly and irregularly. The strength and timing of the Lieutenant's electrical impulses were low and erratic.

Slower and quieter ECG. *Beep...   beep...*

Ferro applied a sterile dressing to his neck wound with gauze and cloth, but it quickly bled through. His body was only jetting out the tiniest bit of blood. I am no medic, but that told me his systems were slowing down. Shipley's face was spattered with blood, and his eyes were frozen and dilated. The boys' hands were covered with blood through applying pressure to the neck wound. Shipley made a strange gurgling sound. At that, Jet burst into fresh new tears, and Rutty bowed his head.

"Hold on, keep trying!" Ferro called to everyone. She ran and retrieved additional gauze to keep the remaining blood inside him.

Jet's crying slowed, and his jaw tensed into a solid right angle. His eyes glistened with tears as he watched Lieutenant Andrew Shipley, his father, slip away. His hand was on his father's ankle, watching him quietly.

The ECG suddenly slowed even further, and then stopped. I glanced down to the gauze and dressing. The blood had ceased to expand through the dressing. There was no movement. Nurse Ferro looked at him, back to the ECG, back to him, looked around quickly as if to consider her options, then back to the ECG.

Finally, she looked at him and exploded in tears. This was clearly too much for her. She was our only nurse. She never had the training that so many before her in her profession had the benefit of. Yet here she was, expected to save a life when she had just lost the one most precious to her.

Nurse Ferro bowed her head and quieted.

The ECG stopped.

We all stood there in silence, with mouths agape and desperately seeking something to latch onto that might convey even a morsel of hope. I walked over to Ferro and put my arm around her, bowing my head on her shoulder. She did the same, bowing her head on mine. Here she was, forced into service and not allowed to even grieve her own father. I turned and hugged her.

Flatline. Solid tone. The boys looked incredulously at the monitor, expecting the machine to suddenly burst back to life and answer their yearning. My heart went out to them. They had lost their mother a few years prior, and now their father. Here, on the very same bed.

Rutty was crying frantically. His legs buckled. Reflexively, grimly Jet reached out and grabbed him, pulling him to his feet, and then their eyes met. Jet's lips quivered, and then he took his brother into his arms, holding him tightly while they both quaked.

While we *all* quaked.

•   •   •   •   •

"I am here for both of you if you need to talk. Please know that," the Captain encouraged them. Private Shipley and his little brother stood before our leader, dejected and bereft of hope. The Private's expression was devoid of emotion, but his eyes shone. The Captain turned to him. "Jet, you're safe. You're alive. Your father gave his life to save you."

Jet didn't respond. He just stared somberly at Captain Stone, gritting his teeth and standing there, numb.

The Captain took a breath as if to say something else, but then realized the futility of words, and stopped himself. He put his hand on Jet's shoulder to console him. The young Private stood there, stoically, staring at his father.

After Lieutenant Shipley died, Nurse Ferro and everyone cleaned him up, and then attempted to help wrap him head to foot. But the boys waved them off, almost in unison, quietly now. They held up their hands in reverence, and tended to their fallen father, silently cleaning him completely and then sliding the cloths around him to seal him for his forever sleep. We all watched them in silence. There were no words.

Jet then signaled to Rutty to give him a minute, placing the last cloth around the Lieutenant's head, covering it entirely. He leaned down and embraced his father's body. After all, Andrew had apparently given his life for him at the plant. Rutty followed suit, signed the cross over his chest, and then bent down and gave his father's covered forehead a silent kiss goodbye.

When they were done, they both retreated, leaving us to clean up the room and encourage Nurse Ferro.

I eventually followed the Captain out of the infirmary.

"Lieutenant threw himself between Jet and a gorgon," he whispered to me as we walked. "Jet saw the whole thing. Ferro lit it up and then Jet took it down, shooting from behind Andrew, but…" -here he took a deep breath and shook his head, putting his knuckles into his eyes as if to scrub out the memory of it- "the damage…had already been done. The thing got him. He crumpled like a deflated balloon, Rosie. It was awful. Right on top of his son. Then…" he looked at me as we walked, "we just ran. Threw him over Jet's shoulder, we covered him, and we all ran."

I thought of Jet carrying the dying body of his father over his shoulder, bleeding out, slipping away, heaving his bulk all the way back to the Blockade, tailed by the enemy. Awful. Traumatizing. But better to carry him back than to let the enemy consume him later.

Shortly, we entered the Pavilion and found the two brothers sitting on the dais at the far end, side by side. Jet had his arm around Rutty. Rutty had his arms up over his knees, with his face half-buried behind them.

We approached them slowly, somberly.

Jet had blood all over his fatigues, his arms, and the right side of his face. Rutty's hands were covered in crimson from compressing their father's wounds. This blood was all that they had left of Lieutenant Andrew Shipley, and they would soon shower it all away forever.

The Captain pulled up two chairs, and we slid them in place and sat, both of us, opposite the two of them. Neither looked up to meet our eyes. The Captain looked at me and signaled. I took a deep breath.

"Jet, Rutty, I am so sorry for your loss. Is there anything you need from us right now? How can we help you?" I asked them, offering tenderness as I leant toward them.

It was some time before one of them spoke. Rutty looked up at me and heaved a great weight from his chest. "Thanks Pastor Rosie," he sniffed through his tears. "We, uh, we just need time, I think."

I nodded. "Absolutely." I offered him a consoling smile.

Captain Stone spoke up. "Private Shipley, uh, Jet, you're on leave for as long as you need," he said. "We have enough teams, men and supplies to perform our recons. You take your time," he said, and he reached out and placed an empathetic hand on Jet's shoulder. Jet didn't look up at him; he just nodded imperceptibly, and mumbled, "Thanks, Stoney." It was little more than a whisper.

"Of course," Stone answered. "Your father was like a brother to me, guys. You know that. I love him dearly. Whatever you need, you have only to name it. We're here for you both," he finished.

"And I'm here for prayer and counseling, of course," I added. Rutty looked up at me and smiled.

"Thanks Pastor Rosie," he said.

I said nothing in return. Just smiled and winked, which evoked the tiniest hint of sober, grateful joy on Rutty's face. I looked at the Captain, and he nodded.

"There will be a memorial tonight here in the Pavilion at 1900. I'll see to it," he said, rising. Captain Stone looked down at me and motioned me toward the boys, allowing me to spend some time with them. He slowly walked off with a heavy heart. After all, Stone hadn't just lost a high-ranking soldier; he had lost a personal friend.

I sat there, remembering all the conversations I had had with Andrew Shipley. About faith. About pain. About receiving. About his wife Melissa's cancer. I remembered teaching him about willingness to receive. In the end, he received.

In the end, he gave all.

He was a good man. I vaguely remember when he and his family arrived here. That was so very long ago, in September of 2026, shortly after the enemy arrived and attacked. He never came to one my sermons or prayer times, but Melissa, Rutty and their daughter did. I couldn't remember her name at the moment, but I know they called her a nickname. She had died here in the Blockade during the one time the enemy got in, killed in the corridor just beyond the Launch foyer. Not long after that, Melissa died from cancer, right where Andrew's body now lay.

It was all so very heartbreaking, and I could only imagine what the boys were going through.

I too had lost family. My husband was still alive, but off in service, and we spoke here and there. We were the reverse: we had lost all five of our children to the enemy, plus my sister. Miguel and I rued our losses, and would always remember our children, but we were determined to go on and make the best of it. But the Shipley boys? They had lost their parents: their *anchors*. It would be no small feat to provide some moorage for them so that they didn't drift spiritually, emotionally, or psychologically.

"Is there anything I can get for either of you?" I asked gently. "Would you like some water at least?"

Jet responded suddenly with a sharp intake of breath, dismissively, almost as if he wished I would go away. "Water would be great, Rosie, thank you," he said in a huff. Rutty looked at me and nodded.

"You bet. Hold tight."

I strode across the lumpy earthen floor to our makeshift kitchenette in the back. Grass was beginning to grow up through the dirt: a faint sign of hope that life goes on even when cut off from the sun. The red and blue LED lights we had stationed down here promoted germination and biomass, along with sward density and root growth. We had managed to sustain life all around us, thankfully.

Pockets of green permeated the floor all around, and now, eleven long years after the invasion, we were starting to enjoy the green floor. The garden was growing nicely as well, with all our hydroponics, tended to by yours truly and others.

The brown and gray walls all around us fenced us in, reminders of our planet above. Composed of gray rock and brown soil, tunneled out long ago by that autonomous Caterpillar drill that was still embedded and abandoned down here somewhere.

I poured two cups of water for them, and returned to my seat. They hadn't moved.

"Here you go," I said, extending the cups to them.

"Thanks, Rosie," Jet said, running his hands through his hair and taking a deep breath. He downed his cup quickly and let out a short gasp for breath at the end. It was then that I realized what the smell was on him: he must have vomited out of sickness and shock when his father was killed right in front of him. His throat must have been burning, and that water must have come in handy.

I stared at him. A memory quickly flashed back to me of when I had first met their family on the way out of the Pavilion, and he had run right into me. He must have been just six, almost seven at the time? That was so very long ago. Rutty would have been only three.

"What do you need right now, Private Shipley?" I asked him directly.

He took time to reply, staring blankly out into the Pavilion. "More water, actually."

Rutty handed him his cup. He hadn't taken a sip yet. Jet thanked him and downed it with equal relish, and then he sat back with his palms flat behind him on the dais. He was staring down at his rifle on the ground.

"I got him, Rutty," he said. "I got the one that got Pops. Blew him away."

I glanced over at Rutty. He didn't answer his brother, but simply nodded and patted Jet on the knee.

"I got him," Jet said again, just above a whisper, but his voice faltered. Rutty noticed it, and looked back over at his older brother. Jet's lips quivered once more, and his face contorted in anguish, slowly, viscerally. His wet eyes flashed up to face me, searchingly, and then over to Rutty, then back to me once more. Not finding whatever answers he sought, he tore himself up, fetched his gun from the ground, and fled out of the Pavilion.

"Private?" I asked him, but Rutty reached out an arm and placed it on mine. I turned to him.

"Let him go, Pastor Rosie. He just-" he faltered and trailed off with a sigh. "Let him go. He'll come around."

I placed my hand on Rutty's, and then stood and opened my arms up wide for him, slowly.

Rutty took a deep breath and stood, looking at me.

"I'm so sorry, kiddo," I said, and then my composure broke. I cared about this kid. After all, I had prayed with him so many times, and he had a good heart…a good heart that was now broken. But somehow, I knew he'd make it through. "I'm *so* sorry."

It was Rutty's turn to have his lips quiver, and then he burst into tears as he looked into my eyes with a yearning for answers that I just couldn't give him.

But I gave him what I could, and that was the strong, loving embrace of this seventy-three-year-old matriarch who dearly loved this fourteen-year-old, his eighteen-year-old brother, his late father, his late mother, his late sister, the late Ray Ferro, the late Nora Jentzen, and all the others we had lost in the late earth we had so loved.

Rutty wept, and he wept long and hard.

•　　•　　•　　•　　•

Tuesday, October 20th, 2037, 1709 hours

I stepped onto the dais, and all eyes were upon me. I looked around. *Lord, give me the wisdom to say the words that give hope, and hold back the ones that extinguish it,* I thought to myself.

As I placed a hand on the lectern to steady myself, I looked back at the tiny lights behind me, two of them, on either side of the stage, blowing up two bluish, waving images of those lost. On the left, Lieutenant Andrew Shipley. On the right, Corporal Ray Ferro. Their projections flanked me, somberly, in memoriam, as I looked out.

Without a word, before I approached the podium, I put my arms out, palms up. The crowd mirrored me. We all knew what it meant.

Receiving.

"Good evening, everyone," I said. "Welcome. We are often in this Pavilion to talk about life. We pray. We talk about the future. Tonight, however, we are talking about the past, and those who have passed on. We will honor them, and the sacrifices they've made."

I turned first to Ray Ferro's image, wavering in the warm air of the Pavilion, regarding it and allowing the audience to look upon him. He had been in his mid-thirties, and the picture that we had was one of him with his daughter, Sarah, wrapping his arms around her. I located Nurse Ferro in the front row. She was sitting next to Jet, and he had his arm around her shoulder, consoling her. Her eyes were red and wet, and she put a tissue to her nose.

"Corporal Raymond Gerald Ferro was born December 12th, 2001 in Akron, Ohio, as an only child. He moved out to Nashville in 2024 with his wife, twin daughters, and infant son. As with so many of us, they have experienced unexpected heartache and unimaginable loss. All members of his family perished in the invasion, save Corporal Ferro and his daughter Sarah, journeying to us here in Clarksville in 2027. He was a valiant member of our recon patrol for many years. He is survived by his daughter, Nurse Sarah Ferro, who is, may I say, equally as fiery as her father." Sarah tilted her head slightly and smiled. "Everyone here knows how much Corporal Ferro loved his flamethrower. He was the surest shot we had with one, and he will be missed. He gave his life to ensure the return of Captain Stone, Private Markus Jentzen, Private Jet Shipley, and the late Lieutenant Shipley. He was a gallant and valiant soldier, and his shoes will not easily be filled. Thank you, Ray Ferro, for your service."

I looked down at Sarah and smiled warmly. The brothers were seated next to her, and Rutty was shifting his feet, hands under his knees on his seat, his legs bobbing nervously. Jet was stoic as ever, grim-set, eyes fixed on me, a smoldering pride in his eyes even before I announced his father's name.

"Lieutenant Andrew Dylan Shipley was born April 3rd, 1986, in Bellevue, Washington. He married his high school sweetheart, Melissa – many of you will remember her – and they moved to Blue Spring, Kentucky in 2022 with three small children: Cameron, aka 'Jet,' Adelynn, aka 'Sissy,' and infant son, Wyatt, aka 'Rutty.' Andrew was a devoted firefighter, EMT, husband and father, and, as many of you know, he had the very best dad jokes."

I don't know what I did, but at that, both Shipley boys let out a pained choke, dropping their heads and crying anew. Sarah Ferro bowed her head on Jet's shoulder. This memory in particular was one that they were apparently most fond of.

"Andrew was promoted up through the ranks here, ending up at the rank of Lieutenant under Captain Stone, performing one-hundred eighty-two missions." At that, the crowd murmured in astonishment and approval. "On his very last mission, he gave his life…to save his son's." I looked down at Jet, who was desperately trying to hold it together. He looked at me, eyes glistening, and swallowed hard.

"Our Blockade, our very lives, would not be sustainable without the dutiful, patriotic, and steadfast devotion of these two soldiers, who gave their lives for this Blockade. Our lives go on because of theirs. Let us take a moment of silence to offer thanks for their service."

I paused, stepped back, and raised my hands once more, standing there, solemnly. I beckoned the crowd to rise. All did, even the bereaved, and I held up my palms as they held up theirs. We did so for four minutes and thirty-six seconds, all of us, for Blockade DN436.

It was times like that where I missed Miguel the most. My dearest marido. He was with the President and the others, of course, but there was so much that he had to go all palms-up there for: some of it truly despicable. I was willing to receive his absence because he was needed, but I deeply missed him. I cleared my thoughts and returned to the service at hand.

"Thank you for remembering them. Please be seated once more." I grabbed my notes and clutched them tightly.

"Where my husband is, I do not know, as he was away in service when the enemy attacked." I hated lying. I truly hated keeping up the guise that I didn't know his location or where he was serving. I longed for the time when I would be able to speak freely, honestly, and repent of this ruse. There was a higher purpose behind it, of course, but that didn't make it any easier. "When I came to this Blockade in 2026, I left with six people: my sister, and five children. I traveled all the way up from Nashville, and by God's grace, I made it here. But I said six people. Only one made it here. I lost all five of my children on the journey, as well as my sister. We traveled forty-eight miles through a zone which was heavily concentrated with the enemy. How in the Lord's Name I am even breathing, I do not know. I will never pretend to understand, except to say that there was some Grace at play, and I trust that I was meant to be here.

"We may never truly know why they are here. We may not be allowed that revelation. What we *are* allowed is the journey. While we know so little, we are always allowed the journey to draw nearer to the One who knows everything. While we flail in despair and questioning, we are always allowed the opportunity to choose to trust that there is One who holds the future in His hands. What our future may become, I simply don't know. But I do know the One who holds it, and that is enough for me. That knowledge is what carries me beyond the present line of sight, knowing that what lies beyond is full of answers. And trust is the bridge I walk down every day, to get to that other side. But it is always a choice.

"For Lieutenant Andrew Shipley and Corporal Ray Ferro, they chose to walk that road. They chose to cross that bridge. The Corporal, by holding the enemy at bay and trusting that his fellow soldiers would return safely. The Lieutenant, by throwing himself between his son and the enemy and trusting that his son would live. The road of trust is never easy, and it is always a choice. But these two," I paused, motioning behind me to their projections, "these two walked that road, they crossed that bridge, not knowing the answers when they passed, and not being allowed to find them in this life. Still," -here I held up a finger to have the crowd lean in to me and listen- "they *trusted*. Trust never knows the outcome. Trust *believes past* the outcome."

I looked down at the Shipley boys and Sarah Ferro. "Just as I have no idea how I made it here, and we have no idea why your parents had to be taken from you, we grieve your loss with you. All of us here believe that there are reasons that will have you walk that bridge of trust. And we promise to walk it with you. Let us pray."

I bowed my head, and I heard the audience do the same. This was always the hardest part, praying, because I knew that some here did not believe. Some would be uncomfortable talking to a God they could not see. Some were uncomfortable even before I got to this point. But praying epitomized trust: it had always done so, and it always would do so.

Heavenly Father, we thank you for the lives of Corporal Raymond Ferro and Lieutenant Andrew Shipley. We thank you for their children that we love. We thank you for your continued protection of us down here in this Blockade, afforded us by the very soldiers we just lost. We commit them to you, and ask that you would help us to always remember them in honor, and to serve one another in love and trust that you know what you're doing up there. Help us to trust you more, especially in times where trust itself is on the line, vying for our attention with doubt. Help us to believe that one day there will be justice, and that one day, this will all make sense somehow. In Christ's Name we pray. Amen.

I looked up at the crowd, and thanked them. "We will have food at the tables momentarily. Please offer your condolences to Sarah Ferro, and Jet and Rutty Shipley, but please do respect their space as well. Thank you for loving them; I am very fond of each of them. Thank you all," I said, stepping down, and I returned to my seat next to Wyatt Rutledge, 'Rutty' Shipley.

The Captain ascended the dais after me, but I hardly heard a word. Something about continued operations and recruiting new recon volunteers. In my heart, however, I couldn't stop praying and thinking to myself. Something I had said when the recon patrol arrived back at the Blockade. Something I was now praying for Jet Shipley, in particular. I knew where Rutty's heart lay. Jet, I was unsure of. All I knew was that he needed to trust, and, like his father, he was far from it. I prayed that God would usher him into trust.

Bring him in, bring him in! I prayed, silently.

2 | MIGUEL

Monday, November 2ⁿᵈ, 2037, 0800 hours

"Yes, Madame President," I said.

"And make sure those flyboys of yours are all ready once we receive the go from our wonderful Colonel Cartwright," she said. "It'll take some time for him to get off his ass with this, and I don't want your guys to drag it along any further than he has."

"Ma'am." I saluted.

"Dismissed," she said, and then she was off.

President Jean Graham was becoming antsier. She had been ever since her son had been lost on that recon mission. No one was ever really properly equipped to go out on any of them. It was all still very much a guessing game. As such, her son had only a handgun and instructions to be quiet. He was only twenty-five, and they never found his body.

Graham had been closing off and getting more irritable ever since. My contact is close with her, but fears he's being pushed completely out. He had been reassigned once already, and that meant that we no longer had eyes on the inside. I understood that, but I wasn't sure how much longer I would be able to receive intel from him. Time would tell.

The things I had heard thus far from my contact defied belief, however. They strained credulity. They baffled and sickened me. It sounded as though she was making progress on a few new referendums, one of which involved the amulets. Of the many thousands we had recovered from the *gorgos*, the scientists were making progress in harnessing their energy and close to weaponizing them. Graham didn't share much about that with me of course, but there were whispers that they would be the first step in us being able to effectively fight back. And, as it turns out, they were the *gorgos'* Achilles heel. They brought them with them, of course.

That was the good news.

It was the bad news that made me and my contact nervous. He had shared things with me about stuff he'd heard her communicating with other international world leaders that has made the hairs stand up on my neck. Terrifying, truly. Conversations about nukes, about final solutions, about taking out our enemy with tactics that most would deem utterly reprehensible.

And it had moved from talk to action. Even now, equipment was being shipped to the middle east, slowly, ever so slowly, on barges where the men were wary and quiet. Taking nuclear materials, supplies, equipment and personnel over to three specific locations in Europe and Asia. For my own protection, my contact didn't share with me where those were.

But Graham was doing all of it now. She was intent on using nuclear action, and my contact was convinced she was preparing to pull the trigger.

The worst part of it was that it was being done behind closed doors, and there were more and more talks like that. President Jean Graham was starting to get a little too *loco in la cabeza* for my taste. This woman had clearly overstayed her welcome, and was about to continue into her fourth term. No one had done that since FDR back in 1933 to 1945.

But in truth, there was no one to replace her, and no elections. No Congress. No House of Representatives. Only Vice President Cooper to ratify the impromptu revision to the 22nd Amendment to allow her to continue. Cooper had been in it as long as she had, by necessity, the day the last president was killed by a *gorgo* at Nashville airport in 2026. He was sworn in as her VP shortly after the last VP was killed in the White House.

But eventually, he, too, had to go.

I wondered when that time would come, because in the eleven years since the invasion, not much had changed. We were still dying, and they were still here, and they owned the planet, and we were all stuck here in the shadows.

All in all, thankfully, my contact was keeping tabs on what was going on from afar since he had been expelled and stationed up at Mammoth Cave earlier this year. After all, he had been asking too many questions, and that was making VP Cooper nervous. It was Cooper who had him relocated there, but at least he had communications there to relay developments and intel where and when he could. He thought he could trust Cooper, but apparently the VP was too close to Graham.

Things were happening. Pieces were moving, and a groundswell of dissent was flowing.

In truth, I dearly missed my wife. I missed her embrace. I missed her calm wisdom. My dearest Rosalita, *mi flor preciosa.* She was stationed in Clarksville, Tennessee, and she was doing well there. I say *stationed*, but of course hers wasn't a military designation, but rather one of spiritual support. When we occasionally spoke, I couldn't relay much, and when I did, I'd have to speak in Spanish on an encoded line.

Thank God that we had someone at that Blockade, and that my contact was in charge of security and communications here in Nashville. That has enabled us to be able to keep her in the loop. And she's been able to keep us in the loop as well. She's echoed news of developments happening in Alpharetta with their science team, and that has mirrored what we've heard from insiders around the President. Sounds as though the team there is about to conduct an experiment on capturing a live gorg.

Man I hate those *gorgos.* They got another two of our men out on recon just two days ago. When my time comes, I hope it's painless. I hope it's not by a gorg. But if it is, I'm not going to go quietly into the night. This old body ain't that old yet. *Es la verdad.* I won't go quietly, and those *gorgos* will feel the wrath of First Lieutenant Miguel Monzon.

But for now, I had to report to Colonel Cartwright.

●　　　●　　　●　　　●　　　●

Monday, November 2nd, 2037, 0902 hours

I found the Colonel on the second floor, in the briefing room with his aide.

"Colonel Cartwright? Lieutenant Monzon is here," announced his assistant. Beautiful young lady named Leah Aponte, and I loved that she was of Mexican descent, though I scoffed at the fact that Cartwright used her. We were down to fifteen percent surviving mankind. *What kind of man needs an Aide* and *an assistant?*

"Send him in!" Cartwright barked, and Aponte smiled at me and waved me in.

"Buenos Dias, Aponte," I smiled back at her.

"Buenos Dias."

"Monzon!" Cartwright yelled, seemingly oblivious that his room was small enough to not necessitate such volume, much less the fact that he forgot that there were still *gorgos* out there. "Come on in, if you must."

I strode into his office, and Barnes gave me the old eyebrows-up. Cartwright was much less courteous.

"Colonel," I greeted him, saluting.

"At ease, messenger boy. I supposed you're here to ensure that we're getting close at BNA."

"Yessir. The President-"

"I know, I *know*. Unbelievable," he waved me away, holding up a gruff hand and snorting. "Don't bother me with *Jean Graham*. You can tell your precious Crusty Commander in Cheat that the guys will be ready on time for the tests down there. You can always count on us flyboys over you mailboys." Cartwright cocked a brawny and patronizing smile at me, and then he looked up at Barnes for approval of his insult.

I felt my shoulders sink a little bit. "Yessir."

Cartwright was my contact's replacement, and was in charge of Embassy security now that the SecDef was dead. Graham loathed him, and despised every exchange with him. There was no way she was going to be lobbying for this Colonel to ascend the ranks to Secretary of Defense. All the more reason for him to hate her back.

"That woman. *Good Lord.* She has to bird-dog every single thing we do. Bad enough she's got eyes and ears on every single floor with Cardona running security. That guy's a weasel and won't amount to anything. But she doesn't trust him or anybody enough to let anyone do their job. You tell her from me that we're *fine* over there, *thankyouverymuch,* and they'll be ready to go as promised. The amulets are all mounted up and they've got the ghetto blasters ready." He sneered.

Ghetto blasters? No one has called them that in like forty years. *This guy is even older than me,* I thought. I had just had my sixty-sixth birthday last June, and could recall a time before the *gorgos*. We even had a joke that anything before the year 2026 should be called "B.G." after the year. 'Ghetto blasters' were called that circa 1985 BG.

Anyway...

"Just run along and tell Queenie that we'll be good to go as promised. And next time, just call, please. I don't need a bunch of looky-loo's dropping in on me and Barnes here," he growled. I glanced up at Barnes behind him, who shrugged feebly.

"Sir," I started reluctantly, and the Colonel whipped up erect in his seat, irritated to hear another word, as if he didn't expect any further dialogue and was itching to be rid of me. "Sir, the President asked me to simply ensure that the subject in custody will no longer be a problem for our troops." I didn't need to add that we had lost four men already to the damned thing.

Cartwright gritted his teeth at me, and then slowly rose. We stared at each other for a solemn moment.

"Run along now, First Lieutenant Monzon," -here he seemed to be reminding me of my lower rank- "and tell *El Presidente* that we know what we're doing here. The gorgon is isolated and contained." He paused. "Okay? That will be *all*, won't it? Yes, First Lieutenant?"

I nodded, eager to move on. "Yessir. Thank you sir."

"Dismissed," he said quickly, trying to preempt me from saying anything else, and glanced over at Barnes as if I didn't even exist.

•   •   •   •   •

Monday, November 2nd, 2037, 0915 hours

Following the meeting, I revisited the President in her room and informed her that Cartwright promised readiness by 1200 hours today. What men we had were ready to test the avionics in the old Amazon Fulfillment Center at Nashville International Airport, virtually a straight shot south of us as the crow flies.

"Thank you, Lieutenant Monzon. You're a good soldier. I hope Cartwright didn't give you any bluster today. I'm considering having him reassigned for an attitude adjustment," she scoffed.

I didn't know what to say to that. I had heard rumors of her having people reassigned, and it was secretly joked about that whoever was being reassigned was about to somehow meet with an imminent end. I couldn't wait to get out of this post, nor this assignment. Hopefully, my time was drawing nearer.

Her smile faded and her expression dimmed.

"Well, it's up to him and his team tomorrow to show us if this damned thing is going to work or not. Right now, it's our best shot at kicking the gorgons to the curb," she said with a terse lip and defiant, smoldering eyes. "We've spent enough time in their shadow. Hopefully, this will see them spending time in ours for a change."

I looked at her and said nothing, but I had to admit I shared her hope, no matter what I had heard about how she planned to ultimately go about fulfilling that hope.

"Dismissed," she said, becoming the second person to send me on my way in less than an hour.

"Yes, Madame President," I answered.

3 | CLARKSVILLE

| Rosie |

Tuesday, December 15th, 2037, 1312 hours

The young soldier was doing fine.

It had been some time since he'd checked in with me, but from what Rutty told me, he was doing better. Rutty himself was improving in spirits, though I suspected that the fact that they were both drawing near to their first Christmas without either of their parents or their sister was weighing on them. They had been stripped down to twenty percent of their original family, and it was a cruel diminishing.

But Jet was doing well, so said Rutty, and was nearly ready to return to recon patrol. That was good. He was needed. They were all needed. We didn't have high hopes that any survivors remained out there except in dark holes like ours, but every attempt to find more was worth it.

"Thanks, Pastor Rosie," said the fourteen-year-old standing beside me, and I put my arm around him.

"You are always welcome, kiddo," I said, giving his shoulder a squeeze. "I'm here to do whatever I can to make sure you can do whatever you can. We're all we have left, so we have to make everything work as much as possible, right?"

He nodded. "Ten days until Christmas. I know he's hurting. We both miss our family, Rosie."

Just as I suspected.

"I dunno. It's just not going to be easy, not that any of them have been easy in here since we came to Clarksville. Just…give us time."

I nodded back. "Of course, Rutty. You take all the time you need. I'm always available if you need to talk more."

He smiled faintly, and started to get up. "Gotta go talk to Captain Stone. He wanted to see Jet and I after you."

"Oh? What about?"

"Didn't say. I'm sure it's some of the same stuff though. He's concerned about my bro, though…mostly. I know he needs him back on recon as soon as possible. I'm itching to be able to enlist myself, frankly."

I looked at him grimly. Such a young man, eager to get out there on the battlefield and potentially lose his life in the name of preserving humanity. So brave. "Well, you have two years, yet, young man. Enjoy this time. You're doing so well in here, and everyone knows it."

He tilted his head and frowned. "Do they? I don't know that what I'm doing really makes any real difference, but that's just me. I want to follow in Jet and dad's footsteps. I'm glad they lowered the enlistment age to sixteen, that's the truth. I can't wait."

The young soldier, ready to do battle with his father's enemies. For a second, a brief flash of the little guy that I had seen so many years before, in the cafeteria at orientation when Captain Stone introduced himself to all of us. He had grown so much since then: flowering into manhood, transforming into a warrior, aching to engage.

I regarded him and clenched my lip. "I'm proud of you, young man. Your service in here does matter, and it's not overlooked, and your presence makes a difference. Never forget that, Wyatt Rutledge Shipley."

Rutty paused, starting to say something in return, but his head just dropped then, and he smiled a quiet thank you at me, turning to head out.

At the door, he turned back.

"You wanna come to the meeting with Stoney with us? I know Jet could use you too."

Those were the words I was waiting for.

"Of course. It would be my honor."

•   •   •   •   •

Tuesday, December 15th, 2037, 1400 hours

"Senora Rosie!" Captain Stone greeted me in surprise, after letting us in past the Sentry. "Can I help you?"

"No, Captain, it's alright, thank you. Rutty had requested my presence."

I looked over at him and his brother standing there. Jet had met us in the hallway, glowering and looking pensive as usual. I'd say it was less pensive than I had become accustomed to seeing him, but you never could tell. He was a closed book…a locked safe…a sealed-off cave.

"Oh! Well, that's fine with me," Stone replied. "As long as the boys here don't mind." He gestured to them and both of them shook their heads. "Well then. Have a seat, everyone."

The Sentry closed the door behind us.

The four of us sat on the folding chairs around his little office. There was a dim light on his desk illuminating a stack of papers, which he always seemed to have adorning his desk. It felt strangely like some kind of family gathering: older male and female, younger males. I wondered if the same thing was going through the Shipley boys' heads. There was a moment of silence where no one said anything. I didn't want to be the first one to pipe up. I would speak when called upon.

At last the Captain cleared his throat, after watching them solemnly for a bit.

"Private Shipley, how are things?"

Jet looked up at the Captain and took a deep, labored breath, holding his air in his lungs so long I thought he might burst. "I think they're fine, Cap. Just…" -here he looked around at us- "emotional. Slow-going." He managed a feeble smile. "It's like Rutty said. Christmas is coming fast at us, and neither of us want it."

Stone nodded. So did I. "I understand," the Captain muttered. "We both do," he said, motioning to me. "We've all lost family as well, and Christmas can be painful."

I looked at him. I didn't recall his story exactly. He had shared it informally in passing at some breakfast. I think he had a wife, but no children.

"We all come from *before*. A time where everyone was with us, and we'd all wake up to a brightly-lit, colorful tree loaded with gifts beneath it. We don't have that down here, and it's more or less emotionally counterproductive to do so anyway. But we still remember, and remembering can be healing *and* painful."

Jet nodded and inhaled again. "I'll be fine in time, I promise." Rutty looked at him. "I'm almost there, Stoney."

"I know," the Captain assured him. "I know. I would never ask you to return until I knew that you were ready, Jet. Please know that. I ache for your loss with a father's heart, kid. Both of you. I loved your dad. You know that. And if your father were here…" I started to say something, but bit my lip. Where the Captain was going might be too painful for them still. But my fears were ill-founded. "He would be very proud of you for working through it in your own time," he finished. That was good. That was allowance for healing.

Both boys nodded. Jet spoke again eventually.

"I should be ready a little after the new year. I promise. I just need time."

That made Stone happy. "I believe you, and that's just fine. Just don't take too long, soldier, or your little brother here's gonna pass you up."

I looked at Rutty. The faintest smile crawled across his lips as he looked up at Stone. His left eye squinted slightly, and then he turned to look at his brother. Jet met his gaze.

"Never," Jet breathed, and then a smile took over his lips. He put his arm around his little brother and pulled him close as Rutty snickered.

"There it is. That's the spirit I know you have," Stone said. "You guys'll be just fine."

"We will, sir. Thank you, sir," Jet answered in a monotone, his smile turning to a proud, smoldering grimace.

Rutty matched him in intensity, showing that he wanted to be every bit the soldier that his older brother was.

"You're welcome. Again, if you guys need anything, you need to talk to an older man for anything, and I mean anything, I'm here. I know you have Rosie for everything else."

Everything else? I wasn't sure what that meant but let it go. To me, the Spirit was everything, and everything *else* was everything else.

"Yep, thank you Cap," Rutty said this time.

"Captain, if I may," I broke in slowly. "Do you have enough men on your recon patrols to allow for Private Shipley's continued absence?"

The Private looked at me in slight confusion. So did the Captain. Pretty sure Rutty did as well.

Captain Stone's eyebrows angled downward. "How do you mean, Senora Rosie?"

I shifted in my seat. "Well, far be it from me to push someone prematurely. But this kid is made of stern stuff. Look at him. He's tough in the fiber. If you need him sooner, I encourage you to let him know now."

"S-sooner?" Jet eked out.

I nodded. "Yes. Sooner. He's a valuable member of our recon patrol, and he's needed. I just want to encourage you to be upfront with him if the need is there, that he needs to hop back in the saddle. Sometimes the best treatment for our broken heart is to get it pumping again."

Stone looked at me, his mouth slightly open. His eyes darted back to the Private and his brother, then to me.

"Pastor Rosie, with all due respect, I…" he stammered. "I agree with you, but you can't microwave the healing process."

"No, you can't, that's right, Captain," I agreed with him. "However, it's been two months since the Lieutenant lost his life, and you need the soldiers out there. Cameron – excuse me – *Jet* Shipley here is ready for you now."

Rutty looked at me incredulously, as if he regretted his decision to ask me to be part of the meeting.

However, the expression on his brother's face was markedly different. There was no incredulity, no pain, no disagreement. No trace of anger at having his hand forced. Instead, what I saw was a smoldering realization that he was who he was. I saw a desire for readiness, and a willingness to receive his duty back into his own hands. Acceptance.

The Captain was still looking at me, and I thought I heard a faint grunt of wonderment. He took a deep breath and then moved his gaze over to the Private, holding his tongue behind his upper lip for a moment. At last he took a swift inhale and asked Jet, "And how do you feel about that, Private?"

Rutty looked back at his brother. And then he looked back at the Captain, then back at me, then back at his brother once more, watching the volley happening between all of us.

Jet continued to look at me for a moment, and I could swear that the corner of his mouth was beginning to crease into a faint smile at the edge. In my peripheral, I could see the Captain nervously shift in his seat, clearing his throat.

The Private and I locked eyes, and for a moment I thought of our enemy. Cold, pale eyes that would lock with ours, sending whatever alien signal from their mind to ours that would force our muscles to freeze, sucking our very life force out of us, and stealing our will. We'd learned that much about them. The Private's eyes were steely as well, but there was not a trace of malignancy. There was a resolve in there that just needed to be tapped, and perhaps he needed to admit it to himself first after being pushed to a place he thought he wasn't ready to go yet. Between us, you could draw a line in the air: past the Captain, past Rutty, connecting me to him.

Not once had he ever set foot in one of my Sunday services, but there was a smoldering passion there. Some raw force of grit, determination, and passion: the same stuff his father the Lieutenant was made of. He was locked in my stare, but he knew that I, unlike the enemy, held no menace nor malice. All I wanted was for him to find his own strength once again.

Jet nodded at me slowly, acknowledging the truth, not once taking his eyes off of me. "She's right, Stoney. I am ready. I can start in two days. I'm needed, and you know it. I can do this."

My lips clenched as I looked at him with pride. I nodded slightly, and he nodded back, this stranger one degree beyond Rutty whom I barely ever spoke with and who barely ever spoke with me. I didn't know him well; I only knew there was a fire there that perhaps he himself was unaware of. Just needed a match. I could be that for him.

The Captain shifted uneasily again in his seat, looking in turn at all of us. "Well," he continued at last with a heave, "Rosie is right. She usually is," he halfway sneered at me with a cold smile, "and we could use you. That much is true. If you say so, you'd be welcome back, son." Jet turned to look at him.

Son. No one called him that anymore of course, not since his own father was taken two months ago. The word might have offended him, and it might not have. But it also lit a match in him, from all outward appearances.

"S-sorry," the Captain said, putting his hands up in self-defense. "I didn't mean *that*," he said. "I…I just meant-"

"It's okay, Stoney," Jet said, and I found he and Rutty both nodding together. "I know what you meant, but I appreciate it."

Rutty glanced at the Captain in agreement, with a trace of a somber smile and a slight nod.

And then, it was time for the three of them to regard each other. A silent adoption was taking place right before my eyes as they both looked at him, and they looked *to* him.

"I appreciate it," Jet said again.

"Me too," Rutty added.

Captain Stone had his hands flat on the desk before him, and he took a deep, cleansing breath, looking at the two of them in front of him: one young soldier, and one young soldier-in-the-making. "You boys are family. You know that. I'd be proud to have you back, Private Shipley. And proud to be here for both of you anytime you need it," he added, and I looked at them with a warm smile, my neck tingling with joy running in waves down my back.

The boys nodded.

Private Shipley would return to service. He would be fine. The soldier in him would be fine.

In fact, both soldiers were doing fine now.

4 | TRUDY

Wednesday, December 30th, 2037, 1238 hours

I, Allison Leigh Trudy…

"I, Allison Leigh Trudy…" I repeated after him.

…do solemnly swear that I will support and defend the Constitution of the United States against all enemies, foreign and domestic…

I repeated after him, as long as I could remember all that. "…do solemnly swear that I will support and defend the Constitution of the United States against all enemies, foreign and domestic…"

I will bear true faith and allegiance to the same…

"I will bear true faith and allegiance to the same…"

…and that I will obey the orders of the President of the United States and the orders of the officers appointed over me …

I repeated the words gravely, my right hand held erect just off of my ear in solemnity.

...according to regulations and the Uniform Code of Military Justice. So help me God.

"...according to regulations and the Uniform Code of Military Justice. So help me God." I took a deep breath, and smiled, then saluted him, and he saluted me back with a deep smile, and then shook my hand.

The Staff Sergeant before me had a low thick southern drawl, but he was handsome. I'd gotten to know Joe over the past year when I joined up. He was the one who welcomed me at the Launch so many years ago after I ran from that Subway, from Holt, from my old life, and made my way through the shadows of Alpharetta to this Blockade.

I missed Holt. He was such a sweet old man. He didn't deserve to go the way he did. That was *so* long ago, but his memory stayed firm in my mind, and his insulin vial stayed firm on my shelf. A really good man.

Joe was a good man as well, and I didn't want to be sworn in by any other. But it wasn't like *that*. He was forty-seven, and I was only nineteen, so that would be icky; there wasn't anything like that between us. He was married anyway, and his wife, Maureen, is one of the most darling women I've ever met. I just loved him in an admiring way. A really good man. Reminded me of Holt. Reminded me of my dad.

My dad. *Man* I missed my dad. I missed Nick, Badge, my mom and my dad *so* much right now. I wished they all could see this, see me enlisting. I wished Nick could have seen it in particular. He was the one who kept me alive, after all. He doesn't lean over me when the gorgs come, then I don't get into that Subway with Holt and have him take care of me. I don't get to Holt, and Holt doesn't take care of me.

I don't leave Holt to go get his medicine, I don't get to this Blockade here in Alpharetta. I don't get here, I don't enlist, become a Private, or get to start putting my science expertise to good use. *Thank you Nick.*

Thank all of you. I felt Holt's vial in my pocket, pressing against my leg. I carried that everywhere I went, still, to this day, for luck. I sometimes wondered if I hadn't gone out to get it for him, would he and I have died together? I'll never know. I'm here now, and I'm alive, and that's what I know.

Staff Sergeant Joseph Bassett leaned toward me and whispered, "I'm proud of you. Let's do this."

"Let's do this," I whispered back through a smile. He winked at me, and moved on to the next Private. I scanned the crowd, and the many faces of my new family beamed back at me. There were Charlotte, Eric, Raylin, and Chance sitting together. On the other aisle I could make out Gage, Brant, and Shelly. Scattered throughout were a few others I knew here. They were all clapping. I bowed to them.

I was now an enlisted Private.

Me, *Allison Leigh Trudy…*

5 I JOE

Wednesday, December 30th, 2037, 1307 hours

She was *filthy* and shaking.

That's what I remember: that little girl had come to us from eight miles away, over the course of several weeks. She was nine, I think, when she got here in '26. So long ago. Maureen and I met her at the front door, practically. Filthy and shaking.

But here she was, all grown up. Clean and confident.

I was so proud of all of them, but especially of her.

I made my way through all our Blockade folks and found Trudy standing with her friends, hugging and smiling between bites of our crappy MRE food packs. That's the best we could do. Oh, for the days when we could celebrate with cake. Our hydroponics farm was getting better and better down here though, so today we had a few extra veggie treats, and Maureen always got creative with how she presented them.

Oh, Maureen, my sweet Maureen. She was in here, somewhere, milling around with our new underground family. I'd connect with her again soon. She was truthfully the only reason I was still alive. That mission. I was so dead-set on choosing that recon patrol, so hellbent on making a name for myself and climbing up the ranks. Yet I had a choice; I could opt for that one and head to the surface, boldly going where no man had gone before as the old *Star Trek* show used to say, or, as she suggested, I could put my name in the hat for the science team. She knew I wanted to make a bigger mark than I would have in a single patrol. She knew that I wanted to be part of the takeback of our planet.

Nearly every single one of our team members from that patrol died: all of them killed by the gorgs. Except for Steph. My sister was as tough-in-the-fiber as they came, and she was no bullshit. I was not surprised in the slightest that she and Donner made it back, but I confess I was relieved *and* frustrated. I was the one who stayed back and opted to command the science unit in the absence of Sergeant Rico who was in quarantine. They were hot on the trail of this new mask tech they'd thought up, and it was headed by none other than our beloved enlistee here, Allison Trudy. Before she enlisted she was always in there, volunteering, spending her time trying to figure out that contraption and how it could be rigged to deflect the gorgons' deadly vision. That girl was committed to the core, and to the corps.

And to her lip balm, of course. She was always smearing that stuff on. I didn't even know they had that down here.

And because I held back at Maureen's insistence, I was alive. I owed my beautiful bride my life. Steph wasn't too upset that I was still kickin' either, though she would never let me outlive her anyway. She could give as much as she took. I loved her.

But then there was the other little lady. The third part of my female triumvirate. My wife Maureen, my kid sister Steph, and now Trudy. It was my job to protect all of them.

And there was my wife. I saw her at the far end of the Rotunda. That's what we called the gathering place in the middle of the Blockade. Not cozy in the slightest, but it allowed for great celebrations like this, and it was far from the danger of the Launch. Our eyes met, and she smiled and waved. I winked at her and blew her a kiss. She grabbed it and quickly inserted it into her bra, close to her heart. I loved that silly spitfire of a woman. I loved her with all my heart.

I smiled and turned back to go congratulate Trudy, but as I turned around, someone bumped into me and spilled their water all over my fatigues. "Whoa! Hold up-"

It was Allison.

"Oh my gosh, Joe, I'm sorry, haha! Forgive me, here…I'll get a towel."

"No need, no need, darlin,'" I said to her, wiping myself off. "Runs right off these old army rags. You'll see," I said, laughing with her.

"Sorry," she repeated.

I looked at her. "Hey, glad I found you. You are something else, you know that? I'm so proud of ya, girl. You've come a long, long way, and I can't wait to see what you and the team do with this new mask tech you're working on with the boro- boro-," I trailed off, not remembering the name.

"*Borosilicate glass,*" she enunciated slowly for me. "Get it in your head, old man. You're heading up the team, right? You gotta know your own tech because your name will be on this too, Joe. I mean, sir," she said, mock-saluting.

"Ha! Alright, alright, enough of that. We'll see how that turns out. You know I'm all for it. I'm just up to my eyeballs in figuring out what we can find out about their anatomy. We're still working on a mission where we can actually get a live one. Until that time all I have are skin flakes and bare samples to go off of."

Trudy had been so excited to see us return from that particular recon with the flesh of a gorgon that had appeared to have died only recently. She knew that this might be a breakthrough. Gage had been studying it closely, poring over it night and day and studying the microbiology of it, craning his neck and looking, yearning for any signs of hope that it might impart. So far, nothing. But that was my department too: biology. Trudy's was science and defense, and for that, she was now going to be heading up the mask tech she was pioneering with her friends. Heck, she might just leapfrog me one day, she moved so fast.

"Yeah, well, to each their own, right? We'll get there. Both of us."

"Both of us," I murmured low, and then smiled at her again. "Anyway, I'm proud of you, and I know you know that, but I wanted you to hear it from the old man. Congratulations, Trudy. Never doubted you for a second."

"Not one?"

"Well, maybe that one time, but it was more like a half-second."

"Oh, good, phew. Glad I made the cut."

I snickered at her. "You always do, kid."

She put her arms out wide. No place for a salute here. I went in and embraced her fully. Trudy felt the closest thing to a daughter that I would have ever had, and I loved this girl.

Maureen and I never had kids, and I've sort of always silently regretted that. Maureen didn't really want any, and I knew that going in. In hindsight however, that was prescient…that would have been hard getting all of us here safely to this Blockade.

But this girl did it all by herself, with no one else's help. Her story of how she had lost her brothers…of that man in the Subway restaurant that helped her and took care of her…how she bravely ventured out to get his insulin for him after he had fallen asleep…how he came out of there calling for her far too loudly…how the gorgs got him…how she stayed under that car for so long…how she summoned up the nerve to pull herself out of there and to make her slow, long, dangerous trek here…how she finally made it and fit right in.

How she was an exemplary little girl.

How she was a brain and a half, devoted to figuring things out and studying, studying, always studying.

How she had graduated at the top of her little class of four kids down here.

How she had worked so hard on those masks, hoping against hope that one day we would be able to walk freely up top again, breathing the free air, firing away and worrying not an ounce about being stared down by a gorg.

Allison Trudy was something else, and she was like a daughter to Maureen and me, and she was going to do great things in this war.

I hugged her and told her I'd see her around, making my way over to my beautiful wife. I took one look back at her as she reunited with her friends: all of them throwing their arms around each other and doing little mini-dances of excitement. Yet as I beheld her, all grown up, I would always remember the scrappy little survivor who first made it to us.

She was so filthy, and shaking all over.

6 | TESTED

| Miguel |

Friday, January 15th, 2038, 1000 hours

No one likes bad news. Graham had had enough of it.

Colonel Cartwright had given the all-clear for the test to begin, and the President, her advisors, myself, and anyone else who wanted to watch – which was pretty much everyone – were glued to the monitors.

It had taken far longer than anticipated. Two whole months longer than anticipated, and Graham was losing patience with him. She was doing something, working on something behind the scenes in her office – away from us – but whenever she emerged her first stop was always the Colonel's office, presumably to bite his head off. She was always nearly silent before him, receiving his scorn and sneering. But she had that look about her – the one that said, *I'm going to outlast you* – and she just absorbed his ire and stuck it in a place deep in her heart to be called upon at the time she deemed right.

I never knew the real story behind it, but there was bad blood between them, and no love lost. When the previous President was killed out there on the tarmac, the Colonel was aboard Air Force One with all of them, and he was one of the loudest dissenters to anything and everything Graham had proposed, including sending those poor planes off to their death as a diversion so that she and everyone else could get away. She knew they would all plummet to their deaths, but she did it anyway. It had been so long ago, but we all remembered that day with a sullen ache in our hearts. Cartwright never forgot it, that's for sure. And he made sure to wear his contempt on full display ever since. But Graham was never visibly ruffled by it.

Now, the Colonel was sitting down in front of her watching the monitors, and she was positioned imposingly behind him. The President looked down at him.

"You have a green light, Colonel."

He rolled his eyes, but she didn't see it. I did.

"Yes, *Ma'am,*" he smirked, scorn evident on the *ma'am.* He picked up a walkie-talkie and depressed the switch. "Cartwright to DTF-1, go code Zero."

"Copy," came a youngish voice in a burst of a reply, and then silence.

DTF. That's what we were calling these things. 'Dissonant Tidal Floods.' The DTFs happen over 35 kHz, fusing the power of high explosives and an EMP charge with whatever they did with those amulets. I wasn't part of that team, though I wish I was. It was truly the most significant development we'd ever seen, and it filled us all with hope. And now, they were going to test it.

It had something to do with what the *gorgos* brought with them. They had all floated silently down with those things embedded into the back of their necks. These little devices that looked like amulets: strange thin silver circlets with glyphs, and some kind of translucent stone set in the middle, about the size of a silver dollar. They had dropped from them when they activated in the attacks of September 3rd 2026, separating from their alien bodies and falling down to the earth. We had collected them, analyzed them, and began experimenting on them.

It was surmised that they had these things on them to help equalize the pressure they experienced in traveling through space, as well as entering our atmosphere. These things helped their 'ears' with that. Probably also helped with mass communication to coordinate the awakening and the subsequent attack. Well, the scientists took them, and turned them around. It became their Achilles' heel. It prevented sound and pressure one way, but if you projected sound and pressure the other way, at certain frequencies, it could potentially be dangerous to them. The thought was, if one side was used to protect and enable them, then perhaps going the other way could be used to injure and disable them. Maybe even kill them. It was worth exploring.

There just needed to be a test subject first.

Baxter was such a good dog. He flew everywhere with the previous President, and he was one of the last canines alive on the planet, to be sure. When everyone fled across Nashville International Airport, commonly known as BNA, over here to the Embassy, Baxter hustled with the rest of them. He had survived the onslaught of the invasion as a two-year-old pup, and was now fourteen and graying. So, that was some consolation to all of the weapons team when it was decided that he would be the first test subject.

Graham decided it, of course. It was cruel and unnerving to see him go through what he went through. But the DTF team were all resigned to the fact that they had to test it on a canine. The frequencies were terrifically high, and if it worked on a canine, then presumably it would work on them, they thought. And so, since Baxter was geriatric and presumably near the end of life, the President gave the final order to use him in the tests. We all begged and pleaded with her to spare him. His kind had presumably been all killed off, and we'd never get another lab-hound-pointer in all of Earth's future if we did.

I can still see when his head exploded from the audio barely three seconds into the test.

It was a success, however, and we acknowledged that as we bowed our heads silently and switched off the monitors. That was two weeks ago, when the search began in earnest for another *gorgo* to put with the first one in containment. There is power in numbers, so they thought, and all of them figured that they would be calmer, and thus, less prepared, for when the blast went off: an exercise simulating a real-world incident as it would out there in combat.

How they got the first one, I don't know. And how they lured the second one in, well, that was done with someone acting as bait. They lured it in, trapped it in a thick net, and blindly felt for its body in order to sedate it. I cannot imagine what that must have been like. They lost one man in the process, I'm told.

BNA had a large Amazon warehouse not unlike a Blockade, only massive. A thousand feet across, it offered relative safety for those charged with the experiments. And they had gun towers on top of it, sure enough.

In that warehouse, now, they had wheeled both *gorgos,* strapped to vertical gurneys and blindfolded, side by side. The fish they fed those things. Constant feeding. There they were on our monitors: we could see them clearly now, stationary, calm, eating the last entrails of what would presumably be their final meal. They could hear, and would occasionally twitch when a human came near, but now all humans were retreating behind the triple pane plexiglass and RF shielding.

In a full circle surrounding the two subjects was a thirty-foot diameter halo of what they were calling DTF emitters. They were roughly two feet wide by one foot high by three feet deep. All of them were positioned on wedge mounts angling them slightly upward. And all of them were pointing at the epicenter of that ring where the *gorgos* were unknowingly waiting for their death.

I looked at the President. Her arms were crossed in front of her, and she was watching the screen solemnly, intent on the two subjects.

The youngish voice came back over the radio. "Command, standby for detonation in T-Minus twenty…nineteen…eighteen…seventeen…"

He continued to count. The *gorgos* were silent and still, almost as if they knew their end was near. Either that or their bellies were so full that they were content and no longer cared about being restrained.

Audio technicians were patched in here for signals that would be captured there, and the signals would be harvested and analyzed in depth for frequency impact, point of dissolution when their craniums might cave in, and any other valuable data that the electrode sensors – which were all over both of the subjects – would pick up and relay.

Ten…nine…eight…seven…

A faint bass crescendo rose in pitch over the speakers as the emitters surged to full strength.

I looked nervously out the small window in our tiny Command Center on the 6th floor over toward BNA.

Four…three…two…one…

"Go for detonation," came the voice.

A blinding light lit up the monitor, and we heard the instant shrieks. How only two of them could generate such noise was beyond me. We felt nothing. The soldiers in the BNA Amazon warehouse felt nothing and reported nothing.

Though the *gorgos* were lost to our sight, the cacophony of anguish and despair, wailing rising to inscrutable and measureless tones, faded to choking cries as the crumple of alien bone sounded in fierce cracks and splinters, resonating loud and clear through the speakers on our end. I could only imagine what it sounded like over there.

We waited. Anxiously, we waited.

"Standby," came the young voice.

The monitors gradually faded back into clarity, and what we saw both appalled and sickened us, and filled us with a surprise hope of immeasurable proportions. Color crept back across the screen and whoever was filming zoomed in.

The smoke cleared. The vents began sucking out the smoke. As the room faded back to clarity, there they were: crumpled and disemboweled remnants of their former glory. Two alien skeletons bent and contorted beyond belief, smoking and bleeding husks beyond recognition, one with jaws wide open in agony, the other with broken off mandible lying on the ground in front of it.

Pulverized into discombobulated chunks. *Ay caramba.* A truly gory sight, but one that nonetheless brought more gladness and hope than we had felt in years.

The amulets could be used against them.

The DTFs worked, and Baxter's life was not in vain.

•   •   •   •   •

Friday, January 15th, 2038, 1315 hours

There was no time.

"Radar inbound, radar inbound, to arms!" came the call across all of our walkie-talkies, and we jumped up from our seats. I was with the President in her outer office, her 'lobby' as it were, on the sixth floor. We knew what to do, and this particular announcement wasn't filled with any more dread than any other time.

I drew my P320 and brandished it by my ear with both hands, looking out the windows which were partially obscured by the curtains.

It was times like these that I wished we were in a Blockade somewhere. Preferably in Clarksville of course, so that I could be with my sweet Rosalita. Those gun towers: they were enviable to a massive degree, and the only places we had in this hotel were simply other rooms. We always keep the bottom floor deserted, and that thick glass and those locked doors afforded some minimal protection. But if the *gorgos* were intent on getting in, they would get in. We were down to ninety-six people in here, including those straggling survivors we'd found over the years in our occupancy of the Nashville Embassy Suites. But we hadn't found anyone in many years, and our numbers were only diminishing now with each loss out in the field. I couldn't shake a sneaking suspicion that we were about to lose more.

That the *gorgos* were here could mean only one thing. They'd been disoriented by the DTF testing over at the airport, and they were now swarming here. They did that to any area where there was a sustained noise, and they smashed it in their fury, rending and destroying in their unabating wrath. Just a few hours ago, we had sent a massive plume of sound outward in all directions, and they had to have heard the anguished cries of their fellow creatures as they were decimated.

Now, they were fanning out all over metropolitan Nashville and setting their horrible sights on us here after having been driven off by the dissonant tidal floods.

The remaining Secret Service detail of two officers quickly escorted President Graham off to a secure room within a room down the hall: her new PEOC, her Presidential Emergency Operations Center, such as they used to use below the White House. It was on this same floor, fortunately, in the center, away from the windows, the ground floor, and the top.

"Securing Iron Maiden, Securing Iron Maiden," chimed one of the agents, using the code phrase for the POTUS. "Sit rep on Ibex," he huffed, pushing Graham in front of him, down the hall. I was running behind her on the sixth floor, and the walkie-talkies squawked again.

"Ibex secure, repeat, Ibex secure," came the answer, confirming the VP was in custody and safe. There was a smaller, similar bunker on the fourth floor.

"Contact, seventy meters southeast, coming in fast! BNA under attack, repeat, BNA under attack!"

The airport.

"BNA taking heavy hits, they're breaking through, repeat, they're breaking through!"

We trudged down the hall and were almost there. That's when the hotel alarm went off. The walls blipped in bright blue LED flickers down the corridor and there was a short, staccato periodic burst followed by a warning announcement.

The agents thrust Graham through the door into the 'Nest,' their PEOC, and I started to follow in, when one of the agents whirled around and put a hand against my chest. My eyes narrowed and my brows furrowed as he stopped me dead in my tracks. "President and top brass only, not until the end," he said in an ambivalent monotone, touching his earpiece and pushing me backward.

"Nice," I grunted.

He shrugged his shoulders, and the door closed.

Maravilloso, I thought. *Wonderful.* But so be it: they would need my gun, and I was a good shot. I lovingly kissed my sidearm for luck. These Sig Sauer P320s were solid shots, and I was solider. The President had enough guns covering her right now anyway, and she'd be locked away and hard to get to. They had reinforced that door, slowly, quietly, with as much ingenuity and outside-the-box thinking that even a few berserker gorgons working together wouldn't be able to get in there, because of its reinforced strength. Oh how I wished I was up there in a Raptor or Lightning to shoot a few of them out of the sky. But that would last only a few minutes for me, and I'd die a quick and probably painful death, thrown out of the sky by a berserker *gorgo* without even getting a missile off.

My mind was racing with these thoughts as I raced back down the hall toward the offices. I ran into Willis and Suzuki who were sprinting toward me, their rifles drawn, ready to post up. Foster and Marone were further down. In two seconds all four of them were perched with their rifles aiming over the ledge toward the bottom floor. Behind me and on the bottom floor were the conference rooms, and if we had to fall back or got trapped somewhere, we would definitely want to be in there, so we would at least have some communications.

My heart was thudding in my rib cage. This old body could keep up, but this was stressful, and they were coming for us. Why didn't we think they would come for us after realizing we now had such a potent weapon to use against them? *Hubris.* That's a weapon they used against us time and again as they beat us back down over the years.

Across from us I espied three low heads peeking behind the stock of their XM5s, aiming down: Sanchez, Frankfurt and Battle. Battle was a good shot, and he was aptly named, but Frankfurt was even better, and we would need her clear eyes. Sanchez wasn't too bad either. They all had sniper rifles over there. They had rehearsed this plan time and time again: the three snipers take the intruders below, and the four on my side would take any from above. Altogether, we were eight guns against who knows how many *gorgos.*

Intermittent chatter was coming from all over the hotel through the walkie-talkies. I snatched mine from my belt. "Central, Central, this is Monzon. The President is secure in the Nest. Sit rep, over?"

"Monzon, radio silence, they're coming, you idiot!" came an answering growl. I recognized that voice. *Cartwright.* I don't know where he was, but he was obviously able to see if they were coming. Hope briefly passed through me that Barnes had gotten to safety and was okay. He was a good guy.

So was my contact. I wondered if I would make it out of this in order to keep him posted of things in here, so we could continue helping each other. I tugged at my dog tags and kissed them quickly, trying to send a mental message to my sweet Rosalita, far away, to offer a prayer for us. She was so good at that.

Silence. We waited. Radio static burst briefly. The sound of a ticking clock in a room nearby. I could hear Suzuki breathing as I perched against a column, preparing to squint my eyes and not let them inside me. One look, and it was all over: we all knew that. All of us charged with the defense of the new White House, the 'Green House,' as we called it, knew that we couldn't look. It was shoot first, make sure you hit it, and then flee around a cor-

Yelling! Glass shattering below. I clenched my eyes and gritted my teeth. I looked briefly over the mezzanine railing at the lobby six floors down. Shapes. Dark shapes swirling amidst that accursed mist they put out, dashing between streaks of gunfire.

They were in! We had always kept the bottom floor fairly deserted so as to screen us off from them should they hover by outside. But now, they were *inside!*

Screams. All around us. Thunder to my left as Suzuki's gun erupted and a screech flew past us. A dark shape whizzed overhead and I let loose. *Adios, muchacho.* A shadow plummeted to the floor far below with a thud. I squinted my eyes and kept my free hand over my brow.

A horrific burst of glass directly above us, over the ninth floor. *Gorgos!* Four or five of them descended straight down through the atrium glass and swirled straight down toward the lobby, enshrouded in their deadly cold vapor. A brief thought of gratitude washed over me that perhaps the rest of them were still at BNA, and we would have to contend with fewer of them. One passed to my right, and I averted my gaze to look beyond it, hiding behind a column. I held still. Movement. I heard the sniffing and the grunting. To my right. I moved to my left. It shifted. I felt it breathing heavily as another shape swirled down from the top of the atrium glass. The thing behind me growled, hovering there, reaching. I moved. Back to my right. It went to my left. My right arm whirled back around the column while I kept my eyes straight forward. *Boom boom boom.* Mark down. Something screeched and flailed behind me, long dangling arms slapping against the railing for purchase, and gaining none. Another shape crashed to the floor below me.

I breathed a sigh of relief and looked over to my left. Willis was just standing there, his gun frozen, trained on a target. "Willis, get down!" I whispered, reluctant to draw any more to me. He didn't answer, and then I knew why. A large mass descended upon him, mouth outstretched, settling into his shoulder and tearing out a large mass. Willis didn't move or change expression, but his eyes filled with tears and something in him forced a reflexive grunt. The thing took another bite out of him. Willis' right arm dangled from its mouth. Tissue flapped loosely from the end of it, and I thought I saw white bone crushed into powder. Still, Willis didn't move.

The hell with that.

I took aim and fired repeatedly, my eyes shut tightly. It turned and sneered at me – I could tell even with my eyes closed – and I fired and fired. A gasp of fright and surprise emerged from its massive jaws, and it thudded to the floor next to Willis, knocking his prone form to the floor without changing posture. I barely opened my eyes to survey his dead form. He was also a good man.

That was almost it for me. I only had four shots left, and one mag remaining after that. I got up and bolted for the office, shutting the door behind me so I could reload. *Poor Willis*. I didn't see the others, but I heard the shots.

Then, suddenly, a concussion blast shook the floor. Someone had lobbed a grenade. Screeching! Wild screeching from outside the office, and a quick blur of wind shot past. Gunfire spraying into nothing. An agonized scream stopping short into muffled grunts…then…crunching: the sound of bone on bone. I knew what that was. Either Willis or Suzuki, since they were nearest to me. I shook my head. I wasn't going to let them all die. Hopefully, the snipers were getting some of them secretly while the machine gunners were making all that racket and drawing them to us.

I wrestled with my desire to stay here and take cover, knowing full well that they would eventually find me. Hiding was never for me. I lurched up, spun around, whipped open the door with my handgun brandished – and stopped short.

Right in front of me was a large gorgon with its back turned, and I stiffened. My arm moved of its own accord, straightening out and reflexively firing into the back of its head. Slime burst in all directions, along with brain matter and chunks of alien flesh. Something large smacked into me, a chunk of something from below its brain. The terrifying shape screeched and batted its hands at the air around it, flailing miserably, and then fell forward with a dull cry. I slapped my last magazine in fast. I kissed my P320 for luck and prayed over those last ten shots.

I looked down the hall to the south. Suzuki's body was right there. Gone. Just like that. He had tried to leap over Willis' body and keep running, but the one I just downed had gotten him first. I looked north. Foster and

Marone were still there, firing angrily in vain at what they thought were the last things they had seen, and desperately trying to avoid being frozen.

Out of either faith or foolhardiness, I ran toward them. I didn't look over or down, I just knew I needed to be there with cover fire, and they needed my good aim. And there is always power in numbers. But I was fleeing from the offices. Our only communication would be our walkie-talkies.

I heard less commotion far below, but that didn't mean anything. They could be fanning out and hunting, and I didn't know the fate of anyone, much less who exactly was down there. All I heard were the screams, and less gunfire.

More *gorgos* kept coming. Filling the air, almost oblivious to the three small figures on our side up above. I glanced over to the other side briefly amidst the mayhem, and all three snipers were still there. Those single shots weren't the rat-a-tat of XM5 gunfire that the *gorgos* were good at zeroing in on. And they were stealthy. They kept picking them off and then selecting new targets. That helped.

"Come on," I whispered to Foster, and he nodded quietly. He lightly tapped Marone on his shoulder, and we quietly got up and made our way into the hallway leading to the PEOC, tip-toeing down the corridor with our guns drawn. I glanced back and Marone was walking backward behind us, covering our six.

I thought I heard a commotion from up ahead somewhere, and I grabbed my walkie-talkie. "Nest, Nest, three at your door, over."

Without warning, the door to the Nest buzzed and burst open. The Agent who waved me off earlier came crashing through the entrance into me, firing back through the portal. He was missing his right leg and was white as a ghost. A horrid scream came from within. Yet he was still mobile! The *gorgo* must have gotten him without freezing him. It must have surprised him from behind.

I fell to the ground to the right of the door, and the Agent fell to the left. My eyes widened in dismay and fear, whipping over to him and raising his weapon back through the door. A streak of black the darkness of which I'd never seen shot through the door and smashed his corpse into the wall next to me, as plaster and splinters flew. I turned and fired. The *gorgo* was down before it could consume the rest of him. He was dead anyway.

At that moment, Marone's XM5 sounded loud and clear, as he sprayed bullets down the hall back from where we came. Bodies and black shapes fell back, and sparks flew all around the hallway entrance.

I jumped into the PEOC and pulled Foster and the other agent back in behind me by their lapels and fatigues. They tripped over the first Agent's corpse. The sound of sniper fire could still be heard out beyond the corridor, and the occasional burst of grenade, which sent angry tremors through the building around us. There was smoke everywhere out there.

"Marone, come on!"

Marone turned and ran toward us. I saw the thing behind him careening after him. I've never seen Marone run so fast. The *gorgo* sailed through the air behind him and had its long snapping arms in front of it, intent upon its prey more than it was intent on me, thankfully. I fired over him and gave it my last four rounds, dropping it in the hallway twenty feet shy of our door, skipping, flipping and sliding clumsily in a tipsy death roll toward us. Alien blood dotted the hallway.

Two more *gorgos* appeared down at the hallway entrance and shot toward us.

Marone crashed into me, almost passing the door. Foster and I pulled him in too, and slammed the door closed. The remaining Agent locked it and then pulled a heavy security wall over that from a hidden position within the closet. It had been hastily mounted to the wall at some point in years past.

Along the window wall were erected iron posts, barring the window from floor to ceiling as with fence posts, so as to prevent any entry from the outside. The President was screaming and pointing, standing in front of a smashed portion of the iron fence. That was where the *gorgo* had come through and gotten the first Agent. Where Graham had taken refuge in that, I didn't know. She was near hysterical, and her hair was in disarray, and she was covered in blood. She kept pointing and screaming something, but I couldn't understand her ramblings. I traced her eyes down to the floor at a small rectangular object positioned on a diminutive table near the window. Graham gave up pointing and fled into the next room which was even more reinforced than the entrance to where we were. Dull thuds sounded from beyond our door. Over and over. They wanted in.

I advanced toward Graham, noticing a spare XM5 lying on the business desk in the room. It was loaded. I moved toward where she was pointing. What was the object? I didn't know, though something panged in me. "Foster, man that door!" I screamed at him. Foster turned and took aim at the suite door should they burst through.

I moved toward the small table by the window. The window was open. I could hear a faint humming. Muffled yet rhythmic, it was putting out a pulse wave that rose and fell, rose and fell, but the volume wasn't very loud.

I heard screeching. Multiple alien voices outside the window crying, wailing, almost pleading for relief.

I remembered. The object! I'd seen it before, though small and a mile away at the airport warehouse. One of the DTF emitters. But why was it here? My eyes flashed to Graham. The screeching grew nearer. *Gorgos* were right outside, and they were all approaching the broken and bent aperture that they had repeatedly bashed through to get inside and cut off the infernal noise they were hearing; the infernal noise that had just taken out some of their own at the airport.

We were hemmed into a narrow place, flanked on both sides by the enemy. Our guns wouldn't do much.

I approached the black rectangle. Cables ran from it back under the bed, plugged into AC power.

Dark shapes moved outside. I could see them through the girders, cutting off the sunlight in their passage. I dropped my rifle and looked it over. One small glimmer of hope hit me.

The volume button, set at thirty percent.

Why thirty?

My eyes went wide. A dark shadow moved beyond the curtains of the room.

I seized the volume knob and cranked it all the way up to one hundred.

The dial spun.

The alien screaming soared to a fever pitch. Shadows fell from above the curtains outside, plummeting below. The dull thuds on the suite door stopped. The Agent, Foster, Marone and the President covered their ears, as I did too.

Dark, screeching shapes zooming toward us swerved aside and clumsily jerked out of view. Some of them exploded. I picked it up and held it straight in front of me. Other shapes all around the hotel fell to their ruin and burst asunder. A rhythmic pounding pulsated out of the small capsule of noise: such a tiny thing, yet utterly destructive to the enemy all around us.

I stared south. There were still other shapes over BNA. The airport was still under siege, but some of the shapes fled, to where I do not know. But they fled. What I was holding made them flee.

Yet how did it get here? Was it accorded to the President as a last measure of defense to protect her in the PEOC? Or was it placed here? If so, why was it only at thirty percent volume? Surely that would not be more than a troublesome annoyance to our enemy? Surely it would not drive them away.

But would it draw them here?

The answer dawned on me. Someone had placed it here, deliberately, to take out Graham, knowing that she would be taking refuge in here.

We couldn't stay in this room. Everything happened in a daze, and our ears pounded. The forms moved slowly around me, foggy. I grabbed Foster again, and the Agent, and we surrounded the President and moved her, slowly, out into the hall, to take refuge in a room across the hall. It was not the PEOC, and it was not reinforced. But the Nest was no longer secure, and we had to move.

I reached down to my waist for the walkie-talkie, in an attempt to radio anyone else I could. "This is First Lieutenant Monzon. Iron Maiden secure. Room 625. Repeat, Iron Maiden secure."

Cartwright didn't answer. I wasn't surprised.

No one answered.

So. We tested them, and then they tested us. We tested our equipment, and they tested our fragility and our patience. They had tested our whole Embassy, and we were found wanting. Heads were going to roll.

It would be a long time before we could emerge safely from 625, that I knew right away. We locked and bolted the door and then took up posts facing it and the window, instructing the President to lock herself in the bathroom.

Cartwright had attempted to assassinate Graham. She had to know. He was in charge of security. She had to know. And now he wasn't answering.

It wouldn't be long before we would find out how many lives were lost, and how many had paid for his assassination attempt.

I could hear Graham in the bathroom, cursing loudly. We whispered to her to please be quiet, but she would not be consoled. She was screaming into a pillow: angry, gurgling, choking cries of desperate rage, blood-curdling and gagging chokes of revenge-craving despair.

Graham had had enough, and Cartwright wouldn't like the bad news coming his way.

7 | MASKS

| Trudy |

Monday, January 18th, 2038, 1527 hours

They were getting close.

In another week or so, the masks would be ready for testing. It was just that simple, and it filled us with so much hope! I just hoped to God that nothing would go wrong. There was a *lot* that could go wrong.

Chance and I traded high-fives, and then we just smiled silently with somber, proud expectation that had all of our hopes pinned to it.

"We did it, Trudy," Chance said, and I nodded.

We gazed down at the crude thing we'd just finished. This was the prototype, and it was ghastly to look at. But it was something, and we needed *something*.

Raylin and Shelly milled about behind us. Charlotte, Eric and Brant were somewhere else. Gage was off with Joe.

Chance and I had been working most closely on this thing for so long now. The Major wanted an update, and we'd be able to give her one.

Major Bayless was a sweet woman. Not the kind of commanding officer you would think to find after gorgs knocked us all on our ass and drove us underground. You'd maybe expect to have hardened, gruff military guys with thick guns and limited vocabularies running around, their minds always on their guns. No. Hers was on computers, technology, science, all of it. She was so supportive of our efforts. And this would be a big stroke.

This was it. This was what we needed. Unless something bigger came down the pike, this was our first step. Right here. In Alpharetta. Our first step in fighting back against the gorgs. And me and Chance were the principal architects. I stared at it, willing my soul into it, willing all of my heart into it, and taking a deep, solid, sustained breath, projecting hope for everyone left, into this little thing.

Borosilicate glass. Would anyone get it? It came from boron oxide, silica, alumina, and potash. Resistance to thermal shock, high chemical durability, adaptability to fluctuating temperature or pressure changes. You could pour boiling water onto it, and it wouldn't crack. You could freeze it, and it would retain its properties. It had this magical magnetic deterrent built right into it, and if it was successful, we'd finally be able to look at one of those damned things and not pay the ultimate price. There was only one question remaining.

Who would be willing to pay that price?

We'd figure that out later. For now, Major Bayless kept in touch with the other Blockades regularly and kept them apprised of our progress, and now we'd be able to give her some real news. I was so excited.

I got up, gave Chance a big hug, and then stole out of there to find the Major.

We were getting close. So close.

8 | DESIRE

| Bassett |

Monday, January 18th, 2038, 1642 hours

There was no way around it. The gorgons' love of power was about to end.

"We have it, Joe. This is it. The Major gave her blessing to proceed ASAP."

I beamed at her. This girl. So fancy pants smart, and she and her team had done it. Her silly pigtails bobbed as she spoke so excitedly. I looked over at Gage, who was also beaming.

"It's time, Sergeant," he tossed at me casually, shrugging his shoulders. "She's right. We've never been this close. This changes the game entirely."

I took a deep breath and then puffed it out, turning back to look at her.

"Who's the volunteer?"

"Me."

"*Hell*, no," I said, without missing a beat. "No way, girlie. You're too important, and you know that."

"What, the others are less important? Gimme a break, Joe," she said, and her pig tails bobbed again. "You *know* I'm right! *I* designed this. This belongs to Chance and me!"

"Private Trudy, you enlisted for the science division, not for recon patrols. Not yet. You'll be able to go one day. Look at this!" I said, brandishing her own mask and holding it up before her. Her eyes darted over to it briefly, but her lips were pursed in frustration at me. "You did this. This might just save us all. If this does what you think it does, then we'll need you to figure out how to make it better. You and Chance."

She exhaled noisily, puffing hair out of her face. "See? *You and Chance.* You just said it yourself. Even if you lost me, you still have Chance. He knows what all of this is about, Joe. He and I worked on this day and night for all this time. He knows what he's doing! I'm talking…about *one* patrol."

"Allison-" I stopped myself. "Private Trudy, this is not something I can grant anyway. And even if I had the authority, I still wouldn't. I barely got Steph and Donner back from the last one. I almost lost my kid sister, girl. So don't think for one second" -here I pointed her own mask at her chest- "that I'm gonna let you march off to your own death holding what could be a touchstone of massive change for us. You're the catalyst." I noticed I was raising my voice. "You're the spark, Trudy. You and Chance started this in here, and in here is where you'll finish it. You got that?"

She looked at me, defiant and bristling. "I'm gonna talk to the Major."

"Fine!" I nearly shouted. "She won't let you go either; I promise you." Trudy started to walk out. "Private Trudy!" She didn't answer me, and then she was gone.

I looked over at Gage. He just shrugged.

• • • • •

Monday, January 18th, 2038, 1803 hours

I found her in her bunk. Steph said she saw her in the showers crying, and that she wanted to be alone. I gave her time and then proceeded to her quarters.

"Trudy, can I come in?"

"Go away," came a soft voice.

Apparently, she had gotten her answer from the Major, and I was right. Not being allowed on recon patrol was something that she couldn't stomach.

"Listen, kid, I just wanna," I fumbled. "I just wanna let you know I'm here for you. That's all."

Nothing.

I gave her a minute, pounded my fist softly against the wall outside her bunk, and then started to say something, but thought better of it. Better leave her alone for now. "Yeah. Okay. I'll see you at chow time maybe."

I pulled away from the door and started down the hall, wondering what that conversation must have been like. Had the Major gotten as heated at Trudy for asking? Had Trudy gotten as heated at Bayless as she had at me?

A sudden click and a sliding of wood on earth made me turn around.

Trudy.

I smiled at her weakly, while she just stared at me.

I gestured toward the Rotunda. "I, uh," I sluffed, moving closer to her. "I was just gonna meet Maureen and Steph for chow. You wanna join us? We can talk on the way of course."

Trudy was holding her left arm at the elbow with her right. She was mad, and I could see her biting her lip in frustration. But something in her softened. I knew she wasn't mad at me – not really. It's not like I had told the Major to hold her back. I think she knew me better than that.

Trudy slowly nodded and then turned and started off, not waiting for me. I jogged up to her. "Whoa, wait for an old guy," I laughed. She didn't.

We took a few slow paces, not looking at each other.

I gave it a moment and then started in.

"Trudy, you know how Maureen and I feel aboutcha. You're like our own daughter, girlie. We love you so much. You know that. This isn't personal. I was just saying the same thing the Major probably said to you. You're too valuable in here. I *know* you wanna get up to the surface. I do too."

I scanned her face to see if any of this was registering, but she was a brick wall.

I looked away and sighed.

"You like my mask?" she said at last.

I looked back at her in confusion. "Like it? Trudy, it could be a game changer. I mean it."

Allison looked at me slowly, blinking hard and tired. Her eyes were red from crying.

"I mean it, Trudy. Game changer. The Major thought so too, didn't she?"

She looked up at me slowly, and gradually nodded at a tempo that would age milk.

"Yeah, she did. She's excited about it."

I smiled. "I knew she would be. You're a spark, Trudy. You and Chance. Those things might just save lives someday. And you did that." She didn't acknowledge me.

I stopped her, grabbing her slightly by the arm.

"Hey. Seriously," I said, looking her straight in the eyes. "This could be the very beginning, girlie. Those guys up there? They're fighting the continuing battle. But down here, you're starting a whole new war. You and Chance have just given us something to maybe – *finally* – make a dent! With all this, this Toro-syllabus blast stuff," I said, waiting for it.

She looked up at me. "You're a geek, Sergeant Bassett," she sneered, and then that corner of her mouth tilted up into a smile. "*Borosilicate glass*. Get it right."

And then she punched me hard in my right arm.

"Ow! Hey! Take it easy," I said, clutching my arm, but I kept smiling at her.

She stared at me. "Thank you, Joe. I love ya, old man."

And there it was. That love for each other, every one of us down here, that would always win out. That love that kept us alive and in unity even when we were mad at each other. It was that love that would keep Trudy patient for her own time up there.

The human power of love would always win. There was no way around it.

9 | BREATHING

| Miguel |

Friday, January 22nd, 2038, 0342 hours

We were still alive, and that was something.

The President was snoring gently in the other room.

We listened night and day. Foster, the Agent (we found out his name was Grimstad), myself and Graham, holed up in Room 625, and we were growing more anxious by the day. Were any more left alive? Were any more dead? Was my Rosalita out there somewhere praying for me? She had to be worried since we'd not spoken. And what about my contact? Surely, he would have heard of the attack by now.

We'd been in here for a week. Thankfully, we had water, but we were all very tired and weak for lack of food.

Our walkie-talkies stopped working two days ago. We were tremendously hungry and growing stir crazy. The last we'd heard, estimates were that we had lost twenty-six souls, including the snipers on the mezzanine level.

Sanchez. Frankfurt. Battle. Gone.

That would mean we were down to seventy people, all told. I was just thankful to be alive, but we'd need to regroup. We needed to keep the President safe, but she was safe, and so were we. The same was true for the folks over there at BNA, though they had encountered heavy losses as well. They did as we were now doing, though they had far more emitters than we did. Last transmission before our walkie-talkies gave up the ghost was that they were doing exactly as we were, and running those *ghetto-blasters*, as Cartwright had called them, at maximum volume. And that had kept off the *gorgos*.

Where they were now, none of us knew, and none of us relished the thought of going back out there until we were certain that the Embassy was free of them.

As for Cartwright, I didn't know if he had made it or not. All I knew was that Graham would most likely have his head. If the *gorgos* didn't kill him, Graham definitely would for sure. Of that I was certain. I looked over at her sleeping there. I had to admit, once I left the captivity of this little room, I wouldn't want to think back on the primal, murderous thoughts that occasionally crept through my mind. I had to do some serious mental battle. If Graham was as bad as my contact said, she herself was going to commit murder on a massive scale. Would I be doing the world a favor by taking her out? Could I make it look like an accident? Would the world care? God forgive me.

The loud, rhythmic pulse continued unabated. On Day Two Foster couldn't take it anymore and started to lose it. The noise punches a hole through your peace and uppercuts your sanity, that's for sure. But for whatever reason, Agent Grimstad, the President and I did better with it. Grimstad had to knock him out. Foster eventually woke up with a newfound resolve to withstand it, and he decided to will himself to endure it like the rest of us. We kept it in the next room, and closed the door between there and here. None of us were willing to turn the volume down from one hundred percent: that might have been precisely what saved us and had kept us alive since then. We had never been attacked so bad at the Embassy. The losses were great.

I can't exactly describe the sound. It's a pulsation beyond the edge of hearing, but maddeningly present. Earplugs would have been nice, but I don't know what they would have offered that the sound couldn't punch through. It was a combination of deep, throbbing, rhythmic bass coupled with frequencies that were far more felt than heard. An assault on the senses, to be sure. What those boys at BNA engineered most certainly had the power to drive off the *gorgos*.

To pass the time we had told bad jokes. Graham had most of them. At times it felt like we were just humoring her, kissing up to her even when the jokes sucked, but it kept us in better spirits than if we were all sitting in silence in fear, propped up against the walls and waiting for our annihilation.

I looked over at Foster and Marone. "Esta bien, amigos?"

They looked away from the window briefly, nodding to me, and then returning to the blinds. Pretty sure they were scanning for any trace of darkness zipping across the skyline beyond our fragile curtains. In the darkness of the wee hours of the morning, they wouldn't have been able to discern any shapes against the night sky. But I guess it gives us humans some feeling of power to keep our eyes on things anyway.

I turned to Grimstad. "How you doin,' Grimstad? You holding up okay?"

"I'm holding up okay," he muttered. "Just hungry. Mention food and I'll punch you in the face."

I shook my head. "No mention of food here."

"Of course, you just said the word *food*, so now I have to punch you in the face."

I looked at him quizzically. "But you just said it too, just now, so I guess we have no choice but to do a Rocky III freeze frame?"

His eyebrows furrowed.

"You never seen Rocky III?"

He shook his head.

"Oh man, what a pity. Best boxing movie series of all time." I thought back. "Ya know, he said something in one of those movies, about taking as much as you can and still moving forward. He said it's not about how hard you can hit; it's about how hard you can *get* hit, and keep moving forward. I think we took a pretty big hit a week ago, but I see we're still moving forward."

"Are we?" Grimstad muttered again.

I shrugged my shoulders. "As much as we can, right? We keep moving forward as much as we can."

He said nothing.

I looked out through the curtains with Foster. "I don't know about you guys, but I'm ready to get outta here. If I don't get some food today, I'm gonna eat all of you guys."

"Now I have to punch you in the face," Grimstad said. "Come here."

"I'm good over here, thanks. Just giving you some food for thought."

Grimstad grunted.

Foster and Marone said nothing.

The President snored the night away, oblivious to any of our banter.

I chuckled to myself. Grimstad was big, but I doubt if he swung at me if he'd even connect without falling over from weak knees and headrush. Besides, this old man was tired, but he had thick guns to still take it *and* dish it out.

And speaking of 'dish,' that just brought food back to my mind. I meant what I said. We needed to get out of here today and get some food in our weakened forms. If we didn't, the next time they came they'd spare no expense and rip us to shreds.

All things in due time. We took the hit. We took a bunch of hits. But we were still moving forward, just like Rocky. And we'd keep moving forward, just like Rocky.

It was something that we were even still alive.

10 | RECON

| Rosie |

Saturday, April 3rd, 2038, 0933 hours

He was alive, and that was all that mattered.

I thought back to my husband being trapped in the Embassy with the President and a few men. It sounded horrible. But he was alive, and they now had technology to defend themselves against our enemy. It brought joy to my heart and hope to my soul. Soon, he said, the technology would be mass-produced and distributed along secret channels to the various Blockades, including ours. It would take a while to get them all done and get them here, but they were working on it. And they were working on other forms of disseminating the signal as well, which included nominal-yield explosives.

For all of that, I was so thankful.

Before he hung up, he told me that they had been unmolested since the attack, and that the new devices – he called them DTF emitters – were continuing to run. The soldiers at the airport had mounted some to their tanks and jeeps and drove them over to the Embassy. None of our enemy wanted to come anywhere near them while those things were putting out their signal. IThis was good news. They had brought *tons* of them to the Embassy.

"I love you, my sweet amor," I whispered to him. "*Ten cuidado,*" I said, urging him to be careful.

"I will," he whispered back. "*Té amo mucho, cariña.*"

He disconnected Zoom.

Gracias, Señor, I prayed. *Thank you Lord, for sparing my husband's life and keeping him safe.*

Miguel was okay, and now they were rebuilding and reinforcing the Embassy – and the airport – under the protection of this new technology.

So, one man was okay.

But he wasn't the only one.

Rutty and I sat and watched the communications in Command with the Halcyon Crew. The Captain was gracious enough to let us hear Corporal Shipley command his first platoon, as he went out on Recon patrol.

Jet had healed nicely. He and his brother were back to their true selves, serving with honor, pride, and determination. He had taken the time he needed, and he had resumed his post just before Christmas last year, and he had come back with stores, ammunition, and even found some straggling survivors.

Since that time, he had been on twenty-six missions, and had recorded six kills for the enemy. For meritorious service in battle, he was promoted to Corporal in March. His promotion ceremony was small, just the four of us in Stone's office. The Captain didn't have any medals to give for the promotion, but he recorded it and sent it up the chain. Corporal Shipley saluted him, and Stone saluted back.

After all of that, the Corporal voiced a solemn but grateful, "Thanks, Dad." I think Stone melted right then and there, and he took him into his arms and hugged him.

Rutty and I looked at each other approvingly. Rutty turned back to face the monitors in Halcyon and watch the mission, but I couldn't take my eyes off this young soldier. He was so alike his older brother, and yet so very different. He was coming up on his fifteenth birthday down here, blossoming into manhood, ready to do battle. Watching him, I could see that he himself was itching to get out there up top and wage his own war.

Both boys wanted vengeance for the loss of their father and sister. That much was clear. However, anytime that came up in conversation amongst the two brothers, Jet would always say something like "you're not ready, bro," and Rutty would scoff and shake his head.

I turned back to the monitors.

Today, here was Corporal Shipley on his first command, out there somewhere on the surface with Markus Jentzen, Sarah Ferro, Will Pettijohn, and Alex Santella.

At some point after her father's death, Nurse Ferro wanted to get out on the field. I don't remember when. The Captain had put out a call for more volunteers to serve in the infirmary, and we had more.

Private Sarah Ferro was essentially now pulling double duty as a nurse and a soldier. But no one really blamed her. I was fairly certain there was a spark of chemistry between Private Ferro and the Corporal.

Today marked her and Will Pettijohn's first patrol. The five of them were a team. A team that not-so-little fourteen-year-old Rutty here longed to join someday.

All things in due time. Safety first.

Corporal Shipley had had some scrapes already, been hemmed in, trapped, and besieged by the enemy. He had already lost men close to him: schoolmates, and fellow soldiers, desperate to go up to the top and make their mark, breathe fresh air, and get out of this underground enclosure, for some of them, for the very first time.

We watched the monitors.

They had left the Launch at 0900 hours and were now threading their way up Wheeler Road after leaving the cover of the forest. We could see them from the various cameras that had been posted in previous missions. Shipley was in the lead. The others were attaching more cameras to trees with zip ties and Velcro straps. Small devices with long battery life. Halcyon would verify the connection was good, and they would move on.

They were about a half mile to our northeast. They had mounted some cameras on a house less than five hundred feet south of them on Wheeler Road, and then a large shop just beyond that. The cameras clicked on, and the Halcyon techs verified connection.

I glanced over at the Captain. He had his fist to his mouth, watching in silence. He was quite obviously nervous. The stakes were high, and he didn't want to lose another good soldier, much less the son of his friend.

The platoon was stealthily nearing a muted-white house with a red aluminum roof that sloped up after a carport on the south.

One of the Halcyon members lurched forward toward his screen and belched out, "Uh, contact, eighty meters, north-northeast, bearing four-oh, four-two, four-six." I could see three dots at the top of his screen, some kind of infrared vision, drifting south toward the dots at the bottom center. Those were our team at the bottom. The dots at the top were clearly the enemy converging on their location.

I heard the Corporal breathe out "Hold!" and then "take cover!" to his team. They all quickly advanced inside the carport and waited. We could see them from a camera mounted over the front door of the house opposite them.

Just beyond where a rusty chain-link fence met a thatched red side wall leading up to the carport, they waited. The grass was six-feet high and bending over. A rusted-out riding lawnmower could dimly be seen through the tall grass in the yard behind the fence.

We held our breath. We couldn't see the team clearly; they were too far away, and the resolution faded as Halcyon zoomed in and around them, but we could hear them over the coms. The darkened room was a solemn environment: tense and foreboding, brightly illuminated only by the small rectangles the Halcyon technicians sat at, watching…listening…guiding.

Rutty cleared his throat, but it sounded like his throat caught. He was afraid.

The camera across the street saw them first. "Visual," said the same Halcyon tech. "We have visual. Incoming. Stand by. Range sixty-two meters. Hold position or take evasive inside."

"Confirmed, evasive," whispered the Corporal. The blurry pixels danced as we heard slight shuffling movement. They were making their way slowly, stealthily, up a set of steps.

"Fifty meters. Heading your way, team. Move," said Halcyon.

More movement that we couldn't see, and some staggered grunts.

"Door is locked, Command, we can't break it or pick it without noise," whispered Jentzen.

"Sit tight," said the Halcyon tech, turning to the Captain for confirmation and direction.

The Captain spoke up. "Alpha Team, they're inbound. Twenty-seven meters. You know what to do. You're ghosts. Just don't become one."

"Roger," whispered Shipley.

They were all holed up, and we could dimly perceive that all of them were squatting down so as to blend into the shadows below the porch at the back of the carport.

"Twenty-one meters, no change in bearing," said Halcyon.

We could hear their breathing.

"Eighteen."

We knew the drill as well as the team did. As well as *all* the soldiers everywhere did. They could not make a sound. If they did, they would jeopardize the safety of the entire team. And if one of the enemy discovered their whereabouts or seized upon one of them, the rest would have to flee.

"Contacts continue inbound, fifteen meters, bearing change, bearing change. Fourteen meters, bearing one-two, one-one, oh-niner. Repeat, coming to your north, down Wheeler. Stay still!"

Their breathing quieted. Rutty's and mine did not. I reached over and hugged him to myself. He had his hands in front of his mouth, balled up into a praying fist. He was barely looking over his knuckles at his brother.

"Team, here they come. Stay still."

The Halcyon tech didn't have to say that. At least not for our benefit. They swiftly came into view, down, down, down to the road, floating by, on the hunt, sniffing. We could all hear the sniffing. Our men made sure to rub themselves down with pine needles and berries, grass and ferns to mask their scent. But there they were, on the left of the screen, drifting south toward our dear friends, our soldiers. It reminded me of the account of Jet's father, Andrew, and the mission where we lost Markus' mother Nora. Sarah Ferro's father Ray and Will's father Adam were on that mission as well. And here we were again, three sons and a daughter of those lost, now on another mission with the enemy closing in. May we fare better this time, I thought, as I squeezed Rutty close to me.

"Nine meters. Seven. Six," said Halcyon.

The team said nothing, pressed down into the shadows and against the wall of the house in the darkened carport.

The enemy was almost upon them. They drifted closer.

"Five meters, team. Four."

Here they come, I thought. *Father, protect them.*

Shipley said nothing.

"Three. Two. Hold tight."

In utter silence we watched three hideous shapes float by, slowly, all seemingly looking ahead, up, at the sky, or to their right, while our team cowered to their left. I heard the ever so slight crack of knuckles as fingers gripped around a gun being brandished. There was no sound beyond that.

The enemy passed our team by as wordlessly as our eyes passed over each monitor, holding our collective breath. Our chests heaved full of air, jaws clenched, hands clasped.

The Captain didn't move.

Nor did our team.

A pin could drop, and we would hear it. Indeed, we could almost hear the fluid in all of their eyes scanning to their left as the enemy drifted by.

Fortune never favors the faithful forever.

The enemy suddenly paused, stretched their arms out, and began arching their necks, bobbing up and down. It was never a calming sight; it usually meant they smelled something or were on to their prey. And then, to confirm what we suspected, they started jetting out their deadly cold mist. A cloud of blue-green haze swirled around their venomous bodies.

"No," breathed out Rutty silently, and his arms tightened.

"No," muttered the Captain simultaneously.

The enemy continued to hold there for a moment, and then they craned their heads around and began sniffing. We could all hear it. They were searching.

Ever so faintly over the com, we heard Shipley whisper, "Command, permission to engage?"

"Granted," said the Command over the com. "Defend yourselves at all costs. And get back here as soon as you can."

One of the enemy hissed. They were moving around, fanning out, snapping their long fingers and cracking their bony arms, bobbing their stunted heads. And hissing. Always hissing.

I saw the faintest trace of movement from across the street inside the carport. One of our team was slowly rising up and taking aim.

"Hold. Hold until the time is right!" whispered Shipley far under his breath.

"Confirm, hold!" whispered the Captain in reply.

They continued to move. They were in search and destroy mode. They were hungry, you could tell, and they wanted our men. One of them, the northward one, was drifting ever closer. My body tensed and my nerves were on fire. This was going to end badly. *Father, please protect our soldiers!* I breathed.

They were almost on us!

Suddenly, one of the team rose up and engaged. The nearest enemy was suddenly aware of him. It made a sound I never want to hear again, even over a tiny speaker. Before it could move in, the soldier sprayed it with gunfire. It's left arm went flying off, pulverized and separated from its body, cut down by machine gun fire.

Yelling. Lots of yelling.

The other two of the enemy circled back, and around, and tried to approach from a different angle.

Multiple overlapping screams and yells, grunts and wheezes.

All of them were now running.

More gunfire. Some of them connected with the camera across the street and Halcyon's vision went to black. We reflexively spasmed as the sound of shattering plexiglass and plastic sounded. Then the video cut out.

But we could still hear them. Running. Running for their lives, all of them. Shipley was issuing commands I couldn't make out, and Ferro was screaming. Or was that Jentzen? It was a high-pitched shriek. I couldn't tell who it belonged to.

The enemy scattered and regrouped from a different angle, pursuing them. It was hysteria and pandemonium, and it reminded me of the attack on September 3rd, 2026, when they all activated. All we could do was run. All they could do now was run. Down the road. Through the forest. Firing behind them in a desperate attempt to connect. We could hear swooping noises and gurgling hisses, coming close to them, followed swiftly by gunfire, flame thrown from an incendiary weapon, and small arms fire.

They ran.

Stone lurched behind me and grabbed a walkie-talkie on a ledge against the back wall, perched next to the giant supercomputer they had in here that they called 'The Beast.'

"Launch, Stone, Launch, Stone, man the guns now! All men to the gun towers!"

The gun towers. Our last hope to keep them away. Soon, across the horizon, those men in their turrets would see springing from the trees five desperate lives hoping for sanctuary, the very warmth of their blood stolen from them as they sprinted for their lives in a cold sweat.

Continued crunching of branches and twigs intermingled with the horrendously close reports of a salvo of gunfire sounded loud and clear over the coms.

I heard Shipley. "Gorgs, overhead, overhead, shoot! Not that way, Markus! Follow me! *Run,* with everything that's in you, *run,* dammit*!!*" he screamed.

"Shit! *Shiiiiiiit!*" exclaimed Santella, and it sounded as though he was spraying gunfire in all directions. We all just watched each other in that small computer room of Halcyon's, desperate to conjure up any kind of imagery connoting victory for our men out there. We were truly desperate.

Rutty put his hands over the back of his head and let out a choking cry.

The walkie-talkie squawked and someone replied. The Captain instantly ran out toward the Launch.

"Halcyon to Alpha Team, you're almost there, move your asses!"

Screams. Punctuated screams mixed with desperate panting and horrid breaths fueled by adrenaline and raw primal fear. Five of them. Coming through loud and clear.

More firing.

Suddenly, one of the Halcyon techs switched his monitor, and there they were. We could see all of them, practically *leaping* from the forest. I perceived them almost in slow motion. Rutty did too. Running for their very lives, and firing behind them, not daring to look and risk locking eyes with those things.

One look, and it's all over. We all knew that rule. We knew it painfully and all too well. We had discovered, by now, that they need to be at least within thirty feet of you to begin their deadly telepathy, but that was thirty feet too close. And they were getting closer.

Our soldiers ran.

"You're five hundred feet from the Launch. You got this. Move!" screamed the Halcyon tech, standing up and still staring down at his monitor.

Suddenly, the ground above us shook. Deep, sustained booming echoed through the earth above us, and silt drifted down onto our faces as we looked up.

The gun towers.

"Three fifty. Move, move, move!"

They ran. We could see them all on the monitors. And we could see the things behind them, lurching up over the trees and preparing to dive bomb. They were getting closer, daring to approach us, though they knew where we were, and they knew not to get too close.

"Two hundred feet! You're almost in! One fifty!"

Boom boom boom. Rutty turned away from the monitor. The sight of his older brother fleeing for his life was too much; he couldn't watch. If things went wrong, he would see all of it. He wasn't prepared to witness that. I held him close as I watched.

Here they came. And then, here *they* came. The enemy. I silently cursed them, squinting my eyes at the tiny dots on the horizon drawing ever nearer to our precious souls, willing vengeance and anathema over them: scourges, plagues, any kind of torment I could muster up in prayer. Yet, still, they came.

"Eighty feet! Halcyon to Launch, open the doors now, now, now!" screamed the tech. Someone answered something on the other end.

All five of them were still alive. It would be utterly cruel if we lost one at the last second. I closed my eyes. All I could do was listen now.

I heard the thunderous reverberations of the guns above us.

I heard the muted pounding footsteps as they sprinted for the doors.

I heard the blood pounding in their veins.

I heard the guns again, and the agonized screech of the enemy being obliterated in the skies far from us.

I heard the Captain down the hall yelling something.

I heard Rutty's soft cries into my shoulder.

And then…I heard commotion and thumps as five bodies flew over the threshold into the Launch.

I heard the tech. "Go for close, seal it up!"

I heard the doors close.

And then I heard rejoicing. Laughter, even. But I wasn't ready to laugh yet. Nor was Rutty.

He tore out of my arms and fled up the passageway to meet his brother and the team.

And I stood there, hearing my own blood pound through my head as I tried to breathe.

Another recon mission with only marginal success.

A few cameras planted and a bit of sundry ransacked from a few houses.

Some fruit picked from the trees.

Such tiny gain at the near expense of five lives. One step forward, potentially five steps back. Would it ever be truly worth it in the end? Would all of this make sense someday?

One could only hope.

They were alive, and that was all that mattered.

11 | HANDS

| Bassett |

Saturday, May 1st, 2038, 1428 hours

I held a few hands up. "You gotta play the hand you're dealt, right?" I said.

Trudy looked at me quizzically, applying her lip balm once more.

"I'm serious! You can't just swap out cards if you get a bad hand, kid," I laughed. "It doesn't work that way. This isn't Go Fish."

Steph snickered playfully and watched, standing beside us.

"What's Go Fish?" Trudy said with a tilt of her head.

"Never mind. Before your time." I looked at her in mock-disapproval as she held her hands up in a helpless posture. We hadn't even started playing the game yet and she was already trying to rewrite the winning strategy. I guess I wasn't surprised. *Little innovator.* I glanced up at Steph as if to say *what's with this girl?* She just chuckled.

I scooped up the cards and shuffled them again like a pro. Trudy smirked at me and put her hands on her hips, watching and waiting.

"Now. Let's go through it again," I said. "The goal of poker is to make the best five-card hand using a combination of your cards and the community cards. The player with the best hand wins the pot."

"I got that."

"Good. Ok, both of us get two cards, we lay 'em face down, and these are the 'hole cards.' K?" She nodded. "Then we keep five cards face up. Those ones are the 'community cards.' These last ones we all share, and you can use them with the hole cards to make your hand. We'll take turns betting on the whole value of our hands in what's referred to as 'betting rounds' or 'intervals.' Savvy?"

"I think so. Sure. Yeah."

I snickered. I think I already lost her. "Anyway, before dealer deals, you have to contribute your initial amount, called-"

"Ante! I know that one," she proudly exclaimed, cracking her fingers.

"Good job! Win for the womenfolk," Steph joked.

"Nice job, girlie. You ante up. Then, during the game, you can fold your hand at any time. Ya got all kinds of hands you can have: high cards, pairs, three of a kind, straights, flushes, and of course full houses. Aces are the highest pair, and a full house, or 'boat,' is three of a kind plus a pair. I'll walk you through it as we go. It's all about keeping your poker face on, even if you got a crappy hand, you never let me know. K. And then after the last round of bets, if you haven't folded yet – which you will, 'cause I'm

gonna school ya proper by kicking your poker ass proper –
then you show your hand, and the player with the winning
hand takes home the pot."

"Right. Okay," she said, "I kick your ass and I get the
pot, which I'm gonna do because you're old and I have that
new poker smell."

I guffawed to myself and shuffled again. This girl
was about to go down.

$$\bullet \quad \bullet \quad \bullet \quad \bullet \quad \bullet$$

How in the world women keep beating me at poker
when I've just trained them, I'll never know. Steph looked at
me with playful pity, as I rolled my eyes, shook my head, and
folded. I looked at Trudy, sitting across from me with her
proud smile and exuberant charm, pigtails bobbing in a tiny
follicular victory dance.

My head drooped, resigned to my defeat, then my
eyes met Trudy's again. She had beaten me soundly, and she
was reveling in it. I shrugged my shoulders. She and Chance
had already been promoted to Sergeant by Major Bayless for
their work on the mask technology. Now she was just one
rank under me. The woman was going places and knew how
to play her cards.

I held my hands up. "You gotta play the hand you're
dealt, right?" I said, smiling.

12 | MAUREEN

| Bassett |

Saturday, May 12th, 2038, 0732 hours

There would never be another, for my whole life.

That's what I said to her, in my vows. I remembered back to the way she looked in her pretty white dress, her done-up hair and god-awful perfume that made us both sick.

I loved her then, and I loved her now. I stroked her hair lovingly and kissed her again.

Rarely did we get a chance to make love in this place, what with all the people passing by outside our bunks, and everyone able to hear damn near everything in here. The times we could, oh boy, what cause for rejoicing. I was forty-eight years old, but I still had it. So did she.

I laid back down beside my bride.

"Remember when we first had to bail and come here?" I asked her.

"I try to forget it," she said, and she scooped the hair out of her face. "I'm just glad we're here."

I smiled. "Me too, hon. I can't imagine how hard it must have been for all those families to bring all their young kids in. Nightmare."

That sent me back to some conversations I had had with a mom at another Blockade. I think it was the one in Clarksville.

"Remember that gal I used to talk with up in Clarksville? They had three kids, and even lost one of them right there in their Blockade after a gorg got in."

Maureen gasped.

"Yeah," I said, nodding and turning to her. "Their daughter. Gorg flew in through their Launch during some kind of malfunction and got her. Horrible. And then, later, Melissa died of lung cancer. She was such a sweet gal. Couldn't believe it when I called up there and got someone else. And then her *husband* dies last year, killed by a gorg, leaving the two sons. They said he threw himself between the gorg and his oldest son. Heartbreaking, yet so courageous.

"Just goes to show you how awful it is wrangling the kids, keeping them safe and staying an intact family unit. And all those years in there, together, just trying to assure them that it'll all be okay someday. How hard must that have been with little ones?"

Maureen didn't reply; she was lost in her thoughts. I knew she was thinking of my desire that we had had kids, but now, probably, even more grateful that we didn't.

"Just crazy," I ended, and then I turned to her and looked deep in her eyes. She had these blue-gold eyes, and one of them had a bit of a darkened wedge below the retina, stemming out from the center. *It's just a slight imperfection* her doctor had said many years before. But that just made her all the more perfect. I could get lost in that wedge and never come out again. I just stared at her.

"I love you, darlin.' So much."

"I love you, babe," she echoed. "So much. I'm so glad to have you, and so glad that you're mine. I worry about you out there too, but I'm glad they're keeping you down here more for science."

We had one of the bigger Blockades. I guess that was the result of Alpharetta – and other cities closer to the east coast – getting so hard hit. More survivors driven underground. There were roughly two hundred of us in here, and they were still digging, to this day, burrowing out more passageways. That thing they used – the big drill – finally gave up the ghost, and so it was manual labor. But I suppose that was the way it was everywhere else too.

As a result, we had more people to spare, so they could use more out on recon and spare some for in here. I wasn't getting any younger. I was approaching fifty, after all. My body was more suited for a desk jockey than high-tailing it away from gorgs up there on the surface. We were making progress down here with biology and these masks.

"Yeah, well, that makes two of us. Every time I go up top, I wonder if I'll ever get to have some of your jambalaya again."

"Oh, is *that* all you'd miss?"

I smiled at her. "Of course not," I assured her, waiting for maximum effect. "I'd miss poker with Steph."

She didn't waste any time fetching a pillow and smacking me upside the head with it. I laughed and tried to defend myself but lost my grip and fell off the bunk. Cold, naked, aging body met cold, naked, aging earth, roughly, as I tried to shush her since it was early. She just kept laughing,

laughing…scooting over to pummel me over the side of the bed even more.

I jerked myself up and grabbed her balancing arm as she tried to swing again, pulling her down on top of me as she squealed. I covered her mouth and held her tight as she softened in my embrace.

"People are tryin' to sleep in here, ya barbarian," I giggled. "Now, I'm gonna let you go, but one more scream, my little Ace Queen, and I'll have to play my final hand."

I slowly withdrew my cupped hand from her lips. Her hair, falling in streams above me, tickled my face.

"Oh, and what is that?" she inquired deviously.

I smirked at her. "I'm gonna flush you royally."

"Oooh, I love when you talk cards to me," she smirked. "Ante up, big guy."

I kissed her, deeply. "You asked for it. Just, let me get back on the bed please; there's a rock or a root or something sticking into my back!"

Maureen laughed. I loved that laugh. I loved her, and that laugh, deeply, forever.

There would never be another Ace Queen, not for the rest of my life.

13 | HOPE

| Miguel |

Tuesday, May 18th, 2038, 0916 hours

Hope is a funny thing.

We can pin it to things, send it all the way up to God for something we need, unify it with prayer, attach it as an addendum to something we're interested in, et cetera.

But here in Nashville, just a stone's throw away from the President, we were beginning to see some real hope.

I hadn't heard from my contact in a while, but I had briefed him about this new DTF technology. It had been four months since the attack on the Embassy. The DTF emitters – now we had tons of them on the roof *and* at ground level – were still running like champs, as a steady throbbing all around us. We were using earplugs now, all of us, except in the innermost rooms, though they didn't completely block out the felt, muted pulsations night or day. It was harder to sleep because of the noise, but it became easier to sleep figuring we wouldn't be attacked again.

The President had formed strategic plans to mass-produce the DTF technology, and those plans were underway. Cartwright had implemented them in January.

And now, we had received word out of Blockade DN282 in Alpharetta that the science team there had developed some new mask technology that was showing promise in deflecting the *gorgos'* deadly telepathy. They were continuing to test it. This was a one-two punch that just might give us the upper hand! The President immediately ordered Alpharetta to perform continued testing on them, and, once their prototypes had been confirmed effective, to get them down to BNA for mass production.

We finally had hope for the future. There was just one problem. *Colonel Cartwright.* No one had seen or heard from him for over a month.

President Graham had gone to his office shortly after the attack, once it was safe for us to come out again. She brought Agent Grimstad and assigned another to her protection detail along the way. She brought me along too. I will never forget her face when she found him hiding in a small side room on the second floor, hiding with Leah. Her clothing looked disheveled. We had guesses as to that. Barnes was nowhere to be found.

She stood before him, arms crossed, jaw clenched in barely suppressed rage. You could have drawn an angry line from her eyes to his. She spoke no words, just staring at him, while he withered in the power of her gaze. You could swear she was a *gorgo*, freezing him there and then. He was practically groveling on his belly when she suddenly barked out some orders and released him from her stare.

Cartwright was sweating. He had been caught, or, at least, he thought he had. Why the President didn't confront him on what she knew to be true – what we all knew to be true – is beyond me. But I got the sense that she uses people, and she was now using Cartwright to spearhead the widespread manufacture of the DTF emitters over at the Amazon warehouse at BNA. He was to get that going, and report back at regular intervals. She also ordered him to amass whatever he could in the way of tanks, jets, choppers, APCs, C-17s, RVs, jeeps, M3 Bradleys, SUVs, M9 armored vehicles, amphibious vehicles, ATVs, motorcycles, etc. *Anything* that could possibly be used in military defense as well as to disseminate the DTF emitters around the globe. Also, she wanted several large-scale DTFs to be developed and shipped off to our friends in Europe, but she didn't say why, and we didn't ask. For now, they brought hope, and maybe that's all that she was trying to do.

That was in January, and Cartwright kept it up through April.

Then, the Colonel vanished.

Barnes was found dead a week after the attacks, on the third-floor stairwell. At least, that was his ID badge lying amidst body parts and crumpled clothing floating in a pool of blood dripping down each stair. Poor Barnes. When I saw Cartwright and Aponte in that office, it only made sense that they had left Barnes to fend for himself. Or, perhaps Leah Aponte had pleaded to her boss to let him in, but he hadn't relented. Barnes was doomed. And, judging by Leah's clothing when she and Cartwright were found, no one was pleading for anything except a quickie.

And now, it appeared, Cartwright was doomed as well. A sweep of the building was conducted, radioing for him on all channels. We never found him. His keys were in his drawer, nothing appeared out of the ordinary, and he had talked to the guys over at the BNA warehouse to see how the manufacturing was coming along. So said the President.

Then…gone.

The search yielded little else.

Except for the note.

Yesterday, I was returning to my quarters on the seventh floor. I opened the door, and there was the note, blowing across the floor with the A/C.

My eyes squinted at it. Obviously if someone wanted to send me a message, there were the walkie-talkies. But that was either on limited channels, or the open one. Or, they could have done it publicly in the cafeteria, or at any of our meetings.

No, this was meant to be clandestine, and was meant for my eyes only.

I quickly closed the door behind me and retrieved the note. Unfolding it slowly, hastily scrawled on crumpled paper, it read:

Cartwright. Graham did it. I saw it. Meet me in Office 520 at 2200 hours.

I knew then what I had suspected, and I knew then what I had to do.

•   •   •   •   •

Tuesday, May 18th, 2038, 2200 hours

Standing outside the office, I glanced both ways. No one up or down the corridor. Cartwright was in charge of the cameras now that my contact was gone, but Leah had been reassigned and there was no Barnes, so I had no idea who might be watching me. I had to go in.

I opened the door, and my hand went for the light switch. In the pitch-black void of the room, a deep, husky voice stopped me.

"Keep the light off."

I pulled my hand away from the light switch.

"Close the door."

I complied, closing the door quietly behind me.

"Did anyone see you come here?"

"No, at least I-I don't think so," I stammered. It was hard to tell. I didn't even know which cameras worked anymore after the attacks.

"Did you tell anyone about our meeting?"

"No, I promise you. Please! What's going on? Who are you?"

The smell of second-hand cigarette smoke wafted my way.

"I'll ask the questions here, if you don't mind."

I put my hands up, though I'm sure he couldn't see me. "*Esta bien*," I said.

"What is your allegiance to President Graham?" I saw the faint signature of an amber cigarette butt as he took a drag, blowing it outward.

I thought to myself momentarily. *My allegiance?* I didn't know if this person knew about my contact, or my suspicions, or my wife, or anything. But I had to play along.

"I follow my orders, sir. I follow the orders of the President of the United States of America and all those above me." I was slowly moving closer toward him. I needed to know who it was.

"That's far enough," the voice stopped me. I stopped in my tracks and put my hands up. *Night vision? Could he see me?* "What do you know of the attack on the Embassy in January?"

"I-I was here. I was here for the whole thing. And then I got trapped in the PEOC with the President, her agent and some colleagues."

Another drag on his cigarette. Another faint amber glow. Another puff of smoke.

"And what happened right before the gorgons fled?"

This man was either in the room with us that night, unbeknownst to us, or watching us on camera, or had been informed about it. How could he know? Surely there was no way he was in the room with us!

I thought back to that night. "I discovered a DTF emitter, at low volume, positioned in the Nest, near the window. It was attracting the gorgons."

"And who put it there?"

"I have my suspicions."

"Who put it there, Lieutenant Monzon?" he pressed me.

I gritted my teeth. "I," I started. "I *think* it was put there by someone who didn't like her very much."

"Colonel Cartwright."

I said nothing. The voice sounded somehow strangely familiar, though muffled.

"And have you confirmed this?" he pressed.

"I've confirmed nothing," I said through the darkness. "The President came to her own conclusions about it and confronted him, though she never accused him to his face."

"And what does the President do with those she doesn't like?"

"What do you mean by that?"

The voice paused. "It was clear, was it not, Lieutenant Monzon, that there was tension between the

Colonel and the President, yes?" *Something* in that voice had the bite of familiarity to it, like a cold slap on the face to wake an uneasy sleeper.

I faltered for a moment, but then answered. "I think that's safe to say."

"So, again," he pressed, "what does the President do with those she doesn't like?"

"I assume she gets rid of them, I-I mean, reassigns-" I stopped in my tracks. *She reassigns them!*

I bolted back to the door and hit the lights, whipping my head back to the corner of the room from which the voice came.

There he was, sitting there, upright, in his fatigues, war-torn, suited up for battle, looking every bit the part of someone who had just journeyed ninety-three miles from north to south, amidst *gorgos*, amidst hot spring days, amidst fear, terror and loneliness.

It was him. My contact.

Captain Vance Cardona.

A smile seized my face and contorted my lips up my cheeks until I thought I would split at the ears.

"Brother!" I whispered ecstatically, running toward him. *"Hermano!"*

He smiled and rose slowly.

I practically tackled him with a hug. I couldn't believe it. My contact was here. How he had gotten here, I had no idea…over all that terrain, sleeping out in the open, using what tunnels had been built thus far, surviving alone, flitting between thousands of shadows along the way…he had done it. I was blown away. But exactly why he had come, I had no idea. Be that as it may, he obviously knew what had happened, and knew about Cartwright. He was, after all, in charge of security and surveillance here. Must have left a back door open for him to keep tabs on us from Mammoth Cave.

"Brother!" I said again.

"Shhhh!" he quieted me. "No one can know I'm here, man."

"I know, I know," I said, giddy as a child, "but – I mean – where – how did you…?"

He smiled again, and I could smell the heavy tar of his cigarette up close. "In due time. Took me two weeks. Me and Hollingsworth. He's here somewhere. Blending in."

"I can't believe it," I said, feeling like I was looking at a ghost. "Is everything okay up north?"

"Fine, fine, I assure you. Things are in motion. Me getting reassigned? Best thing that could have happened. Now I can do everything I need to do without Graham bird-dogging me and looking over my shoulder. This way she doesn't know anything about anything."

I beamed. "I cannot begin to tell you how glad I am to see you, brother."

"The Resistance is growing far and wide, Miguel." My heart pounded with joy to hear that. "It's spreading exponentially," he said again, and then he looked at me sternly. "I watched as she snuffed out the Colonel, Miguel. Obviously, her beef with him was strong enough so as to take him out. That's what she does. She sent Grimstad. Her Agent. Him and another guy."

I nodded. I knew Agent Grimstad.

"The two of them, at her orders and while she watched, took him out and tied him to a pole not two hundred meters from here. They attached something to him, some kind of claxon or something, must have gotten it from BNA. Dead of night while no one was watching. That drew them in. They froze him and then tore him apart, Miguel."

My stomach churned.

Even as my stomach revolted at the thought of what she had done, my heart filled with hope. Here before me was the catalyst. The enigma. The nexus to deliverance. It was bad enough we were dealing with the *gorgos*; we also had to contend with a President who had dangerous and nefarious intentions and motives. She was desperate to hold on to power. Conspiring with her precious counselors. And now, eliminating dissenters. And here before me was the man who had discovered all of it and had started a groundswell of uprising against her while we worked on an uprising against the *gorgos*. Two missions, two enemies, one hope: deliverance.

Hope is such a funny thing.

14 | RUTTY

| Rosie |

Saturday, June 12th, 2038, 1427 hours

The song swirled through the heart of the Pavilion.
Happy birthday, dear Rutty, happy birthday to you!
There he was, this young man, one year older, and now fifteen. In a year, he could enlist, and join his brother up on the surface. He would also graduate next year from the feeble impromptu schooling system we had down here. It was schooling, sure, but not enough academically to equip you to become anything other than a soldier.

That may have been Rutty's plan all along, however. From the traces and bits of our conversation where he talked about his older brother Jet, he always seemed to perk up, envious of Jet's valor, regard, position and esteem. He longed to prove himself.

He was living in his brother's shadow.

Today, however, was all about him. Several of his classmates surrounded him, showering him with makeshift gifts.

The new teacher, Mr. Arnold, was a rather stoic, bristling figure. Hard to read, robust, and stern. But, on the rare occasion he would actually smile, it could light up a room. I had had one or two counseling sessions with him and always encouraged him to smile. For now, he kept up his smile, and he gave Rutty a firm handshake and congratulated him, handing him another gift to put in his pile.

Baking had been relearned down here. We didn't have wheat, but we did have rice, potato, almonds, soy, lentils, oat, barley, and the like, from the hydroponics. So, that's what they used, and they baked Rutty a cake. What berries they could find up above – what berries actually made it back to the Blockade and didn't fill the stomachs of the soldiers on the way home, that is – were pressed into jam, and then smeared across the top. Our cakes were more natural, less synthetic. They were filling!

Today, there was a huge one. Rutty was an important figure down here. He ran errands for the Captain, just like his brother. He replenished ammunition from the gun towers. He helped serve in the mess hall. He was on cleaning detail. He sat and encouraged those in solitary confinement and in medical isolation when they were sick. He was every bit a missionary in here, communicating worth and encouragement wherever he went. I was so proud of him.

The Captain came up to me, wiping his hands free of the piece of cake he had just devoured. I was standing on the periphery, arms crossed, watching all of our youth cavort with and celebrate Rutty. His older brother, Corporal Jet Shipley, was sitting further up on the stage at the end of the Pavilion with some of his patrol cohorts.

"Afternoon, Señora Rosie," Stone greeted me, and I turned to him.

"Hola, *Capitan* Stoney! Nice to see you. Our little man is fifteen today."

He shook his head. "It's so hard to believe. He was just three when he came here."

"Mmm-hmmm. And next year he'll graduate and enlist, just like the rest of them."

"Yes, he will," the Captain said, and then he fell silent. I looked sidelong at him. He was watching Rutty intently, and I could see that he was second-guessing himself. Perhaps images of the late Lieutenant, Rutty's father, were passing through his mind, and he was unsure whether he wanted to commit Andrew's youngest to the battlefield. Or perhaps he had other aims. One could only guess. 'Stoney' was sometimes stone-faced.

"That is, if Jet lets him," Stoney said. The Captain turned to me. "Not gonna be easy having both of those boys up top," he said.

And then I knew I had guessed right.

One of Rutty's classmates offered a song for him, something that she had been working on. We had an old, beat-up guitar down here for those times where we could gather in worship and music, but I didn't know this song.

Fight on, fighter. Don't let anyone steal your fire. Fight on, fighter. The Spirit is alive inside ya, yeah... I was there on the day that you were changed. You were scared and prepared for the heartbreak. Everything you knew faded out of view, stole a piece of you. If I could, oh, I would be a hero. Be the one who would take all the arrows. Save you from the pain, carry all the weight. But I know that you're brave. Fight on, fighter. Don't let anyone steal your fire. Fight on, fighter. The Spirit is alive inside ya, yeah... There's a part that you hold that you lock down. Let it breathe, give it wings, set it free now. Time to make ya walk, break the prison bars. Show them who you are. Fight on, fighter. Don't let anyone steal your fire. Fight on, fighter. The Spirit is alive inside ya, yeah...

Rutty beamed as the words were sung his way. We all sat captivated as the girl serenaded him. The Pavilion was darkened and lit only with candles all the way around, and we felt the reverberation of hope, worth, and valor swirling around all of us. What were we all, if not fighters? What was Rutty?

The Corporal got up, strode over behind Rutty, perched on an upturned log as his friends were, and wrapped his arms around his little brother from behind. He put his head against Rutty's, and then patted his chest, as Rutty smiled and patted Jet's arm in turn. Jet turned his head and planted a huge kiss on his brother's cheek. Rutty scrunched his face as his friends laughed around him.

The Corporal released him and then slugged him in the shoulder. Rutty turned to try and fire a return hit, but lost his balance and fell from the log perch. All of us laughed in earnest at the brothers' love and playful antics. It was whole. It was needed.

And all the while, the girl continued to sing.

The song swirled through the pavilion of my heart.

15 | LEAPFROG

| Bassett |

Tuesday, August 24th, 2038, 1427 hours

It was inevitable. I should have known.

The Major presented the news to me on a thin sheet of paper with a red stamp at the top. "What's this?" I asked, sitting up, standing, and then saluting.

"Read it," she said.

I looked down and there it was. Sergeant Allison Trudy, along with Chance Davis, had been promoted to Lieutenant, effective immediately, by order of the President. Trudy's mask had been sent up on a recon op, deliberately designed to be tested in the field. Steph volunteered. I strenuously opposed it, but the Major allowed it. Maureen and I white-knuckled it the whole mission, watching on the monitors.

They only went out ten feet from the Launch and rang the dinner bell with an air horn. A gorg heard it of course – any one of them would have heard it from a mile away – and it flew down and posted up in front of her. She just stood there with Trudy's mask on. She slowly opened her eyes. The thing looked at her and came up close. But my kid sis was still alive and breathing.

That was all they needed. The others opened fire and blew it to shreds. Steph collapsed, weak in the knees and heavily nauseated. They brought her back in and closed the Launch doors. Aside from feeling mildly queasy and a little stiff, she had made it. *She had made it!* We now had something that worked, and my kid sister survived.

Oh, I was angry that they let Steph volunteer, but I was relieved that she was okay. She was now in medical, recovering. I visited her, and she was doing fine. The Major reported the news to President Graham, and Graham ordered the promotion of her and Chance two grades up. So, Allison Trudy was now a Lieutenant.

Pigtailed Girlie had leapfrogged me.

I took that paper and handed it back to Major Bayless and, though my male pride took a bit of a blow, I truly was beyond happy for her, and that trounced all.

"Major, you got yourself a winner in that girl. This is utterly deserved beyond all doubt. Where is she?"

"Weps," she said. "Congratulations. I know you're close to her, so this is your doing too. You and your wife took her in, Staff Sergeant Bassett. I commend you." She smiled at me, though I wasn't sure why she reminded me of my rank, which gave my male pride one more blow.

Weapons. "I'll go see her now. Thanks, Major Bayless," I said.

• • • • •

Trudy smiled at me, biting her lip. "I wanted to tell you. I swear. I just found out myself." She put her hands up in self-defense. I had put on my best grim, smoldering look of displeasure. "I promise."

I just stared at her and tried to keep it up, but I couldn't hold it in. My poker face failed me. A grunt transformed itself into a seeping burp of a laugh that escaped right out of me, and I guffawed heartily, holding my belly.

"Girlie, if it had been anyone else," I said, coming over to her and wrapping my big meaty arms around her. She sunk into me. "Come on, kiddo. You're like my daughter. I'm *so* proud of you. *So* damn proud of you, Trudy. You have earned this, and you deserve it."

"Really?" she said, pulling away and snickering.

"Yeah. Really. I said it before, and I'll say it again: *this* is a touchstone of massive change. And you and Chance were the spark behind it. *You* were the spark behind it. I always knew someday you were gonna be huge."

"Excuse me?"

"I mean huge in the *war*. You ain't got nuttin' to worry about for yourself, darlin.' You're gonna make an impact and drive somebody crazy, if you don't already."

"Yeah, well, Chance is gay, and I don't see anyone else around here that's ever suggested they'd even be remotely interested in me, so…"

"You'll find somebody someday. Or they'll find you," I said, smoothing some hair out of her face and back behind her ear. I took her by both shoulders.

"You're way more important than a crush, woman. I should be calling you *that* instead: *woman*. I'm proud of you, woman."

She beamed at me. "It's really gonna work, isn't it? Does the President really want it, and they want to mass produce it?"

I nodded. "That's what Bayless told me."

She breathed a huge smile through her nose, her eyes twinkling. "Wow. Just…wow."

That's all she could say. It was inevitable that a development like this would get her promoted, get her noticed. Inevitable that she would come up with something that could turn the tide of this war.

I always knew that with her, it was inevitable.

16 | EVIL

| Miguel |

Thursday, December 16th, 2038, 1802 hours

Things were now moving faster than my wildest imaginations.

After staying here for a few days completely undetected, Cardona had returned to Mammoth Cave with his partner, whom I never even saw. That guy seemed to blend in so well not even a *gorgo* could have found him even had you strapped a live jet engine to his back and slathered him with ketchup.

It was *so* refreshing catching up with Vance. He was the invisible leader of our little Resistance. He had been working hard and moving chess pieces behind the scenes, unbeknownst to the President. His Resistance network was spreading far and wide, and dissent for Graham was growing. Sparks were turning to campfires. Campfires were turning to brush fires. Brush fires to forest fires. And soon, infernos would be blazing over the earth, all crackling against injustice, burning with desire to oust this corrupt dictator.

Cardona shared things with me that made me lose sleep. I had always suspected that Graham had embraced the nuclear option, but now, hearing rumblings of what she was plotting with her counterparts, and all that Cardona had shared with me, stamped out any last shreds of hope for her goodwill. He confirmed it: she was willing to take out her enemies along with the *gorgos*, just to secure her political post and eliminate any international dissent. And she was doing all this right under the very noses of her allies: those who suspected no ill will of her. The woman was evil through and through. I wondered when that really began: when that first seed took root in her. I wondered if it had been there all along.

And now, I had been living with the knowledge that Graham had personally had Cartwright killed. Every day in her presence was a revulsion. I had to purge the loathing with frequent, yet secret, calls to *mi cariña* back home, *mi flor preciosa*, Rosalita. Oh, how I missed her. Anytime Cartwright's name was mentioned, I could see the President feign ignorance at his demise. One of those times I almost blew up at her. But that would be dissent, and then I would be tied to my own pole somewhere in the dead of night with a claxon. I had to maintain calm and keep up the ruse.

I knew what she was planning in Europe, at the three locations. It wasn't just one man she had thought of killing…no. It was hundreds of thousands of straggling survivors as collateral damage, simply so that she could wipe out her international adversaries. How a person can become so depraved was beyond me, but it was not without precedent in the annals of history.

One of her own science team members had killed himself recently. His name was William Gibson. He was the one who had proposed the Behemoth Gorgon initiative. Those laboratories nearby where they had biological preserves in cryogenic freeze: they had the DNA of angry animals like honey badgers, gorillas, and pit bulls. That was many years ago now, and we all know now how spectacularly that failed, thinking that the *gorgos* would actually attack their own. They had only created thirteen behemoths, but there were far more berserkers out there, and they were killing off our straggling survivors faster than the regular *gorgos* did. They were *muy malo*. *Diablos* for sure.

Gibson couldn't live with himself. They found his body in a small room on the fourth floor with a note apologizing to his wife and kids, if they were ever found. His note began with *I doubt you're even alive or will ever read this, but...*

It was loaded with a profound sadness and regret that he would never be able to undo. I felt for him.

Beyond that, I wasn't sure why I was here anymore. We all knew what we needed to. Already, Graham's plans were in motion. Sure, she was conducting ops that were actually benefiting the planet: the DTF emitters was one such operation. And now, she was also championing the coordination of the mask technology in Alpharetta. But she was double-dealing, certainly. The time would come where she would be unmasked, and she would reveal her true intentions. I wanted to be with the Resistance.

However, I needed to stay here, because we couldn't let that happen. Cardona insisted that I remain at my post; that I was highly valuable and *needed* on the inside, so that he could keep tabs on Graham from afar, and know what she was doing, to possibly preempt her. I reluctantly agreed.

Sooner or later, the President and her minions would catch on. They would discover my intentions, and the jig would be up. And then I would suddenly be 'missing.' Like Cartwright.

I would do my duty and stick it out. Hopefully, the day of my demise was still far off.

My wildest imagination couldn't keep up with how fast things were now moving.

17 | DIPLOMA

| Rosie |

Sunday, May 15th, 2039, 1629 hours

This was a major development that changed things, certainly.

Wyatt Rutledge 'Rutty' Shipley graduated! He was about to turn 16 next month, the point at which he would be able to enlist, finally. The day was almost here, and he couldn't wait. I was excited for him.

There he was, standing on the stage in his ordinary clothes with his fellow graduates. There were the four of them. Though no caps or gowns, we still embraced the solemnity of the moment, gazing in reverence at the newest alumni. These Blockades are hard places to learn. Deep underground, stuck here, pretending that life is normal when it's not, forced to eke out a living in the shadows and not run free upon the grass. Maybe it made it a bit easier to study when they didn't have the temptation of grass and sun outside their window. I didn't know. All I knew was that it was the same for his older brother, and for every other young person in this Blockade.

I glanced over at Rutty's brother, Corporal Cameron Shipley. *Jet.* He and Rutty exchanged views, and Jet had been crying softly and proudly. The older brother looked like he had a lump in his throat.

I traced his line of sight back to his brother up there on stage with his diploma, and they just looked at each other.

In the brief moment I had looked away, Rutty's face had transformed. Previously, it had been joy. Now, I couldn't quite read it. Grief? Resentment? Regret?

Of course. His mother was not here. His father was not here. His sister had been killed. None of them were here to celebrate with him. He was a studious scholar of a young man, and this was an important moment. He had only Jet to celebrate with, and that was something, but nothing quite like the love and affirmation of the parents who gave him life and raised him. His stoic face showed it. My heart ached for him in his loss.

•　　•　　•　　•　　•

"I'm so proud of you, kiddo," I said to him, taking his face in both of my hands. "You have worked so hard for this, and your future is bright. You did it." I released his face from my hands and just looked at him endearingly.

"Thanks, Pastor Rosie," he said. "I appreciate it. Not bad, eh?" he said rather comically, holding up his diploma.

He was smiling, but I perceived the grief that lay just behind that smile.

"Not bad at all, Rutty. It looks great. They even got your name right on it!"

"Yeah, they did." He stopped. "Rutledge is kind of a hard name anyway. I could never spell it growing up. That darn *d-g* together always threw me."

"Haha, I'm sure! Tough for a little guy! Your parents named you well. I looked it up. It means 'loud noise' in some senses. And that rings true. Your personality shines through like a loud noise…a *beacon*. I also found that there was a British publishing company named Routledge, specializing in academic books. And who likes books and is our little scholar?" I asked, leading him on.

He didn't answer. His smile faded.

"What is it?"

Rutty still didn't answer. He just clenched his lip and forced a smile, looking around.

Oh, dear. I've done it. I mentioned his parents.

"Rutty. Look at me, kiddo."

He turned his eyes back to me.

"Your parents would have been here. They are with you every day, in every bit of you that remembers them and every bit of you that keeps a piece of your heart reserved for them. You know that, yes?"

He slowly nodded.

I noticed the Corporal striding over. He stopped short of us and waited for us to finish. I was grateful. I didn't want to risk offending them both. My eyes returned to Rutty.

"I know you would have liked them to have been here. Captain Stone, 'Stoney,' as you call him, will never be your dad. And I'll never be your *madre*. If anything, I'll settle for your diminutive interracial *abuela*." I caught a twinkle in his eye amidst his fighting back tears. "But your parents live on. They are both still down here with you, kiddo, in so many more ways than you could think of. I'd be glad to accompany you to their graves later if you'd like, so you can show them your diploma?"

I put my hands on both of his shoulders. He looked at me sadly and took a deep breath. "I'd like that, Señora Rosie. Thanks. I love you, Abuelita."

Little Grandma. He had obviously learned that word somewhere along the line in his books.

"I love you too, kiddo." I squeezed his shoulders. "*So* much. Congratulations on your graduation, Rutledge, our little scholar. I'm so proud of you."

Rutty came in for a hug, and then he smiled, turned away, and left for his friends. Some of those friends would end up being on recon missions with him, certainly. Next month would be even more meaningful to him. I hoped that even *some* of my words at this achievement conveyed even the smallest bit of reassurance. His parents' absence would no doubt be even more acutely felt by him during enlistment.

He strode away to the other side of the Pavilion. My eyes were drawn to his older brother approaching me.

"Hey, Pastor Rosie," the Corporal greeted me.

"Hello Cameron. Good to see you. Congratulations on your brother!" I smiled heartily at him.

"Thank you," he said abruptly, moving right along to other matters. "Look, I need to talk to you about something."

"Oh?" I asked him. "What's that?"

Shipley paused for a moment. "Rutty. It's about his enlistment. The Captain says I'm coming up for a promotion, and he said I could have anything I want; I just have to name it."

I smiled at him. "Hmm. I understand completely. You want Rutty on your recon team."

He shook his head and furrowed his eyebrows.

"No, not exactly. That's not it. I've spoken with the Captain," -here he glanced back at his brother as if to make sure he was far enough out of earshot- "and he agrees. Rutty won't be on my detail."

My eyebrows dropped and my head tilted. "I'm not sure I understand. Why not?"

The Corporal looked sternly at me. "Look, I know you're close to him, and he's close to you. I'm telling you this in advance because he's not gonna take this well, and I need your help in…helping him understand."

"He won't take *what* well?" I wasn't following.

"Rutty won't be allowed to enlist next month. At my request. That's what I asked for."

Uh-oh. This would not sit well with Rutty. My smile faded as I looked up at the Corporal.

This was a major development that would change things, unfortunately.

18 | DRILLS & KILLS

| Miguel |

Thursday, November 3rd, 2039, 1527 hours

For years, we had been tired of being trapped, and all of us were cut off from one another, wanting to see progress. Little did we know that was about to change.

And so, 'change' was the order the President handed down. That was in early August.

The Big Bertha drills used to create the Blockades were ordered to be repaired. They would be reactivated and would create underground tunnels: passageways, to facilitate travel between the Blockades.

Geodetic surveys were conducted across surrounding terrain in thirty-mile diameters. Maps and geographic data were studied and ideal routes of passage charted and explored above ground as best and as safely as possible for everyone. The drills would run remotely, so no loss of life would occur.

Word traveled fast over whatever Internet streams still remained. The President had her own channel on X that was used to communicate instructions. There were plenty of naysayers at first, voicing dissent and expressing displeasure with the current state of things.

Then I was asked to take over. VP Cooper had given me the task, and it kept my mind off the daily doldrums.

The DTF emitters continued to sound night and day, throbbing in our ears, and maintaining their steady pulse of defense. They were being made smaller, and more modular. We thought we had it good over here at the Embassy. The boys over at the BNA Amazon Warehouse – now known as *The Lab* – those boys had hundreds of those things all around them. The Lab was Ground Zero for innovation…for mass production…for the genesis of fighting back.

As far as that mask technology from Alpharetta, the schematics were sent to the President from Major Bayless, the officer in command at DN282. They were studied, approved, and handed off to the guys over at The Lab for mass-production. It would take some time to obtain the necessary elements and get borosilicate glass panels on an assembly line. Additionally, they would need to be adapted, able to be retrofit over vehicle windowpanes, office windows, and all kinds of helmets. Soldiers would need them, but so would airmen and those charged with aerial combat or surveillance.

The President was especially interested in the aerial aspect of it all, and she wanted to ensure that she was in touch with pilots who would be charged with disseminating the DTF signals.

Today, I was once again summoned to her office.

"Lieutenant Monzon to Headquarters, Lieutenant Monzon to Headquarters," came the announcement over the walkie-talkie.

"On my way," I said calmly, belying the terror that coursed through me. Had they discovered that Cardona was here? Had he been eliminated? Would they interrogate me about the Resistance? Would I break?

No. Not this old guy. I was *muy potente*. It would take a lot to break me. Nonetheless, my nerves were on fire. I approached her office on the sixth floor, hesitantly, and was greeted by Agent Grimstad. He asked me to leave my weapons with the President's secretary, and then waved me through. The Agent looked at me without the slightest trace of gratitude for the fact that I had saved his life in the attack, pulling him back into that room. He could have been frozen. Whatever. I didn't ask how he'd been.

There she was. Sitting at her new desk in the next PEOC, further down the hall in an equivalent suite such as she had prior to the attack, retrofitted with all those solid panels of protective cover.

I saluted her and felt a wince of grotesque revulsion wash over me. Grimstad walked me in, and there was another guard stationed opposite her. I instantly recognized him as Marone.

"Hey Marone, how you doin,' my friend?" I asked him. He nodded to me and was about to answer.

"Agent Marone, will you leave us please? I'll be fine. Thank you," she said, acknowledging his questioning look.

Marone looked my way, nodded, and then went out.

And then, I was suddenly alone with the President of the United States of America, Jean Graham.

If my sweet *esposa* could hear the thoughts that passed briefly through my head right now, she would slap me in the face. Here I was. I had my chance. No one would be able to defend her. I was sixty-nine and full of muscle, still fit and agile. I could pounce on her and strangle her before anyone was aware of it. Cardona would have called me a hero at my memorial. To all those members of the Resistance that I was hitherto unknown, I would suddenly have a valiant name. I would be gunned down, surely, once the Agents got back in, but I would go down in the history books as the one who stopped another holocaust. As long as those history books were written by those loyal to Cardona, that is.

I passed a hand swiftly in front of my face to clear the air and abandon such murderous thoughts. Graham was the murderer, not I. I would not stoop to her level.

"Feeling alright, Lieutenant Monzon?" she asked me.

"Y-yes Madame President. Sorry…sometimes these damn DTF emitters just get to me."

She grimaced. "Tell me about it. They are a needed torment, are they not?" She leaned back in her chair, fiddling with her pen and pen cap, taking them off and on. "How have you been? I haven't seen much of you since the attack on the Embassy."

"Yes, that was something. Don't remind me," I said, managing a feeble attempt at a feigned laugh.

"True enough," she said. "You're no doubt wondering why I asked you here. You were a pilot, and a damned good one. I've seen your record. And you were instrumental in the aerial operation we conducted from Patrick Space Force Base in '27 with the SR-72 and all those jets."

I blew out noisily and shook my head briefly. "Forty-one souls, Madame President. I'll never forget that."

"First time we saw that damned queen."

"Yes, Ma'am," I said slowly, not relishing the memory.

She paused briefly and studied me. Most uncomfortable ten seconds of my life. Then she got up and started to walk around me. More discomfort.

"I'm wondering, Lieutenant Monzon," she started, as she changed course and walked over to the window, looking out over the horizon. Then she stopped and snickered, shaking her head. "There go three more of them. They'll never leave, damn gorgs. One day we're gonna pound them hard, eh Lieutenant?" she said, turning back to me. "I've got Norfolk lining up as we speak. Rear Admiral Evelyn Lynch and many others are readying the fleet there. It'll be a long while, but we're gonna hammer-punch them off this planet so hard they'll warp out of here," giving off a fiendish cackle as she looked at me.

I smiled meekly. "That's certainly the goal, Ma'am."

Graham studied me again for a moment. That was becoming an irritant. She began to pace back toward and around me.

"Lieutenant, if I wanted to harness these DTF signals, *focus* them if you will, channel them from a single, powerful source and conduct aerial sweeps with the signal, herding them into a corner so we can take them out, what would I need?"

"*Herding* them, Ma'am?"

She reached her desk again and nodded swiftly. "Mm-hmm, yes. A powerful signal, drawing a line, as it were, across the earth, and then having that line slowly sweep across the planet, so focused that the gorgons will have to comply, and we would herd them to a kill zone. Could that be done?"

My eyes widened. I had to admit that it sounded revolutionary, although I felt somewhat steamrolled by all her quick details. "Wow, Madame President, that truly sounds exciting," I said, and I wasn't kidding, because it did. "You would need something aerial, certainly. There is equipment that you could use, already out there. AN/ALQ99s. They are basically jammers and the like; they're specifically attached to jets and mounted in pods on the fin tips, and then you have equipment that transmits from pods under the wings. They can intercept and jam signals. But they can also distribute."

"Fascinating," she said, looking at me intently. "It's the *distribution* side of this that I'm interested in, of course."

"Yes, that makes sense," I said. "Well, there are several planes that could handle them and probably already have them equipped. Growlers: those are the EA-18Gs, and then the EA-6Bs and EF-111A Ravens. All of them could handle them. But you'd need to coordinate it and really go back and forth for these controlled sweeps, with a fleet of jets. Earth's a big place, Ma'am."

She was scribbling all of this down furiously on a notepad, but then she stopped and looked back up at me. "But it could be done?" she asked, pointing her pen tip at me, and I wondered if she would ever use that pen to stick in someone's neck.

"I don't see why not, Madame President. It would take some coordination, but it could definitely be done."

A faint trace of a smile curved upward across her lips. "Thank you, Lieutenant Monzon," she said at last. "You've given me food for thought, and I appreciate it. So begins the hammer-punch."

I had to admit I was genuinely interested in this plan. If Graham was going to sweep the gorgons to a specific place and kill them with DTFs, that would be a formidable response that might actually hand us a victory. It would take tremendous coordination of the signal sweeps, but it could be done. Maybe there was a seed of good in her after all. Maybe she was genuinely trying to give us a chance.

"You're welcome, Madame President, of course. Is there anything else I can help with?"

"No, no," she answered abruptly. "I've kept you long enough. This is exciting. I must get to work with the coordination. I've taken some notes and will talk to Cooper about it and get a plan in motion. Thank you, Lieutenant."

"My pleasure, Madame President."

"That'll be all, Monzon," she said.

I turned and walked out. Grimstad nodded at me on my way out, emotionless and cold. It was almost as if the air warmed the further away you got from Graham's quarters. The icy coldness seeped away, and the warmth of the world returned, full of promise. It was tangible.

This was a new development that gave me hope. I had to contact Cardona. Nonchalantly, I made my way to one of the secure offices on the bottom floor, and sent him an encrypted message.

POTUS has a plan. Aside from the drills and tunneling allowing further networking, plans are underway for large scale dissemination of DTF signals conducted by aerial sweeps. Emitters mounted on planes with jammers. Global sweeps. Novel idea, to corral all the gorgons together and herd them to kill zones. More information as it becomes available. She found me indispensable in providing my knowledge of aerial equipment and corresponding gear. Maybe we might win this war after all. It has filled me with hope.

I waited for a reply.

Briefly I had a thought that I might not hear back from him. That was always a chief concern. Had someone revolted against him? Had Graham planted someone there to take him out? She had to have heard from Cooper by now that he was suspicious of her. *Strike the shepherd, and the sheep will be scattered.* The Resistance would falter. My heart was filled with hope at such new strategies to rid ourselves of the *gorgos*, but it was admittedly occasionally punctured with thoughts of Cardona's demise.

Soon, however, my fears were allayed. Here came an encrypted message back to me. As I read it, my heart chilled once more.

Wouldn't it be great if that were the truth? he replied.

My eyes squinted. *Meaning?* I fired back, and waited eagerly for his reply.

Things are never what they seem. Ignoble aims cleverly concealed in noble cloaks. The sweeps will work, of course, but watch out for the double entendre, my friend: they will be used as pretense for a greater strike. The kill zones are the same as the nuclear strike zones. She'll take out all her enemies in one fell swoop. Use caution and keep watching. Sometimes foes can inadvertently undo themselves in the process. That's my *hope.*

My shoulders sunk. Of course! How could I be so naïve? She would use these sweeps to herd them all to the nuclear strike zones that Cardona had mentioned, and she would propose this strategy to unwitting supporters. They would be as ignorant as I apparently had been. She would lure them all into specific areas under the pretense that she would use DTF emitters on them. But then she would nuke the *gorgos* – as well as all those international leaders in the vicinity who were opposed to her.

She would position it as 'let's kill the gorgons; but if we happen to get some oppositional world leaders as well, oh well, we'll call it collateral damage.' But really, it was 'let's kill off the world leaders that oppose us, and if we happen to take out the gorgons too, bonus.'

And I had just helped her do it.

Sick. My stomach lurched. I wished Cardona well and signed off. The cold truth was staring me in the face.

Using this new method, we could finally be free of the *gorgos*. Perhaps all of them. But it would be used as cover for something far more nefarious, calculating, and murderous. I had always had hope that we would be free, but I never expected it to come at such a ruthless cost.

Graham, like the rest of us, was tired of being trapped, hoping to start connecting to others in the name of progress.

But the Resistance was already connecting to others in the name of progress. Little did she know that was already happening.

19 I RAGE & CHANGE

| Rosie |

Wednesday, March 7th, 2040, 1527 hours

He charged at him in anger now, desperate for revenge.

I had run after Rutty, telling him to think rationally, to not take revenge, to think this through. But he was young, and I was old; I just couldn't keep up with him. He had flown up the stairs of the Launch faster than you could say *ay caramba*. His brother had just returned from the Launch with his team and was now descending the ramp.

Jet never saw it coming.

Rutty tackled his brother and they both flew back. His team, surprised beyond belief, startled and stepped back.

Rutty hammered his fists into his brother. Jet put his hands up in defense and covered his head. Rutty's fists slammed into his brother's gut and shoulder, and then his head. I heard Jet cry out in pain.

"Rutty, what the hell- oof!" he exclaimed, as his brother socked him in the chest. "Ow, stop! What are you *doing*, bro?"

Rutty seemed possessed. Jet probably didn't ever anticipate such injury to his twenty-year-old body by sixteen-year-old fists, but Rutty's hands had been balled up with the power of resentment. Jet took a pelting right punch to his neck, and his face erupted into anger.

Nonetheless, Rutty's wrath proved the greater. He struck again, and kneed his brother right in the abdomen, tossing him backward. Rutty advanced again.

The Captain should never have told him that Jet held him back.

Hearing the commotion, Stone stumbled down the hall into the Launch. He looked around wildly as a crowd from Jet's patrol mingled with Rutty's friends.

Thankfully, the Sentry had closed the Launch doors and kept the noise from escaping out into the listening ears of the enemy. But even through the Launch, anyone could hear this. Rutty had been denied by his own brother, and now he would have his say.

"Why?!" Rutty cried out angrily, and then his brother kicked him off himself, right in the stomach, and Rutty flew back. I heard Rutty gasp for air, but then he was right back up. He lunged at Jet, but his brother sidestepped him and tripped him. Rutty fell into the dirt.

"Why *what*? What are you *doing*, bro?" Jet railed.

"Don't even pretend like you don't know!" he shouted, and he flew again at his brother. Jet once again tried to dodge it, but Rutty struck wide and Jet accidentally moved his face right into Rutty's left fist. Jet toppled backward and stumbled against the ramp railing. Rutty was on him in a heartbeat, tearing him off the rails and wrapping his left arm around his brother's neck.

"I-I can't br-" Jet started.

"Boys! Stop this at once! I order you to stop!" yelled the Captain. "Boys!"

But Jet wasn't finished, and they weren't boys anymore. Survival mode kicked in, and Jet planted his feet firmly and threw himself backward. Rutty received the full weight of his brother, four years his senior, in his stomach. The collision knocked the air out of Rutty. He wheezed.

Jet whirled around with amazing speed and pinned Rutty underneath him. There were now tears in his younger brother's eyes, flooding his view and streaming down his cheeks.

"You held me back! You told the Captain to hold me back! To not let me enlist!" he yelled amidst choking tears, and everyone heard it. "Why, Jet, why?!"

Jet gritted his teeth in frustration, and his mouth was bleeding. It was supposed to be a secret. His eyes flashed up to the Captain. Betrayal framed his features. Stone, realizing that he had been outed, closed his own mouth and clenched his jaw in grim defeat. He raised his hands, helplessly, as Jet continued to pin his brother under him. Drops of sweat fell from Jet onto Rutty's face, mingling with Rutty's tears and fusing with the blood running out of his nose.

Jet looked back down, and his countenance sunk.

Rutty continued to squirm under him. And then, it wasn't just sweat. Jet was crying too, hovering over his little brother.

"Bro! Stop it. Just relax," he fumbled. "Relax!" he screamed at his younger brother, and Rutty, sensing the conflict was nearing its end and he had landed enough hits, he growled, softened, and tore himself away from his older brother.

Jet simultaneously ripped himself away from Rutty, holding his hands out to stay his brother's wrath.

Rutty rolled over onto his side, coughed, and erupted into tears. There were painful, dejected howls of despair. He had longed so much to prove himself up on the surface, and had been denied by his own brother.

Jet looked around helplessly. Now, everyone knew. He had intentionally held his brother back from enlisting, and Rutty was deservedly furious.

"Rutty, listen," he said, panting, wiping the sweat and blood from his face. "Listen to me, bro!" he yelled. "I," he stammered. "I just couldn't let you go out with me."

"No!" Rutty suddenly exclaimed, and then struggled to his feet. "That's not it!" he said, clutching his side, the light of battle filling his eyes once again. "What's the whole story, bro? Tell everyone here! You couldn't let me go out *at all!*"

I wanted to say something to calm both of them but I bit my lip.

Jet looked at his brother, and then turned away.

"Say it!" Rutty demanded loudly, his young voice cracking in the process from both puberty and scorn.

Jet said nothing. He looked up and sighed resignedly. Jet brought his hands up to his face and clasped them both behind his head. And then he slowly turned back around, and his eyes were red. His cheeks were flushed, and his face was contorted into painful knots of guilt.

We all listened.

"Fine, Rutty," his voice squeaked, and he cleared his throat, holding up his hands in helplessness. "You're all I have left, bro." And with that, the floodgates were opened.

Jet lost it. His body quaked, and the tears fell freely as he broke into sobs. "You're all I have left, Rutty. I," he stuttered, wiping his eyes and heaving out a grunt. "I… can't…"

Rutty's panting slowed, and he watched his brother intently. We all did.

"Dad came out on my first mission because of *me*. He died because of *me*. He died out there by a gorg right in front of me, bro!" he screamed. "And there wasn't a damned thing I could do about it!" Now he was railing. "And there's no way in hell I want to see that happen to you, Rut! Do you hear me? I can't go through that again!" he wailed, and the bars of the Launch railing shook under his intensity. "I can't… lose… you!" he said, and he buried his face in his hands.

Jet's vulnerability was on full display, and he collapsed to the ground. It was now clear. For four years he had been carrying the guilt of his father's death – his sacrifice for his son, entirely of a father's own volition and love – and it was eating him up inside. Jet was consumed by guilt. He hadn't held his brother back out of competition or jealousy, but out of protection and love.

Rutty stared at him intently.

Jet knelt before all of us, bawling uncontrollably. The outpouring of his soul tapped into all our collective grief, mirroring what we had all felt for so many years, purged unfairly of our loved ones, left to survive underground with nothing but memories of them. The well of his soul called out yearningly for those loved ones he had lost. Ours did the same as we watched and took in his mournful cries.

"You look so much like Mom…like Sissy…I-" he couldn't finish, and then he collapsed into a motionless heap on the ground.

Rutty watched him while leaning on the railing, his lip quivering and his body quaking, still breathing hard. And then, with nothing to hold him back, he began to weep uncontrollably.

He turned to the Captain, his eyes shining. "Sorry, Dad," he said. "I understand. It's alright."

Captain Stone was crying as well.

Rutty turned back to his brother, lying on the ground and holding nothing back.

"I love you, Jet. I understand, bro," he whimpered, releasing his grip from the railing. And then, brotherly love seized him, knowing full well why Jet had done what he had done, and longing to connect in empathy.

He ran toward his brother and threw his arms around him. I heard Rutty loud and clear, whimpering through tears to his brother, as he bawled into Jet's shoulder. "I love you. *Every day, more and more, over and over.*"

My heart welled, and there was a lump in my throat. That phrase was something Rutty had said his parents had frequently said to each other. It was written on his mother's grave.

Jet echoed it. "I love you. Every day, more and more, over and over." The tears fell freely.

We all charged toward them in empathy now, desperate to show our understanding.

20 | STEPH

| Trudy |

Sunday, May 13th, 2040, 1037 hours

"We are never assured of a tomorrow. All we can do is make the most of today."

The Pastor concluded with those gracious words, and they settled over me.

I heard Steph, Bassett's sister, voice an *Amen* next to me. Maureen and Joe did as well. I wasn't used to the word, but I nodded along.

"Let us pray," said Pastor Finn. We all bowed our heads. I knew to do that much at least. "Dear Lord, we do not know what you want from us sometimes. We don't even pretend to understand why we're living down here for all these years, stuck here while the world you gave us above is overrun by creatures who have killed off four out of five of us. We've endured for almost fourteen years. But we do know one thing. You are good. You love us, and have always loved us, with an everlasting love. And though we don't understand your plan, we rest in the knowledge that one day, all will be made clear. Until that tomorrow, we are resolved to serve you today. In Jesus' Name, Amen."

Amen came the various echoes throughout the Rotunda. I brought myself to say it this time. "Amen."

Pastor Finn smiled, and then excused us until next Sunday.

•   •   •   •   •

Sunday, May 13th, 2040, 1114 hours

We were all sitting together, chewing softly, reflecting on Finn's words. No one said anything, which I thought was odd. Joe was always the first one to pipe up and lighten the mood.

But this was a different message from Finn. The words were heavier. The message was heavier. Yes, it had meaning, and yes it meant that we needed to continue to trust and be patient, but it was different from any of his other messages. We needed hope. We always needed hope for a tomorrow.

I couldn't take it any longer and cleared my throat.

"So," I started. "Big words, eh? No tomorrows for any of us. So full of hope," I finished with a nervous smile.

Joe let out a faint chuckle.

"What? Aren't I right? It was kind of depressing."

He shook his head. Maureen looked at Joe. "Trudy," Joe started, "I don't know what's worse: expecting a tomorrow and not getting one, or knowing that one isn't coming and waiting for it anyway." Joe turned to Maureen. "I mean, I had no idea my tomorrow would include this fine young lady right here, but I waited forever for it, only to see us stuck down here for all time."

"Hmm, but we're stuck down here *together* at least, right?" Maureen asked him.

"You got that right, lady," he winked at her.

I smiled at the both of them.

"And now we have more hope for tomorrow than we've ever had before," Joe said to all of us.

Steph looked at him. "What do you mean?"

"Well, look what's happened just in the last year. Trudy's masks are being mass produced over in Nashville, and they've got those new sound deterrents to send the gorgs scampering. And Bayless has heard whispers that the President even has something else going on, bigger than those things combined. It's gonna be epic. I think we've finally got hope for a brighter tomorrow."

"Hell yeah," said Steph, and returned to her food, joyfully. "Hell yeah," she said again.

Something in me wanted to believe him, but that just wasn't enough for me, I had to admit. Looking at the two of them sitting there, cuddled up close, Joe's arm around Maureen, *that* was the hope I really wanted. *That* was the tomorrow I wanted. For all this time it's been all about service, duty, survival. Love was out of the question. Or, at least, it had been so far.

"Well, if you believe that, I'll support you in your belief. I just kinda need to see it," I said weakly. "Otherwise, it's just hard for me to accept it."

Before I even knew what was happening, Steph was laughing uproariously at me. I sat back in surprise.

"Ha! A bona fide *gotta-see-it-to-believe-it* kinda gal right here," she said, slapping the table hard and turning to Joe and Maureen. Joe smirked at her. "You sure are a scientist. Girl, did you even *hear* Finn's message?"

I looked at her incredulously. "Of course I did."

"Well then," she began again, "think about it. I'm not trying to be an ass, Trudy, I'm really not. But all I heard from that message was hope upon hope."

I looked at her, confused, waiting for her to go on.

"Tell her, Steph," Joe said, and I glanced over at him. Maureen was smiling at me sweetly, as if she knew something I didn't. I looked back at Steph.

"If you knew half the things I've been through, you would be right over in the belief column right quick, like nobody's business, slicker than snot. All I've ever been able to cling to has been hope. What year is this?"

I winced in confusion. "Uh, 2040?"

"Yeah. 2040. Twenty-one years after I should have left this good green Earth. But for some reason, I'm still here. And that was just the first time. By my math, that's seven thousand, six hundred sixty-five tomorrows. That driver hit me so fast I saw stars for a month. When they pulled me out with the jaws of life, my right lung was outside my body. All I ever had was hope for a tomorrow.

"And then I tried to cope for eight straight years. All those AA meetings. All those Twelve Steps. And a freakin' alien invasion on top of that, girl! Yahoo. Good times! No tomorrows in there. I just hoped I would make it through to the next bottle on the next day."

She stopped, and watched me. "Think I'm done?"

I slowly shook my head at her.

"No. I ain't done. My lung hoped it would be able to still work too. And then, by God's grace, guess what happened. Cancer! I don't know how I got it, but I got liver cancer. Now where could I have gotten that. Hmm. Gimme a minute."

Joe chuckled.

"Oh, *that's* right," Steph stopped with sarcastic aplomb. "I did it to *myself* with my drinking! Did you know that I never hoped for a tomorrow more than during that time? HCC. Hepatocellular Carcinoma. The doc said I had a thirty-five percent chance of surviving up to five years after my diagnosis, as long as I received treatment." Her voice was raising in volume. Obviously, I had tapped into something.

"And ya know what?" she nearly yelled. "God gave me a tomorrow *there* too, because I hoped and prayed for it, and that damn cancer didn't spread to any of my other organs, let alone my lymph nodes. If it had? *Twelve* percent chance of survival. And if it metastasized? *Three* percent chance. And ya know what? I did it alone. I didn't tell anyone about my cancer, except for the doc. I did it freaking alone, girl. *Alone.* And why? Because I had one thing that drove me along the river of all that torture. The motor that pushed my survival boat. *Hope.*

"And ya know something else?" she shouted at me. "Hope is what I had when I tested out *your* prototype at the Launch doors, girl. Yeah. That's right. I didn't have a gun. I had *hope* that your mask would save my ass before the gorg froze me. We've all put *one little thing* in your mask, those DTF emitters, our guns, these Blockades, in living another day. It's called 'hope for tomorrow,' Trudy. You might wanna embrace it, like, I dunno, before *tomorrow*."

She got up and stormed out.

I watched her exit the Rotunda. Others did as well. Her voice had carried in the mess hall, and now everyone was staring at me. I turned back to Joe and Maureen, who were looking at me with clenched lips under their raised eyebrows.

"She…kinda feels strongly about tomorrow, Trudy," said Maureen, tentatively, walking on eggshells.

My eyebrows went up. I shook my head to clear the air. "I guess she does."

Others were staring at me, but eventually they returned to their food. I got up and went in search of Steph.

•　　•　　•　　•　　•

"Hey," I said.

"Come on in," she answered in an impatient huff.

There she was, in her bunk, lying face up with her hands clasped across her stomach, eyes staring into the void.

I stood there, surveying her, considering all that she'd been through.

"I didn't mean to offend you. I'm sorry," I offered.

She turned to me and smiled with a sigh. "It's okay. I can get heated. I know. In case you didn't notice I have an opinion."

"Really? No. I missed that part."

"Yeah," she joked back, smiling at me. She took a minute as she stuck her tongue in her lower lip. "The future is all we got, Trudy. It's all we got. Today, we're stuck. But someday, we'll be free. Someday, we'll kick those bastards to the curb. And you, I mean" -here she sized me up and down with her hand- "look at you! For crying out loud, you just went and invented something that knocks out their primary weapon against us, girl. I can't believe that wouldn't give you instant tomorrow-itis."

I slowly walked over and sat at the foot of her bunk, my hands under my thighs. "You're right. I know you're right."

"I *am* right," she quickly agreed, sitting up. "You've been slaving away at that thing for so long, and now look? There it is. Off to the presses. It's gonna change everything, Trudy. *That's* your tomorrow. That's *all* our tomorrow."

I sat there, and slowly filled my lungs with air, licking my lips and holding there as I tried to let it sink in.

"Oh, I get it. You want more," she said pointedly as she watched me. "You want the one thing we all want more than survival. You want love."

I looked at her quickly, and a nervous laugh escaped me. *Boy if* that *wasn't a dead giveaway*, I thought. "Is it that obvious?" I asked her sheepishly.

Steph cocked an eyebrow at me. "Does a gorgon float in the air?"

Silly substitute for the 'bear' thing, but I got it. I laughed. "Yeah," I breathed.

She shook her head at me, with a half-smile still on her lips, her elbows up on one raised knee. "Girl, you're hope-*less*. Wanting a tomorrow *and* a guy. Asking for too much. Take it one day at a time, woman!" She watched me, and nearly laughed, as longing must have been pouring out of me. She could read it. "Slow down, woman. Appreciate what you got all around you, and let hope be the current that keeps you afloat. The world ain't gonna give you a man on a silver platter. Takes time. The right guy's out there. I mean, granted, the pickings are slim anymore, but…he's out there."

She placed her hand on my shoulder for a moment, squeezing it. Felt very 'big-sistery.' "I appreciate it," I said.

And then, strangely, she began to sing. Slowly at first, but then more theatrically as she went along. "Tomorrow, tomorrow, I love ya, tomorrow. You're only a day away." She repeated it.

I'd never heard that one. "What's that from?"

She looked at me in amazement, incredulous that I didn't know the source. Her smile faded to a grim stare, shaking her head again. "Hopeless." And then she laughed.

The source didn't matter, I guess. She was right: tomorrow was only a day away. And no matter how I felt, that was the truth. Right there I figured, if Steph had been through so much, maybe I could go through my own stuff too. I grinned back at her and squeezed her hand. "Thank you, Steph. And," I nodded to her, "I'm sorry you had to go through all of that."

"Hey," she answered instantly, waving me away. "I went through the love part too. Left me angry, lonely and sad. Never again. I'm better off giving my love to hope. 'Course, if I found a bottle of Jack Daniels, I'd give my love to that right quick instead." She chuckled.

I laughed with her, nodding along. I understood. It's what the Pastor had said. That's what Steph had been doing all this time.

We are never assured of a tomorrow. All we can do is make the most of today.

21 | AMASSING

| Miguel |

Monday, May 28th, 2040, 1403 hours

We were preparing for war, and the numbers kept growing each day.

More tanks. More jets. More choppers. More APCs, C-17s, RVs, jeeps, M3 Bradleys, SUVs, M9 armored vehicles, amphibious vehicles. More ATVs. More motorcycles. Everything the President had asked for and more. BNA's runway was filling up.

Operations were underway within five hundred square miles to bring in every sort of assault vehicle or military hardened vehicle we could find. Most made it. Some perished along the way, attacked by *gorgos*.

The word was spreading, and brave souls answered the call.

For air, there was Arnold Air Force Base in Tennessee, Sabre Airfield at Fort Campbell, Dobbins Air Reserve Base in Georgia, Scott Air Force Base in Illinois, US Air Force Base in South Carolina, Maxwell Air Force Base in Alabama.

For the Army, every single Blockade within a thousand-mile radius was put on alert. And then there were Tennessee Army National Guard, Camp Frank D. Merrill, Hunter Army Airfield and Moody Air Force Base in Georgia. Camp Shelby in Mississippi, and army bases in Oklahoma.

For the Marines, there were Marine Corps reserve centers and bases in Tennessee, Georgia, North and South Carolina, and all the way up to Ohio and Indiana.

For the Navy, as much as they were inland, there was the Naval Surface Warfare Center in Indiana, the Naval Air Station Joint Reserve Base Fort Worth in Texas, Naval Air Station Meridian in Mississippi, and Naval Weapons Station, Joint Base Charleston, South Carolina. Up and down the Cumberland in all directions, throughout the Mississippi and Tennessee Rivers, any stops along the way with naval vessels or those sturdy enough to be retrofit with DTF emitters and other weaponry, they were all directed to set sail toward Nashville. The Cumberland northwest of BNA was filled with ships, blowing bridges as they went in order to clear passage.

Word spread as far as Naval Station Norfolk in Virginia and up along the cost to Naval Air Station Oceana.

Civilian ships were commandeered as well. Cruise ships that could barely function were moored at piers all over the world, and they began recruiting crews locally to work on cleanup operations from oil spills from ships that had been knocked around in storms and hurricanes against the piers. Refineries were kicked back into overdrive to harness crude oil and get it ready for those big beasts, for the engines to run well. Once that was finished, they'd load them with as many DTF emitters as they could and distribute them up and down the coasts. It would take years. Gigantic cruise ships such as 'The World,' once luxury cruise liners only for super-rich, were now filled with steerage and everyday folks who just wanted to say *adios a los gorgos.* They were now filled with those who would never otherwise be able to afford such accommodations, committed not to a life of luxury, but a life of labor, of love, for liberty.

Half of the fighter jets that could be quickly routed to Nashville were dispatched, sparing an equally-sized contingent to remain. These fighter jets and C-17 transports would be equipped and loaded with more DTF emitters in order to fan back out to their original destinations and retrofit all the other jets on base. The jets were critical, the President said, as the *gorgos* were aerial. We would need to be able to meet them in the skies. We also knew about that craft, that ship, or whatever it was, up there in our atmosphere, and that they were stealing our water through the funnel out over the Atlantic. A final confrontation and assault on that structure was inevitable. We needed everything that was aerial souped up with these DTF devices.

It was a horrendously complex operation, amassing all these weapons of war. Now, though, it was actually happening. Fourteen years after the invasion, it was happening. In six days, we would solemnly reflect on the anniversary of their invasion. *Their* 'D-Day,' it was observed, because June 6th was our anniversary of our landing on the beaches of Normandy, France in 1944 to liberate Paris and Western Europe. We would hopefully someday have our own again, driving them off this planet for good.

It was exciting news, to be sure, and impressive to see the mobilization underway. Nonetheless, I knew now what Graham's endgame was, and shuddered at her duplicity now that my eyes were opened.

As soon as I could, I moved to one of the secure offices and sent two encrypted messages. First, to my dear wife to let her know that I was okay and that I was continuing to monitor, and wishing her well, telling her I couldn't wait to see her beautiful face again.

And next, to Cardona.

Operation Deep Breath underway. That's what she's calling it. Word has spread. Mobilization initiated for 1000-mile radius. Vehicles and fighters being gathered and equipped with DTF emitters all across southeast. Shipments underway to carry equipment to farther reaches, i.e., Norfolk. We might just win this thing, my friend. These devices have given us all hope.

Again, the fear seized me that I would not hear from him. That somehow, he had been compromised, exposed, and killed. Momentarily, however, there came an incoming message from Mammoth Cave.

'Deep Breath.' That woman and her strange monikers. I suppose it's the deep breath before the plunge, but still... I guess the plunge is coming. Rest assured, my friend, that this is good. If there's one thing that will be credited to our 'friend,' it's that she used her military, for once, for good. But that, sadly, is not where it will end. Contacts in Europe report the three construction sites are well underway and approaching completion in under two years' time. Then, it'll be game time. She'll use those sweeps to herd them in, sure. She'll bomb them with that new technology – we're scheduled to receive some here soon by the way, thank you – but then she'll say 'it's not enough. We

must eradicate them entirely. The fallout will be great, yes, but this is a necessary evil.' And no one will oppose her, because she's holding the triggers, and they know they're next if they do oppose.

I thought to myself. *Her Illuminati.* The six other nations that were in league with her. Her secret advisors, by whom she initially ran all these plans so long ago.

Cardona continued.

That will be a very sad day indeed – unless we can arouse every last one of us to action first. Rest assured, plans are underway on our end. The Resistance rises, amigo.

I hammered out a quick message in reply.

Be safe, my friend. Be always safe. There is no telling what she will do to you once she finds out you've headed this up. And I don't know how much longer I'll be safe in here. I'll be the next domino to fall once she tags you, to be sure. Watch your back. We're getting close to the end of the line, it seems.

But then he replied again, just before signing off. *The gorgs end, our end, or her end? I pray that it's only two of those. One thing's for sure: the Resistance is preparing for war, and our numbers keep growing each day.*

22 | SERVICE

| Rosie |

Tuesday, June 12th, 2040, 1003 hours

It was a 'Private' matter, to be shared and celebrated.

Not a volunteer matter, not a human matter, not a simple helper matter, but rather a Private matter.

Wyatt Rutledge 'Rutty' Shipley was now a Private.

Here, on his seventeenth birthday, at long last, he was receiving something he had once been denied, and deeply craved: *enlistment in the armed forces.*

In a private ceremony with only the remainder of the patrol contingent not presently out on recon, here we were with Captain Stone, Sergeant Shipley and a few other soldiers in the Pavilion. Jet – now his senior officer and squad leader – brought him his fatigues and his hat. He handed them lovingly to his brother, and winked at Rutty. Rutty smiled faintly back and nodded. There was no trace of animosity in him this time: he was too consumed with pride and gratitude to receive what was his due. I was so happy for him.

Cameron had turned twenty-one last October 16th, and here today, Rutty, our young Wyatt, was turning seventeen. Cameron was now an adult. It was unbelievable to me to see the two of them together: one of them a grown man, and one of them flowering into manhood, yet both having come from the same place of trauma as fragile little boys so long ago.

Six days ago, we solemnly remembered when the enemy had come, fourteen years earlier. I dimly recalled it from the recesses of my aging mind: a family of five, coming down the Launch. The parents were holding their phones and chargers in a tumbled mess in their hands. The mother cradled a three-year-old boy in her arms, his diaper flap peeking out from under his Spiderman jammies. It was the last one they had, used only for the long journey here while he slept.

The diesel generators were everywhere then. The Launch still smelled like grease, and the sound of the guns overpowered all else in their thunderous defense. Engineers with blowtorches welded right at the entrance as the family rushed past them, into their new life in our Blockade. At one point, I had gazed out through the gun tower windows some years ago, and seen their Toyota Sienna parked in a row with the others. Rusted over and the glass smashed out, dented in and covered in pollen, it was the last remnant of the life they had known.

Such a long time ago. Yet look at them now! They had made it. They were soldiers, and they were fine ones. They made sure that we were safe down here.

They ensured life would go on.

I thanked God for them in the silence of my heart, knowing full well that their father – the late Lieutenant – and their mother, would be so proud of both of them.

•   •   •   •   •

Thursday, January 10th, 2041, 0900 hours

"Why do you like that thing so much?" Jet asked.

"What, this?" Rutty asked, lovingly stroking his torpedo shooter. "It's a freaking rocket launcher, man, what's not to love?"

Jet shook his head. "Hard to carry. Give me my Beretta and an M5 any day. See this thing? Beretta 92. Look at it! And when it shoots? *Nice.* Plus, you got fifteen rounds in the mag. You gotta take forever loading just one torpedo. Mine's way easier to transport. You need legs of steel to be able to haul that thing around."

"Are you kidding? You ain't seen my legs?" Rutty asked him incredulously, lifting his left pantleg above the calf. "See that, bro? That's not a calf, that's a *cow.* Don't you worry about these bovines. Just get movin' there, Sergeant."

All Jet could do was shake his head again, and mutter "moooooo!" I watched them banter, laughing with Rutty and shaking my own head.

"God speed, boys," I said to them. Sergeant and Private Shipley both turned and looked at me, and I saluted. They smiled and saluted back.

"Thanks, Pastor Rosie," said Rutty jubilantly. This was now his thirteenth mission, and though he was all joy down here, he was all business up there, and he had proven himself able to keep up with his brother the Sergeant.

The Captain nodded approvingly at both of them. "Good luck, guys. You too, Santella? Jentzen? Ferro? Come back, all of you. Good luck, Beta Team."

Privates Markus Jentzen, Alex Santella and Sarah Ferro all nodded as well. Ferro went up on Jet's left side and locked arms with him. They were a cute couple. I had watched them out on previous missions. No funny business. They were always careful. Besides, all four of them had lost a parent out in the field. They were all too acutely aware of the risk.

Per protocol, we all cleared the Launch while they ascended to the top, accompanied only by a single Sentry at the door, and those manning the gun towers around the periphery. It was still winter, and that meant greater danger. I took a deep breath and wished them well in the quiet of my heart, praying for their safety.

The enemy had always been more prevalent during the winter. It was colder, and they seemed to prefer that for some reason. During the heat of the summer, they would be found in more limited areas such as the nearby Cumberland, their heads submerged in water thoroughfares such as that. Why they did that, no one knew. I suppose it comforted them, because they would stay there for hours, apparently to mitigate the effects of the summer sun.

It was during the winter – as well as any evening – that they were to be most feared. Naturally, living in a Blockade with gun towers overhead meant relative shelter, and so, we felt safe down here. We'd outlasted their decimation for fourteen and a half years now, but for how much longer?

Our residents weren't exactly reproducing like bunnies. To compound things, we didn't have any kind of neonatal or maternity ward down here, so I didn't blame them. We encouraged relationships of course: we needed to preserve our race. One day we'd emerge from this hole, and we'd need to start all over. But you couldn't force it.

Nonetheless, we had high hopes for Sergeant Shipley and Private Ferro. Time would tell.

All of this reminded me so much of my dear *cariño*. It had been months since we had spoken.

For now, we retreated from the Launch back to Halcyon to watch the five of them start their patrol. They all paused and catalogued their blood in the sensor at the door that they affectionately dubbed the *lick n' prick*.

A silly name.

•   •   •   •   •

The coast was clear.

"Move out," ordered the Sergeant, and everyone followed, lifting themselves up from the berm and heading south. The Captain had given them D-Range a little further to the southeast. Another team, Alpha Team headed up by William Pettijohn, was handling A-Range in the zinc plant and beyond.

To date, I don't know that anyone had gone into either E-Range to the north of the spur, or F-Range to the far south yet. The further away the patrols got, the longer it would take to get them back, and sometimes they would be out there for days.

This time, they would be heading east down Zinc Plant Road, through the cover of the forest, down to intersect with Cumberland Heights Road to the southeast. There was a slew of houses and buildings, even a church and cemetery that they could visit and investigate for supplies or survivors.

The snow crunched lightly under their feet. As always, they had empty knapsacks on their backs to bring back any recovered goods.

I stood next to Captain Stone in Halcyon. Among our crew was Pete Beckinsale, one of the newest members of Halcyon. He was a bit talkative, but otherwise very skilled at his craft. I had known him as a child growing up in here: he was very intelligent and beyond qualified to help with computers and tech, which was not my purview.

And now, he was monitoring the team as they headed south. They silently advanced south into the cover of the trees north of Zinc Plant Road. The trees were draped in white from recent snow, and the signal diminished with the interference, but at least they had cover from unfriendly eyes above. We all knew the enemy could see us better if we moved.

They passed Potters Court to the south, and I wondered how Markus Jentzen was doing at this precise moment in time. His mother had been killed in a house not too far north of him on a previous patrol when he was just a boy. I wasn't certain which one it was, but I prayed for his strength.

Suddenly, Pete exclaimed a little too loudly, "Hold, hold!" The Captain shushed him. They were supposed to whisper even through the headsets. "Sorry," Pete quickly corrected himself. "Hold, everyone. Six signals, passing south-southwest, range seventy-five meters."

There was only one camera mounted in the woods, and it was pointing east; we couldn't see them. But we could hear Shipley relay to his team to hold tight.

Up the screen crawled a red mass of infrared signals moving swiftly to the west. They were headed toward Pettijohn's team at the zinc plant.

"Winston, connect me to Pettijohn. Now," barked the Captain in a monotone voice, watching the monitors.

"You're on, sir," said another tech.

"Alpha Team, repeat Alpha Team…Pettijohn. Come in, over?"

"Alpha, go ahead," whispered a husky voice coming in on a different channel.

"Six signals coming your way, moving west fast. Get under cover. Pete, send them the coordinates."

"Roger that," echoed Beckinsale. "Contacts bearing two-six-nine to two-five-three, range two hundred meters and closing fast. Wait, hang on."

"What is it?" said the Captain.

"Satellite interference, but I thought I saw something north. Standby."

We waited. Shipley's voice came through. "Are we clear to proceed now?"

"Negative, standby," said Pete. "Just passing you in a moment, heading west." Pete continued to watch his monitors. They had frozen: scratching its way down the screen came a bit of magnetic interference, causing a blip in the signal. Momentarily the signal returned, but then he stood up.

"Contact, contact, hold," he said again, and realized that he was still on Pettijohn's channel. "Shit!"

"Pete, get a hold of yourself – switch to 42!" growled the Captain. "Alpha Team, Pettijohn, ignore that order.

Continue to find cover. Contacts still en route to you. Evasive."

Just then we saw what had made Pete so anxious.

"Roger," came the husky voice again. "Move, team."

Beckinsale switched back to his own channel, 42. "Beta team, Beta team, new signals coming from the north, uh, two signals, range twenty-five meters, musta been asleep, I don't know if they were hiding or doing their river dance thing, but-"

"Pete!" growled the Captain.

"Sorry," Pete stopped. "Uh," he scrambled over his monitors, trying to assimilate the new information and provide correct intel. "Hold tight, Beta Team. The southern band has passed, you're clear, but two signals are coming in hot, north thirty east, and north thirty-two east, range fifteen meters. Hold."

"Roger," Sergeant Shipley whispered calmly, in stark contrast to Pete's frenzy. I took a deep breath to settle my nerves. I thought I heard the cocking of a rifle. "Rutty, load a torpedo."

"Roger," echoed his brother the Private.

And then, silence. We could hear someone's breath catch over the speakers.

My heart was pounding in my chest, as I'm sure theirs were. In ten more seconds, Jentzen's voice came over the com in barely more than a whisper, "Visual. Contacts overhead and passing south. Standby."

Beckinsale knew enough not to say anything in return for fear his communications burst would generate a sound short from the static, and thus attract the enemy to their location.

I could just imagine the tension in their fingers as they flexed them around their rifles, flamethrower and rocket launcher. A few more tense seconds passed.

"Okay," breathed Pete. "I, uh, I think you're all clear now, Beta Team. Winston, how's Alpha?"

Winston turned around and put his finger to his lips, then motioning 'low volume' with his hands. The enemy must be passing close to Alpha Team.

We continued to wait, anxiously. Alpha Team had five members on their patrol. There was Will Pettijohn, Tommy Wilkes, Evy Myrtle, Shannon Hickey, and Celeste Frye. All of them had come up through the Blockade schooling system, and all were initially schooled under the former teacher, Christopher Jackson, and then either transferred to Mr. Arnold or graduated out.

The nice thing about these recon patrols, so said the Captain over dinner in the mess hall on one occasion, is that it was easy to mix and match patrol personnel. Shipley was the highest ranking, but Pettijohn was a Corporal now, so he was leading Alpha Team. However, they would fall in line, and in the event that there were two commanding officers on one patrol, one always deferred to the higher-ranking soldier.

Now, however, everyone deferred to Sergeant Shipley. He was gaining notoriety with the most patrols and the best instincts. He was still stubborn and thick-headed and would sometimes get in heated arguments with the Captain about how to run operations. But, in the end, Shipley usually prevailed. Captain Stone called him a 'loose cannon' at times, which would then accord Jet what the soldiers referred to as an 'Alpha Charlie,' aka, an ass-chewing. Vulgar term.

There was murmured chatter here and there that the Captain would never go out in the field again out of cowardice. But I knew him. That just wasn't the truth. He was much needed in this Blockade to maintain order and keep things running smoothly. Being a Captain didn't mean being just Captain over the infantry, but over *all* the operations. He was part soldier and part desk jockey, so the soldiers said. I think that's one of the reasons they called him 'Stoney.' There were crude jokes at his expense that his butt was made of rock, and he could no longer move well out in the field, and was thus more suited to a desk job. Also, he didn't fare well with any technology and was accustomed to his own way of doing things. So, 'Stoney' had a double-entendre, because he was 'stuck in the stone age.'

However you sliced it, I never heard Shipley tease the Captain, who he and Rutty would often call 'dad' out of respect and honor…and love. Sergeant Cameron Shipley and Captain Maurice Stone had a kinship. They understood one another well. The same was true (more or less) between Rutty and the Captain.

Stoney nervously watched the screens now, waiting for the 'all-clear' from Winston. It finally came, and the Captain let out a noisome exhale.

"Roger, teams, move out and proceed with caution," he instructed, and then he turned to me in an aside. "I know they hate it when I say that. Of *course* they're going to proceed with caution."

He chuckled, and I echoed it. We were equally relieved that both of our teams – all ten soldiers – were now in the clear.

We breathed easy – at least for the time being. Breathing easy came fairly naturally for us in here, but for them out there: they had to hold their breath whenever possible, and for as *long* as possible.

•   •   •   •   •

Thursday, January 10th, 2041, 1147 hours

Lunchtime. Our Beta Team had just made it into the local Montgomery Child Advocacy Center building, now abandoned, and silently closed the door behind them. We could see them from a camera mounted on an outbuilding in a cluster of offices off Cumberland Heights Road. They had all just left the edge of the forest, advanced across the asphalt, and entered the rear of the building.

"Clear," said Sergeant Shipley after a moment.

It's always been said that inside the buildings is where the teams felt safest. Sound isolation, relative removal from unfriendly eyes, shelter, all of which made sense.

For now, we could hear them talking lightly amongst themselves, quietly, trying not to elicit any undue attention. That was always the name of the game, and their banter always helped you understand them more.

Jet piped up first. "Rutty, put that thing away. Don't you ever take a break? It's time to eat, bro."

"Nah, a good part's comin' up," his brother answered. He was clearly in the throes of another book, and we could hear him munching while he read.

"Always hate going through the forest, man," said Jentzen. "It's like a jinx is on-deck. We're supposed to be shielded from them seeing us above, but I always get a bad feeling one's gonna pop out from behind a tree, or maybe they built some kinda nest in there."

"You always say that, Markus, you always say *I got a bad feeling about this forest*, ya goober," teased Ferro.

"What?" he protested. "I do. I mean, one of them out there has my number someday, right? Might as well accept it. Helps me sleep better at night."

"Thinking a gorg's got your number helps you sleep?" asked Jet.

"Yeah, doesn't sound very encouraging," Rutty chimed in. "Tell ya what, I see a gorg floatin' towards you with dog tags that look like yours, I'll introduce you first, and maybe you can take her out to pizza."

"Oh, man, don't say that. You don't say pizza. *Ever*," whined Santella.

There was faint laughter amongst them as we listened. Too true. We had two rules down here: *No matter what, you just...don't...look.* You never look at the enemy. And two: *You never talk about food we can't have.*

But they still talked about it. Maybe that helped them cope, thinking about life before the enemy.

For right now, however, they were munching on whatever they had in their MREs: meals ready to eat. No one ever reported back that what they found in their MREs did their stomach any justice whatsoever, and all were famished by the time they returned.

"Anyway," Markus continued, "we got enough to deal with in bees' nests and ant hills. Did you see that one we passed? Five feet tall. Covered over by the snow, but dude. Massive."

I had not, of course, seen one myself, but previous recon patrols had spoken of bees' nests and ant hills that had grown, unmolested, to the size of small cars. Each year the insects would return and continue expanding. Without human interference or exterminators roaming these woods, they had freedom to do as they pleased.

Someone sighed, and then Jet spoke again. "I've been in this building. But not to the church just southeast. Any of you guys ever been in here before?"

"Nope," a few of them echoed.

"Yeah," Ferro chimed in, and she could be heard close to Jet. I imagined her nestled in with his arm around her. "It was a while ago though. One of my first out here. I went with Will. We…didn't like what we found."

Pettijohn. I hoped he and his Alpha Team were doing well. We had not heard anything from Halcyon, and Winston was all quiet up ahead at his monitor.

No one spoke. The Captain and I could see the latest satellite images overhead, and we knew full well under all those white humps in the parking lot were cars that tried to make their escape: employees and visitors who were in the process of leaving when the enemy attacked. Some humps were smaller than others, and we knew those were bodies: skeletal remains of those poor souls who just couldn't get away.

My thoughts went to my husband, my sweet Miguel, relatively safe and secure back at the Embassy in Nashville, and hoped he would never be attacked again. There were a lot of people in that building, and it would be a similar mayhem.

Jentzen pressed the issue. "What did you find?" There was a pause, and it was as if Ferro shot him an angry glance. "Seriously, I'm just curious," Jentzen said.

"Whaddaya *think* we found, Markus? *Seriously*," she mocked. "Bodies. Children. Lots of them. It was awful."

"No way," breathed Santella.

"Yes. Horrible. They were all strewn around. We gathered them and buried them in the octagon outside and then lit it. There's a cemetery not two hundred feet from here, but we didn't want to bury them outside. Too much noise. They were half-eaten, some of them."

Ferro's voice grew softer, quieter, and you could hear the others leaning into her. "Almost like some kind of 'throwaway killing' on the part of the gorgs. Awful. I held a tiny skeleton in my hands. Must have been three years old."

Again, silence. Jentzen's quiet regret at having asked was deafening over the com.

The team continued to chew their food in silence.

Rutty finally spoke up. "Man. To die so young. That's awful." He didn't have to say it, but I knew he and his brother were thinking of their sister, Adelynn, who they called Sissy. She had died at only ten years of age. "I hope I live to see those piece-o-craps gone."

"Aw, Rutty, we'll take care of 'em for ya while you've got your nose in your book," his brother teased.

I wished there were a camera in that building so I could see them.

"Any of you remember your first trip to the Blockade?" asked Santella.

I couldn't tell if anyone nodded or shook their head.

"Well, I do," he said. "Most frightening six days of my entire life."

He paused, recollecting, and they listened.

"My mom and dad, and my twin brother Caleb. We used to live over on Hawkins Road, close to Oak Hill. We stayed in our house for a month following the attacks in September. The sky was so dark with them." His voice fell to below a whisper. "We thought we were so lucky because we were so close. My mom did *not* wanna go. She wanted to ride it out, ya know? Thought we'd actually be able to ride it out." He laughed grimly to himself.

"We all know now that would have been futile. They came through our neighborhood, and like, everybody was running in the streets, ya know? So we stayed inside and locked everything up. They got our cat, Simon, and our dog, Macy. Froze 'em and ate 'em right up.

"They were coming for our pool. I don't know why. Macy was barking her head off at them, and she was done for. We had a little patio, ya know those ones with the aluminum tops where the rain patters down on them? Simon was sitting in there, watching it. We were inside, and I could see the gorg whirl and just…freeze him. So weird. I didn't think they could do it to animals, but they do them too."

The others were listening intently to Santella as he shared his pain. I had not heard his story either, so he had a greater audience than he was probably aware of with all of us listening. My heart went out to him.

"Well," he continued, "Dad got his way, and we left. He had a map with where the Blockade was. He had me carry it. That was early October. I don't remember the date, but dad got his gun, and he gave mom one. He had a few of them. Caleb and I each got one too. We'd both shot them before, but they were still scary. We were only nine.

"We crept from house to house. We weren't gonna use a car of course: too much noise. We made it all the way to Southern Parkway, but…" he trailed off.

Silence. "But what?" said Ferro, and then she gasped. "They got your mom, didn't they?"

"My dad. He was the first to go. He was last in line, and it was night. One just shot out of the sky and pulled him up off into the distance. Mom tried to yelp after him, but we covered her mouth. Took us a day just to get her to move again. Begging and pleading. She was catatonic. She didn't last another block. She started to move out with us the next night, and they got her on Cumberland Drive. She tripped and fell and smashed into an abandoned car there. All kinds of cars with their driver side doors open, right? People fleeing. She just gave up. Said she wrenched her ankle. We told her to shut up, keep it down, get up with us, but she wouldn't stop screaming. We had already crossed to this building and were outside an old, dilapidated barn. Just north of the sports complex, remember that one, Sarah?"

"Mm-hmm," she said softly. She and her father, the late Corporal Ray Ferro, had evidently lived nearby Santella's family.

"Yeah. Well, mom wouldn't come. And she wouldn't shut up. We couldn't run back for her. She just laid there. Didn't even fight it. It descended on her and made that stupid hum that they do, bobbing its neck. She didn't even move. Just chomped her up. We didn't watch. Caleb threw up silently. I think I did too, but I don't remember anything else.

"We stayed there one more day. We had to reach the Blockade by the following day, or we'd be toast. By that time Caleb figured they were mostly out at night, so we moved slowly by day, across the corn field beyond Cumberland Drive, all the way down to the river. It was getting a bit colder, but we could swim it. We were both in shorts and were pretty good swimmers. We just had to keep our guns above the water," he laughed nervously, and then he stopped.

"What is it?" Rutty asked when Santella fell quiet.

Alex didn't answer right away. We heard a thick sigh come through his headset. "We were down to just the two of us. Just two. Us twins. We were determined to get there. But," he paused, "Caleb couldn't make it."

"Oh, no, Alex, I'm so sorry," said Ferro.

"Sorry, man," Jentzen agreed. "Did they get him in the river?"

Heavy, labored sigh again. "He died in the river. But not by a gorg. Caleb drowned. He was nine years old. My twin. He was the best part of me. He's down on the bottom of the Cumberland somewhere."

They all fell silent. As did we. The Captain bowed his head.

"Well, I sat on that riverbank, crying under my breath. I never saw my brother go under. He just…wasn't there anymore. But I know he drowned. He was swimming after me. I just kept facing ahead, telling him that we were almost there. I turned around once and saw his head above the water, and he was about twenty feet behind me. I climbed out through the weeds and branches on the west side, and there was a nice little bank there leading to River Road. I turned around, and, he just…" he trailed off.

"I'm sorry, Alex," Rutty said, and someone clapped him lightly on the shoulder in consolation. I heard sniffing and sighing. Alex Santella was crying.

"That wasn't the worst part. My best friend, my doppelganger, had just drowned right behind me, and I could have turned around and saved him, maybe. I sat on that bank for almost another whole day. I wanted it all to end. I was all alone. So, this nine-year-old little boy stared down the barrel of that gun, probably thinking about the deliverance that might lie beyond it. I thought, pretty easy way to go be back with my entire life that had slipped away in only three days' time," he chuckled feebly through tears. "Crazy, huh? I just sat there, looking at the water. It was a beautiful day.

"And that's when I saw them."

My heart was in my throat as I waited for Alex to continue.

"The gorgs. Three of them, drifting right up the river, heading north. Staring down, like they were looking for fish. I don't think they expected me to be there. They never looked my way, but I watched them the whole time, my eyes dried and cracked from silent tears. Floated right by me. They were…beautiful. Haunting. Something about them just so mesmerizing and captivating to a little nine-year-old's mind. That's when it hit me. *Fake.* It was all a counterfeit. They were eerily beautiful on the outside in an undiscovered way, but full of murder and malice. My eyes were opened, I looked down, and the truth hit me like a cold bite. So was that gun: full of murder and malice. Just a counterfeit. I couldn't give in to the gorgs, and I couldn't give in to the gun. I had to make the journey now: for Caleb and me both. I *had* to. So, I trudged through that forest for a mile and a half, right past this place we're in now. I remember it. I remember that little octagon building you burnt down, Sarah, right outside of the main building here. I just mumbled to myself the whole way, tried to pray, hummed 'Herman the Worm,' whatever. Anything to keep my mind alive and pass the time. I don't think I ran one bit. Just stumbled through the forest, that wide swath of forest from the Cumberland to where we are now. I finally found the Blockade, and they took me in, this little ragged nine-year-old holding a Glock." He laughed again and sniffed. "I made it. That's how I got here."

I could sense they were all looking at him with a profound respect.

"Glad you're with us, Alex," said Jet, needing to imbue confidence as his leader on this particular recon. "Glad you made it, brother."

"Thanks, Sarge," he answered softly, numbly.

The time passed slowly as they all pondered their own individual journeys. And then it was time to go.

"Well," said Jet finally, "thankfully, that octagon is one place we don't have to recon. We'll leave that area alone. I've been through the west wing here, but not through to the east. Sounds like you went that way before, Sarah. I know there isn't much left. Let's gather what we can. After that, we can search the building to the east, and then make for the church just down the way. Either one should be uneventful since we've already been here."

"Copy that," said Rutty.

"Affirmative," said Jentzen.

They all moved out, silently. All of them were struck, reflecting on Alex's story. The truth was that all of us were struck by it in here as well.

•   •   •   •   •

Thursday, January 10th, 2041, 1319 hours

"Roger, heading out," said Jet, and they all collected at the western end of the building next to the Montgomery Child Advocacy Center. "Command, we're proceeding to the church southeast. Sign says, 'The River Church,' over."

"Confirmed. Use caution. No signals inbound," Pete replied.

Another camera picked them up from the south side of the Montgomery Child Advocacy Center, heading west, threading single file, looking up and around in all directions, quiet as a mouse. I took a deep breath, as I did anytime they were all out in the open.

They proceeded across the parking lot, weaving between the foreboding humps of snow, and finally made their way to the church building about two hundred feet southeast off the corner of the advocacy center.

The Sergeant was the first one to open the door. The camera saw him, hovering at the door, but then he stopped, and proceeded to back up. He just held there.

The Sergeant could be seen lingering at the door, looking in. Markus was looking over his shoulder, and Sarah Ferro was beside him. And suddenly, one of them turned away and doubled over, retching. A trail of vomit spewed out of Markus Jentzen's mouth.

"Let's go," Sergeant Shipley said, and turned them around, closing the door.

"What is it?" Rutty asked. He had been last in line and hadn't seen what the others had. "What?"

"Nothing. Let's just go. Come on." He grabbed his brother's arm and moved him away from the door.

His team gasped and stifled cries of grief. We heard them. All of them, except for Rutty, who had not seen what they had seen. One of them swore. One of them cried out to God. One of them sobbed softly. Yet all of them saw something so unsettling that they backed out of there and made for the Blockade on an immediate return trip.

"Command, Shipley and Beta Team returning to base, over." His voice was quavering.

The Captain tilted his head and pressed his com right away. "Sergeant Shipley, you have not been cleared to return. What are you doing?" he growled.

No answer.

"Shipley, you are ordered to perform your recon. Confirm," the Captain snarled once more.

The Sergeant said nothing.

The Captain said nothing in return for a moment. Then he turned to the other members of the team, "Private Shipley. Private Ferro. Private Jentzen. Private Santella. Report."

Nothing. Only huffing and caught breaths and the sound of snow crunching underfoot as they raced for the Blockade. I thanked God there were no infrared signals coming their way. I watched the monitor Pete Beckinsale was glued to. Mercifully, nothing nefarious appeared.

The Captain asked them once more for a situation report, which they couldn't give; they were too shaken up by what they had seen. Except for Rutty, of course: he was at the back of the line whispering requests for clarity.

"What did you see, Jet? Tell me!"

"Rutty, dammit, forget about it and just come on!"

The team followed him. The Captain asked once more for a sit rep, and Shipley didn't give him one.

"Damnit!" cried the Captain, tearing off his headset, and heading for the Launch. I heard him mutter *loose cannon* under his breath.

Something had freaked all of them out, that much was certain. What they had seen had terrified them.

It was a private matter, never to be shared.

23 | SCIENCE

| Bassett |

Wednesday, August 29th, 2041, 1003 hours

Sometimes things were just a major pain.

We had been commissioned to work on a plan to capture a live gorgon, but no one could come up with a feasible idea on how to do it. Committees were formed and we kept meeting, but we weren't getting anywhere. The order came down from the President herself, straight through Major Bayless.

We were all gathered in the Rotunda at a round table, talking over semantics and procedures of how we would manage to get this done.

Trudy and Chance had whipped up a few more masks now, so it's not like we were going in blind – Maureen would appreciate the pun – but every time we thought we had set a good trap, they just avoided it entirely.

And that was the weirdest thing. We had never *ever* wanted them *anywhere* close to us. And now we were trying to wrangle one? *Good Lord.*

Steph had lured that one to the Launch doors with the original prototype mask, and then they had blown the gorg to smithereens. It had proven effective. But we still needed to test it out up close, and for a longer duration.

"Steph, it's not gonna be easy, sis," I said. "You had us all covering you, and we had twelve gun towers on it."

"So?" she argued. "We go out with a much larger patrol this time. Overwhelm them by superior numbers."

"And risk turning one small, unnoticeable blur on the ground into one giant, noticeable one," said Trudy.

Donner was on a previous mission with Steph, and he was equally as brave – or as foolhardy. "No, Steph's right. We get double – no – *triple* the crew. Like twelve of us. Split it evenly. Six to wrangle it, and six to form a protective perimeter. We bring Robertson. He's a big guy. Dude could just lay on it and squeeze the life out of it. Then it'll be easy to bring back."

"Ha! See if it can float with Robertson's three hundred twenty pounds on top of it, much less any of the rest of us," Steph jested, eliciting laughter.

"Yeah," I shot back, "but we need it alive of course. And we have no idea how long it'll stay unconscious."

'Well, time isn't an issue where we have masks," Trudy objected. "We have enough for a team of that caliber."

"Time is *always* an issue," I asserted. "The more noise that thing makes, the more noise we make trying to subdue it, the further away from the Blockade we are, the more time it'll take to get it down our stairs and into containment. All of that adds up, Trudy. And that brings up another point: the isolation booth. What are we lookin' at for that, Gage?"

Gage nodded. "Well, you've seen it, it's nowhere near ready yet. We've had to fabricate protective shielding, separating it from us, of course. And that's taken time. The booth itself has had to be reinforced. No active factories anymore, man," he said, shaking his head. "All we can go on is plywood, more plywood, and steel or iron bars at decent intervals like studs to give it some structure. But if that thing gets free while we're working on it…" he ended with a wide-eyed look of fear.

"Yep, game over," I said.

"Well, quarantine has a pretty strong containment quotient," said Trudy. "We could just reinforce that and use what we already have. Medical can relocate somewhere else sufficient to treat any wounded, and isolate any sick cases for the interim, at least until we're ready to-" she stopped short.

"To what?" Gage asked.

"To dump its sorry ass," Steph said. "Once we have no more use for it. I don't know if you're holding a raffle, but I call dibs on putting the final bullet through its brain."

Good old Steph.

"And when will that time be?" Donner asked. "How do we know how long we keep it for? And what are we even looking for while we have it?"

I looked at Donner matter-of-factly. "Well, obviously the goal is to test the masks for a prolonged period up close, but mainly to see how the new ones can stay on without getting knocked off. Trudy's got one going in a 3M-type housing that should be more secure than the first one. That's Priority One. Priority Two is to examine it, find out what motivates it, what triggers it, how powerful its senses are, and what other weaknesses we can find."

"'What other weaknesses?' I'd say sound is the biggest one now that they have those new sound gadgets to knock 'em back," said Donner. "It's the first thing someone's found that actually *works*."

"Yeah, well, we wanna find other ways to kick their sorry asses. And faster," Steph put in, and mocked an uppercut. I smiled in agreement. My kid sister was no joke.

I thought to myself for a moment, remembering something. "Look, everyone," I replied, "we have to start thinking outside the box. That's what they did down in Nashville. They thought outside the box and figured out what the amulets were. They were their Achilles' Heel. And now we're using it against them. We have to be smarter than them if we're going to beat them. We know they don't like sound. But what about sunlight? They largely disappear during the heat of the summer. They're head down in rivers, usually, or at least that's where they congregate."

"Hey, yeah!" Gage sat up and blurted out. "Remember before the attacks, how they were all just hanging there, staring upward, and they were sweating in the sun? It's almost like they were enduring it, but it was clearly having an effect on them. Some people even reported that they were, like, *steaming,* or something."

"Right, okay, sunlight or heat could be a weapon. Maybe they have some vampiric qualities. Maybe their home planet is mostly darkness, further away from a central star, so they don't have as much heat. Maybe their planet's made of ice, and that's why they're more active in our fall and winter," Trudy replied.

"If they even have a home planet," Gage answered. "Maybe they've just been out there floating in the cold of space, and that's all they do, going from planet to planet, and eating everything in sight."

My turn again. "Well, aside from figuring out more weaknesses, we just need to analyze them. We need to get into their microbiology. We got the sample from the dead one, but living tissue is another thing. We need to get behind their eyes, crack open their skull, figure out how they engage their telepathy. Figure out how they float, why they're so fast, how they do that misting thing. All of it."

Everyone was silent, pondering having a live gorgon in captivity among us. What havoc it could wreak if it ever broke free of containment. I looked around at all of them.

"Donner, Steph, you're in charge of the capture plan. Trudy, Chance, you're in charge of giving us your best masks, state of the art, to keep us protected out there. Gage and I are in charge of the lab, along with anyone else who wants to chip in with monitoring the subject, analysis, and whatever other aid they can lend to our studies. Right? Let's start planning this thing. The order came down from President Graham, so let's make her and Bayless happy."

At that precise moment Major Bayless walked into our meeting.

"Make Bayless happy about what?" she asked.

We all rose and saluted.

"Major Bayless," I greeted her. "Good to see you, Ma'am. We were just discussing protocol and planning for the capture and study of a primary subject."

She looked at me blankly. Her eyebrows went up. "And?"

"Uh, and we're, uh, working on it. Won't be easy."

"Nothing ever is, Staff Sergeant Bassett. The last fifteen years haven't been easy. Let's get to it. Let me know what you need, people, savvy? President wants this done as soon as possible."

"Yes, Ma'am," I replied. "We've got to first create a contained environment, or we don't have anywhere to put it. Do we have your permission to move medical to new quarters and use the existing medical as an isolation booth? Quarantine has the strongest antimicrobial protections in case they're loaded with cultures harmful to us. It's also got the thickest walls and best containment environment in terms of restraining it."

"Permission granted. What else do you need?"

"We'll need time to make more masks, Ma'am. Better ones. No one here has ever wrangled a gorg, and I only know of the two they had in Nashville. Do we even have tranquilizers in Weps, Ma'am? We'll need those."

"We've never needed them. Only live rounds. But I'll put in a requisition order right away. I think I have an Amazon Prime account somewhere."

The team chuckled. I did as well. "Yes, Ma'am. However long it takes to get them, we'll need those."

"You got it," she said. "Just get a finalized list to me in two days' time and I'll send it up the chain. It'll take time to get it of course, but they're mobilizing at BNA airport in Nashville. *Operation Deep Breath.* I know, funny name, but whatever," she said, waving it away. "Lots of vehicles being equipped with those sound emitters. They're bringing new supplies, ammo, equipment, medical, scientific equipment, and more. You'll have what you need, but it'll take time. No promises on any expected timeline. Keep at it, savvy?"

Savvy.

"Yes, Ma'am," we all said, and Bayless exited.

We would have a big grocery list, I was sure. She would have to deal with our list and get us what we needed if we were to accomplish this crackpot mission.

Must sometimes just be a pain being a Major.

24 | TRAUMA

| Rosie |

Wednesday, September 3rd, 2041, 1016 hours

Fifteen years had gone by so slowly.

We were all gathered in the Pavilion, and they looked to me, their Pastor, to provide them a bit of solace. Solace was really the only thing I could provide sometimes.

We all stood in silent reflection, as was our wont, lining the perimeter of the Pavilion in our Blockade with only our tower gunners absent. They maintained a constant vigil, and they were needed.

The rest of us stood there for fifteen long minutes of silent reflection. Each minute that elapsed, the young girl who had sung at Rutty's birthday played a single note on a flute that someone had brought down. A chilling single note lasting seven seconds, filled with the undulating vibrato of memory for nearly seven billion souls lost.

It was somber beyond belief.

All across the world, similar memorials were playing out in the pavilions of other Blockades. Also, I'm sure, in the hollowed, quiet recesses of ramshackle housing where the scattered survivors still dared to dwell above ground, eking out an existence in the shadows.

We remembered.

•   •   •   •   •

We dismissed, and everyone dispersed to their assignments.

Several people thanked me, including Sarah Ferro and Cameron Shipley, who for some reason had been drifting apart. I think neither were particularly well equipped to handle their sorrow and trauma from that frightful mission, and there was just no spark anymore. Healing needed to happen for them, individually. Right now, there was no fire in their relationship; their wood was wet.

After the Beta team returned from that mission, I had had multiple sessions with all of them. No one wanted to talk about what they saw. They all continued to serve, and were on different missions together and apart, but every one of them became more stoic and less conversational.

Except Rutty, of course. Whether from being desensitized from reading everything under the sun in those books of his, or from quietly putting to rest his own demons over losing his mother, father, and sister, he endured. He had a stalwart will, that one, and an unquenchable joy that had translated well to others. Whenever someone needed encouragement, they would go to Rutty, and if Rutty was out on mission, they would go to me. I so admired his spirit…he pressed on, and would always do so.

After individual sessions, the ones that became most productive were when I would have the entire team together, all five of them: the two Shipley brothers, Jentzen, Santella, and Ferro. The Sergeant was the most stoic and lockjawed out of all of them. He just sat back and glowered with that thousand-yard stare of his. Ferro was the most articulate with how she felt.

And finally, at long last, the Captain and I learned the cold truth.

Babies. Mothers holding their young, frozen in rigor mortis and bodies wasting away together, fused. Elderly. There were bodies innumerable, piled up, mangled, thrown together, in various stages of undress, their clothing bitten through. Missing limbs and bones. Decapitations. Limbs that should have been attached, but several feet away, dangling. Rotting flesh, chewed through in a gruesome, twisted gnarl.

But it was the blood, they had said. The floor was a sticky, darkened, dried mess of coagulated fluid at least an inch thick. The pews were awash in crimson. The windows were splattered. There was a single skeleton up on the stage, leaning over its podium, bitten through and staggering against it, frozen in time. It was the preacher: forever doomed to stand there and deliver his own poetic, haunting eulogy to his deadened flock who would never be allowed to hear, because aliens do not repent.

The powerful stench had hit the Sergeant first, and a wave of nausea crashed over him. Jentzen followed him and vomited. The rest of them were retching, their stomachs lurching. They had bolted back for the Blockade, the eerie disquiet gnawing at them and biting their heels the whole way home. When they fell through the Launch door, they were bawling in each other's arms. A few of them reeked of vomit.

It was the most traumatized I had ever seen a Recon team upon its return, and they all were in a state of catatonia. What fate had befallen all the parishioners of that church was so morbid and macabre, they would never be able to unsee it.

Never.

The Alpha Team, led by Will Pettijohn, was instructed never to go to that location. It would, one day, be burned like the octagon at the other side. But, for now, it was hallowed ground filled with hundreds of souls who never had a chance, taking refuge in the one place they thought the Father would protect them.

All this time I wondered about Cameron. I remembered back four years ago when they had brought his father in, dying. He was only eighteen then, and Rutty was fourteen. They were both so visibly scarred and disassembled at the passing of their father, their only remaining parent. All they had left now was each other.

On the days following their father's death, I had prayed that the Father would usher Cameron into trust. *Bring him in, bring him in,* I had prayed. And where was he now? There were times where I felt he was advancing closer. Certainly, having his brother serving by his side was good therapy, and their jocularity and fraternal teasing was good for them. But all of them had been traumatized from that patrol, and it had already been an emotional patrol with Alex Santella's account of his journey to this Blockade.

I withdrew after the service today. I needed time to collect and reflect, and to be alone.

Sergeant Shipley would be in my office for a counseling session at 1100 hours. I needed to regroup and pray.

Reaching my office, I collapsed in a heap. I don't know why, but right there and then, I started to weep. I could not hold back, and I did not want to. The floodgates were opened, and I mourned fully.

I wept for the lives of every human lost to those things. Those accursed things that had stolen so much from our planet.

I wept because we hadn't heard from the Lord on when we would be delivered.

I wept because I was also not hearing from my husband, my sweet Miguel.

I wept because we were stuck down here, away from the sun, away from freedom and green grass, from the wind blowing on our faces and the sound of music.

I wept.

It was cleansing, yes, but I needed to show strength. These people looked to me, and I needed to remain the pillar – a diminutive pillar, to be sure – of strength that they needed during these dark times.

Good thing I didn't wear any makeup, I thought. The truth was that strength isn't strength unless its put to the test. They counted me strong, but I was still human, and I had not had a good, vulnerable cry in a long time. Fifteen years of being strong gets to a woman.

I wiped my eyes, and took a deep breath to re-center myself, praying for strength, wisdom and clarity.

The Sergeant would be here momentarily. From the little I had heard from Miguel, colossal developments were taking place all over the globe. These new emitter devices, these new masks that had been developed; I sensed a war coming. Cameron was going to do great things in that war. So was Rutty.

But the stoic one was Cameron, and he would be the greater challenge. He would need wisdom, and focus. He would need *my* wisdom, and *my* focus.

It was time to get to know Andrew's oldest son better.

•   •   •   •   •

Wednesday, September 3rd, 2041, 1102 hours

A knock at my door.

"Hello, just a moment," I said, getting up from my little desk. I paced over to the plywood door that was anything but a privacy screen, and opened it up.

There, standing tall and proud in his fatigues, his rifle slung over his shoulder, was Sergeant Cameron Shipley.

"Hello, Cameron. So good to see you. Come on in."

"Thank you, Rosie," he said, and offered a forced smile. His brow was furrowed, and he looked like he was carrying something on his heart…his shoulders were a bit hunched. He sat on my couch, and I sat across from him in my little chair. No one else fit in it but me.

"Thank you for coming," I offered. "Would you like some water?"

"Sure, that would be great. Thanks for all you said at the service. Hard to believe it's been fifteen years."

I shook my head as I got back up to pour him some water. "Hard indeed. They say a watched pot never boils. We've been watching this pot since 2026, haven't we?"

"Yes, we have," he said in a huff.

I handed him his water. I didn't get any for myself, and then sat down once more, folding my hands in front of me. I looked upon him. He looked grimmer than he usually had, and his shoulders were still hunched. Yet something shone in him, and I wasn't sure what it was. I smiled.

He looked up at me, and his eyes slid away with an awkward, momentary smile. "Uh…what is it?"

I laughed as I spoke. "I must admit I usually have your brother in here. It's quite different. You remind me more and more of your father every day."

He smiled. "Well, I suppose that's complimentary. He was a good guy. I was a tough kid to have, that's for sure. He was, uh, pretty patient. So was mom."

I smiled and nodded. "I can imagine. They were wonderful people. Always will be."

He nodded.

"So," I started. "Let's chat. How are you doing since the incident?"

He thought to himself for a moment, and then rolled his eyes. "Ya know, Rosie," he said, leaning forward on his knees, "I don't know what to say to that. That was eight months ago. I mean, at some point you move on, right?"

"And have you?"

He looked like I caught him by surprise. "Well, I mean, you have to. Right? Otherwise, you're stewing forever."

Kid, you have no idea how much I was mourning twenty minutes before this session, due to my own stewing.

"Well, yes, I suppose so. But every once in a while, it's important to let the air out," I said.

"Air?"

"Of the tires of life. You have to let the air out and sink down a bit. Sit. Reflect. Pause. Not be so go-go-go. That's, more or less, the way your father Andrew was. At least, that's what I remember from the few sessions I had with him. And then, after you've taken the forced rest, you get pumped back up again and get back out there. But, without the rest, we're driving forever on a very long and weary road with tires bound to pop."

Cameron fell silent and looked at the soft earth under our feet.

"Rest," he said, and then he scoffed. "Seems like an alien word. I lie down to rest, and I can't get to sleep. It's hard enough having to live down here, but then having to pretend that this is the life we want, that everything is okay when it's not. Man," he said, shaking his head. "You mention Rutty. My bro's got his head on straight. And mine? Sometimes I feel like my threads are stripped, ya know?"

I nodded. "I do know." *I certainly did know.*

He sat back. "These walls all around us," -here he motioned to the green earth carved out by that giant drill, granting me this makeshift ground full of ants and bugs and grass- "I remember when dad had to help put up those girders up by the Launch so it wouldn't cave in. Remember that? This place always feels like it's gonna cave in somehow. The Pavilion especially. Such a big place. But," he faltered, "that's the way life kinda feels sometimes. Like it's always caving in on us. It definitely caved in on me and Sarah."

"Oh? Tell me about her."

He paused. "Well, I like her, still, I mean, I *think* I like her. I dunno," he said, shaking his head. "Thought we had a good thing going. But she kept getting nightmares all the time and became kind of haunted by that place. That's when we started fighting out in the field. She couldn't sleep either. She got pretty irritable, and that's why we haven't shared any patrols for a while."

I nodded once more. The Captain had separated them after Ferro questioned his direction, angrily, on a recent mission. You cannot do *anything* angrily out there on a mission, for fear of creating noise.

"Anyway," he said, breathing out a big jet of air, "I think that's all over with. That's really the only thing bugging me, I guess."

"The only thing?" I asked him.

He looked at me quizzically.

"You just listed several things. Not knowing what to say, trouble moving on, difficulty sleeping, walls caving in, your unthreaded head about to fall off. That last one might require a trip to the nurse. Nice gal named Sarah Ferro."

He giggled. "Yeah. I guess. That would be awkward, for sure."

I smiled at him. It was nice to see him softening.

"Cameron, can I ask you a question?"

He nodded.

"Have you forgiven yourself for your father's death?"

I don't have thermal vision, but I swear his face darkened a shade of red and he flushed.

"Forgiven myself?" he asked dismissively.

"Well," I said in a big breath, standing up and pacing over to the wall. "I've listened to all of you in here recounting what happened in that church with the bodies. Markus was hit very hard by it, as was Sarah. As was Alex. I know you and your brother were too. With Alex in particular, it was *very* hard for him. Sharing that story of his past – about his twin brother – that brought some things to the surface that were very painful for him to remember. You're in here for healing. You may have moved on from – or been able to stuff entirely – the memory of that church.

Consider yourself fortunate. But I'm remembering another incident a while back."

"Which is?"

"You and your brother. At the Launch. For your big, exciting rumble." A smile teased at the corner of Cameron's lips here, remembering his tussle with Rutty. "You were carrying a lot of unforgiveness toward yourself for what happened to your father. Do you remember that?"

"Of course I remember it. I was the one who said what I said about dad. I was bawling, Rosie." His tone took on a slight air of injury and offence.

"Understood. And have you forgiven yourself for what happened with your father?"

His eyes darted around. "I don't know why we're talking about this."

"So, you haven't then."

"I didn't say that."

I looked at him over the rim of my glasses. My mother used to do that to me, giving me her best *I-know-you-better-than-you-think-I-do* look. It bugged me then. Look at me now though: I was repeating my mother. "It's what you didn't say, Cameron."

"Okay, fine," he said, throwing his hands up. "What exactly didn't I say?"

I paused, walked back over, and sat down across from him. "Cameron, I am not trying to agitate you. I give you my word. What you didn't say is 'Yes, I forgive myself.'"

"I forgive myself!" he cried out immediately, clearly irritated.

I tilted my head and just looked at him.

"I mean, what do you want me to say, Pastor Rosie? It was a long time ago. I realize he did it to save me. I'm fine with it, and I'm thankful. It's just taken time to get over it, that's all."

"Well, I mean, you have to. Right? Otherwise, you're stewing forever," I said, repeating back to him what he said earlier.

He didn't like this at all. Cameron rolled his eyes and sat back against the wall, his face reddening, his hands behind his head, slumping. "You think I'm still stewing?"

"I know you are. You carry guilt with you. So much so that you kept your brother from enlisting. So much that you feel bad for leading the team members into the church. So much, that you feel responsible for you and Sarah Ferro breaking up. I predict that, someday, you're going to do something massive that you will carry tremendous guilt for, and you will have to work your way through that as well."

And now he crossed his arms, firing daggers at me with his eyes.

"Again, I'm not trying to agitate you, Cameron. I just call them as I see them. You are very walled-off and stoic, much different from your brother."

He continued to stare at me. "My brother."

"Yes? What about him?"

"It's because of my brother that I backed us out of that church."

"Oh?"

"Yes. I didn't want him to see it. He was off taking shelter when Sissy was killed. He never saw her. *I* saw her, Rosie. When the coast was clear, I ran up to the Launch and I saw her. She was cold, stuck, frozen, all of it. Her eyes were glazed over, and her veins were blue. You could see them running through her skin. That's what all those people looked like in there at one point, though they were skeletons.

They are all of them frozen and haunted. I didn't want Rutty to see that."

"So, you were protecting him."

"Yes. That's what I was doing with all of them."

"But wasn't that what you were doing by keeping him from enlisting? 'Protecting him'?"

"Oh, no, no, don't try to tie this up and blame me." He got up, and looked like he was preparing to leave. "That wasn't my fault. *No one* needed to see what I saw in there. Markus did. Alex and Sarah did. Look at them. Look what kind of havoc its wreaked on their consciences."

"But not yours."

"I didn't say that."

I looked at him intently. "Do you know your father sat on this very couch with me, right here, many years ago, after your mother was diagnosed with lung cancer? We had a talk, he and I. It was good."

He looked like he was softening again. "What was it about?" he asked, quietly, curiously.

"Receiving."

"You mean that thing you do with your palms up?" The way he asked it did not sound altogether approving.

"Yes, more or less. But his was a bit different. You see, where the willingness is great, the difficulties cannot be great. Niccolo Machiavelli said that. Perseverance comes from a strong will. Obstinacy comes from a strong 'won't.' That one's from Henry Ward Beecher," I said, patting his leg, and he stifled an annoyed chuckle.

"Your father wanted to persevere for your mother, but he was obstinate in how he was going about it. You are wanting to persevere for Rutty, but you're obstinate in how you're going about it. I want to encourage you to persevere in trust. You are cynical in how you protect Rutty, as if he doesn't have the mental stamina to withstand what you do. You don't trust him enough to be able to face the horrors that you have. Am I close to the mark?"

"There is no mark," he murmured in a grunt, looking away, his hands now folded across his chest.

I couldn't repress a giggle. "Cameron," I said to him, "look at me. Please."

Cameron turned his eyes to me.

"You can be the *will*, and not the *won't*. Rutty is the *will*. There is a war coming. You've heard murmurs of it with all this new fancy equipment and masks. We won't stay down here forever. When life begins anew on the surface, Rutty will need you to trust him enough to land on his own two feet and thrive without your protection: to persevere. Do you trust that he will be able to do so?"

He looked at me, looked down, and didn't answer.

"Can you try to trust that he can take what you think he can't?"

Cameron took a deep breath. "Yeah. I can."

"Good. That's a great first step, my friend. Rutty is much stronger than you think. You and he are going to do great things together. You already have, both of you. You're going to be very important in the coming conflict, I know it."

"We are, huh?" he said, melancholily. "Okay."

A laugh snuck out of my nose. "You might not see it now. This whole *walls-caving-in insomnia breaking-up-is-hard-to-do* business, all of it is drudgery. For you, tip-toeing around up there in the sun amongst fear trounces stomping around down here amongst friends. You're a warrior. But there will be a time where you can stomp without fear up there. And you have to trust that you and Rutty will stomp together. He has far more power at his center than you give him credit. That center is his faith. His trust."

Cameron stared at me, lightly scraping the faint whiskers of his five o'clock shadow, pensive in thought. He eventually nodded.

"I'm so sorry you had to experience what you did out there. But as someone who lives in this Blockade and fears for all our safety every single day, I'm so grateful knowing that you are who you are, and that you do what you do. All of you. Thank you for your service."

"You're welcome," he said, after a pause. "Thanks, Pastor Rosie." He forced a smile across his clenched lips as he got up to leave. "I've, uh, I've gotta get back," he said, giving me a meager wave and a smile.

I nodded. It was fine.

It would take time with Cameron, but he'd come around. I was sure of it. He was too close to Rutty not to. Something in me told me that Rutty would leave such a mark on him that would open the door for the Father to bring him in to full trust and faith. He was about to be twenty-two, and he was a deep thinker. Something would happen: a catalyst, or something in their service together, that would propel him, eventually, into the Father's arms. I just knew it.

When exactly that would be was anyone's guess.

After all, fifteen years had already gone by so slowly.

25 | MURMURS

| Miguel |

Monday, January 13th, 2042, 0727 hours

Rumors were spreading, and she wasn't safe.

There were now threats against the President's life, and more were coming in by the day. Someone in the underground, Cardona thought, although he didn't know who. Someone who wanted to make their own mark against her, and there began to be bomb threats and other intimidations posted to her X account and sent via private message from an anonymous source. Then the phone calls started too.

Secret Service said they needed to start moving her around, 'shuttling her.' So that's what we were about to do.

There was a lot of movement on our planet; more so than there had been in a decade and a half. Frigates were shipping out with DTF emitters all over the world, equipping other Blockades, and survivors everywhere, with their own personal DTF emitters.

The boys over at The Lab at BNA had also developed projectiles…high-powered bombs and EMP-like technology, coupling powerful sonic bursts with the *gorgos'* own amulets to create deafeningly powerful DTF explosions that could radiate outward for a few miles. Because they were coupled with electromagnetic pulses, any technology in the blast radius would need to be shut down, or they would risk frying their own equipment. These were powerful new weapons that could be detonated with manual triggers. They would now be tested in the field.

However, some of those materials – in fact, a lot of those materials – were headed to three distinct locations in the East. One in Iran, one in China, and one in North Korea. Those were the zones that the President had established in order to conduct her nuclear strikes. Those areas housed her detractors, and she wanted them eliminated, along with the legacy of their cities. Tehran, Pyongyang, and Beijing. Those were her targets, and things were in motion. Conscripted workers were almost finished constructing massive jetties to lure in the *gorgos* with bait food. Then, not only hit them with huge DTF emitters gathered en masse, but then nuke the areas which housed the lures.

However, as yet unbeknownst to President Jean Theodora Graham, Cardona was moving too. He reported a strong undercurrent of dissent growing and multiplying exponentially. He was able to convince those higher up in the chain that Graham's plots were in fact terrifyingly nefarious, and that they were in fact well underway. Incredulity fueled anger. Anger turned to revolt. And the Resistance ballooned. Even now, Cardona was commiserating and strategizing with admirals, colonels, majors, captains and the like, planning.

Preparing to subvert The President at every turn. But advised, of course, to feign allegiance to her until the time was ripe and we could no longer deny our treachery.

And, apparently, that's what created the crazies. Someone out there didn't have enough faith in Cardona to pull it all off, evidently, and they wanted Graham out of the picture now.

So, we had to move. Today. We were in a fleet of suburbans loaded with DTF emitters. They would sound a pulse every two seconds, again, more felt than heard, pulsating all around us. It was like traveling in an urban street fair in Chicago, the rhythmic thumping reverberating like an undulating dance beat. These suburbans were over a decade old. They had kept them in the covered area out in front of the Embassy Suites since their drivers tried to rescue the previous president during the invasion, ready to go at a moment's notice.

We had an old guy named Walt who kept up the maintenance on the suburbans. Strong believer in the Lord. He and I had occasionally conversed and he was always a friendly face. I was so overjoyed to know that he had made it through the attack on the Embassy. The man didn't fear death. *Un hombre duro.* Very tough. Walt kept them shipshape and assisted with the retrofitting of the emitters. And now, we were in those old suburbans, traveling south on 155 to The Lab, the BNA Amazon Warehouse.

She would be safest there both from *gorgos* as well as humans. It was heavily guarded by gunners and DTF emitters.

"I want to get into an actual sub again," Graham said to Agent Grimstad seated to her right. "Love those people tanks! But, hell, look at all of this. I would stay out on top just to see all of this every day." She motioned outside the window to the east, and I could now see it so much more clearly. All those military vehicles, jets, planes, and other ground transports were lined up in nice little rows on the tarmac and off into the grass between runways.

She had been in the Navy, apparently aboard a sub, but I didn't know what rank she held in her service. That longing for days past was now bubbling up to the surface. Maybe one day would see us traveling around in one. And then I swallowed hard. *With nuclear missiles and firing triggers at her fingertips.* I silently prayed that that day would never come. My thoughts went to my dear Rosalita.

BNA was absolutely overrun with military vehicles. The massed fleet served two purposes. One, continue disseminating the DTF emitters and masks. And two, prepare for ground assault and incursions once Graham's master plan had been fulfilled, and we had to root out the remaining *gorgos* that had evaded her signal sweeps.

I looked over at her as she gawked at all of it in amazement. She had really done it. For a moment, she seemed beautiful. The sun was on her face, and golden pride framed her. The President was a septuagenarian, long past her prime, having overstayed her welcome, corrupted by politics, embattled by criticism, embroiled in controversy, embracing catastrophe. Was she really evil? I had seen it, of course, and it was indisputable. But was there a seed of promise there that could be redeemed? Only time would tell. For now, here, across these sprawling airport runways, she was readying our planet for a massive counterstrike. We were all behind her in that. It was her nefarious subplot that made me sick to my stomach. If only we could stop her after she killed the *gorgos*…or find another way.

Come what may, she would take shelter at The Lab, and they were preparing quarters for her, until it was safe for her to return to the Embassy. She left Cooper over there to run things while she stayed here, only a mile away.

If she wanted to get on a sub, that would come somewhere down the line. I just hoped it would bring me up the Cumberland to my sweet Rosalita someday. Didn't know if the Cumberland was deep enough for a sub, anyway.

I had not heard from Cardona in a month, but I know they were busy outfitting the cave mouth at the Mammoth Cave Blockade, DN312. One of the last things he had reported was that they had received a large number of infantry and personnel, along with computer equipment. This was completely under the radar. All Graham was told was that a battalion of tanks and SUVs made their way north to the cave to deliver the equipment. She was never told about the personnel. They were now at least a hundred strong in defectors, allegiant to Cardona and devoted to seeing Graham dethroned.

He also reported that Wright-Patterson airfield was now with the Resistance, working clandestinely with the Colonel there in conjunction with several military bases. He was in communication with Rear Admiral Evelyn Lynch at Norfolk, and she was appearing convinced. He said she had required some persuasion, sure enough, but was no BS.

All in all, this is where we would be now, at The Lab at BNA. All over the world, support for the Resistance was growing.

Rumors were spreading, but so far, the Resistance remained safe.

26 | SANTELLA

| Rosie |

Saturday, February 8th, 2042, 1331 hours

It's not every day you get a priceless treasure.

Rutty held it up to the camera for all to see: a green laser pointer. That would come in handy in case the recon patrol was split up for some reason. He and his team, which included Ferro, Jentzen, Santella and Corporal Pettijohn, were in a neighborhood in C-Range. His brother Cameron was out on a different patrol in A-Range.

Santella sneezed, and they shushed him. He thought he was coming down with a cold and had said that the back of his throat felt a little tight. But the lick n' prick didn't come back with anything strong enough to report, and he was cleared for the mission.

They had been out for a few hours since leaving this morning, and it was still cold out, which meant more of the enemy were about. But now, they were relaxing in a house, taking food and drink until it was time to bring back to the Blockade all that they had managed to collect.

They continued to mount cameras in as many places as they could. Cameron's team wasn't installing cameras at the zinc plant; it already had plenty on the premises. Halcyon was able to hack into those and add them to the surveillance feeds. We needed more cameras everywhere in order to gain usable intel of the enemy's whereabouts. Especially for us nail-biters in Command, it was important to know where our teams were and how they were faring. Each recon was always like watching a scary movie.

However, there were rare moments of joy in the field. Rutty finding and proudly displaying his laser pointer was one of those. The kid was almost nineteen, but he was still a kid. They had to tell him to cut it out because he kept playing with it.

Ferro teased him and bantered easily with him while they were taking a break, sheltering in a house along Skelton Drive. The house next door had burnt down, presumably from someone who had been frozen while cooking something…or ironing something…or lighting their wood stove. Who knows. That was probably done by thousands more inhabitants of houses just like the one that had been reduced to ash here. Seeing it on the camera was disconcerting. They all had died, or had already been killed by the enemy. But, of course, the fire burned out of control, and there were no firefighters to put out the blaze.

In the midst of all of that, however, it was a pleasant contrast to see Sarah and Rutty talking freely, at ease. I wondered if a spark of love was developing between those two. I wondered how Cameron would feel about that. In my talks with him, he had moved on.

In watching them, I feared for mi *cariño*, Miguel. My *Miguelito.* My mind was flooded with memories. I had known him for so long. I was in my twenties and he was in his teens, in the throes of forbidden love back in the late seventies and early eighties in Mexico. It was taboo, but we were honorable. My mother always used to tease us because he was nine years younger than me. However, I had not entered school on time because we had emigrated from Guatemala, and we didn't have the same schooling; it just didn't translate. It didn't help that I always had my head in the clouds back then as well, so I flunked a few grades. As a result, I remained in school long after my peers had graduated. Miguel and I got together, and despite the age gap, Mama was happy for me.

He was still in *escuela secundaria* in Matamoros just south of the border with Texas while my mom and I lived close by.

We fell in love and made plans to get married in 2026, before the invasion altered everyone's lives. We were not together that fateful day as I had been visiting with my mom in Nashville. Upon my entering the Blockade, we communicated through encrypted emails that Miguel's contact – the hardy and insightful Captain Vance Cardona – set up for us. I am so grateful for that man, and for what he has begun, though I wonder how much longer he'll go unnoticed by the President. When it became clear that she was as murderous as they suspected, Miguel feared the worst. He wanted to leave. I don't know how I convinced him to stay at his post, but he remained. He was the only link to the inside, once Cardona was restationed. Vance echoed my sentiment. Therefore, we kept our marriage, and our children, under wraps.

I remember when I finally got to see Miguel for the first time after the attacks: eight years ago in a Zoom call. The year was 2034, and he looked a bit grayer, but there was *mi cariño,* healthy and well. He asked me to marry him again in that call, and I burst into tears. A volunteer in Halcyon helped us conduct the ceremony over a Zoom call privately.

I said yes; I couldn't contain my enthusiasm and joy. He hadn't even finished his proposal. Our marriage had never been formally certified, but all things in due time. One day we would meet an ordained minister who could certify it.

I hated keeping up the lie that he had died in the attacks. I couldn't let on that I was married, let alone married to Lieutenant Miguel Monzon. There was too much at stake. Such was the price of being a committed member of the Resistance. But there would come a day when we would be free, and we would journey back to Matamoros together.

My thoughts were interrupted by the sound of Beckinsale hailing the Captain with the snapping of his fingers. Stone had been watching both teams simultaneously. Another Halcyon tech named Cody had been watching Cameron's team, and he kept on them.

Pete Beckinsale held up three fingers.

Three targets. Oh no. Here we go again.

The Captain mirrored him and signaled for him to relay the intel to Beta Team, which was Pettijohn's patrol.

"Beta, Beta, this is Command, volume zero, over."

Pettijohn whispered a confirmation, awaiting orders.

Beckinsale quietly relayed the intel. "Targets inbound, repeat targets inbound, three of them, three hundred twenty meters, heading southwest, bearing four-two, four-four, and four-eight. Take cover."

"Roger, evasive. Go, team, go."

The infrared images could be seen on the top right of the spur heading diagonally down to them.

"Move, move. Rutty, move your ass," ordered Pettijohn. I could see Rutty fumbling with his rocket launcher as he emerged from the house. He was caught in the doorway. Something had snagged him while the team ran ahead. Ferro looked back to see him trying to break free, and she ran back to him with a cry.

"Ferro, stow that shit, soldier," Stone ordered over the com. "Both of you, haul ass!"

We could see Ferro reach Rutty. She whipped out a tactical knife and cut through a strap that was tied up in the broken door frame. Rutty could be heard grunting. "Got you," said Sarah.

"Targets moved and now heading west, range two-hundred sixty-seven meters," whispered Pete.

"Come on," Santella pleaded quietly. We could see him on the edge of the forest just beyond Skelton Drive's south bend. There was a major swath of forest cover directly after that, and a straight run south by southwest to return to the Launch doors. "Come on, you guys, hurry!"

I wondered if Santella could see them from where he was.

Rutty and Sarah dashed across the snowy ground southwest, darting in and amongst crumbled buildings which littered the property, along with a few rusted and scattered vehicles.

A sudden and unexpected sound short came through Santella's headset. *A cough. And then another one!*

"Santella!" demanded the Captain. "Shut that down now!"

"Roger," coughed Santella. "Just a cough. Sorry, Stoney."

The Captain shook his head, and I think I did too. Our team fled. All of them. But too late! The damage had been done, and the sound of Alex's cough had exposed all of them now.

"Uh, targets, targets!" Beckinsale's voice had risen in volume. "Move, Beta Team! Targets veered back southwest and closing fast. One-hundred eighty meters. One-fifty. One-ten. They're haulin' ass, move!"

The grunts and panting could be heard through the headsets. The team took evasive action. They started sprinting through the woods. They were all past Skelton Drive now. We could see their thermal images running south on a split-screen of one monitor, while the other half of the screen showed the infrared of the enemy, which was cold-blooded, and thus, didn't show up on thermals.

I clasped my hands together and began to pray. Santella's cough had summoned the enemy! And now they were fleeing, fleeing, as fast as they could, making an accursed racket as they plunged through the woods.

We couldn't see. There were no cameras in the woods there. Someone fell with a thud and a grunt.

"Sarah, get up, get up!" cried a voice, and I recognized it as Rutty's.

"Eighty meters. Sixty-five. They're gonna see you, move it! Fifty!" Pete pleaded.

Sarah grunted again and got back up.

"Crap," Rutty exclaimed. "Not gonna make it. Permission to engage, Captain?"

"Granted," said Stoney through clenched teeth. "Everyone beat it. Rutty, you hold them off."

Oh no. That meant Rutty would die! That was the rule: if detected, one person holds them off so that everyone else gets to safety.

"Thirty-eight meters. Twenty-seven! Here they come!" Pete practically shouted as he stood.

And then, metal clinking upon itself, grunts and wheezes, and then the sound of something being heaved. We couldn't make out the thermals clearly because they were now under the cover of trees. My hands clasped at my face, and I could tell I was sweating. My brow furrowed.

Please, Father. Please let Rutty return to Cameron. Cameron needs him. Please let them all return.

Then, a whoosh. A quick jet of air filled the com followed by a dreadfully long pause. I thought it would never end.

The thermals lit up white at the edge of the forest back by Skelton. The infrared targets were just entering the forest when Rutty's rocket launcher detonated against a building. A fireball erupted in a giant expanding circle, and we heard the distant, frenetic and angry screeches of the enemy. One infrared signal went dark and lay still, fading to black.

"Rutty, come *on!*" screamed Ferro. "There's no time, let's go!"

"One more, just one more," screamed Rutty. And as if he was brandishing the next one in his teeth, ready to go, he slapped in one more rocket, and launched it with his signature gritty determination.

The infrared signals swerved aside, attempting to avoid the thermal plume. One of them flailed about, but composed itself, and began to move again. Two of the enemy were still left.

Run, kids, run, I pleaded through my teeth.

"Go, just go!" Ferro screamed.

They headed toward a lake. And then I realized, *no they weren't*: Pettijohn and Jentzen were already *in* the lake. But where was Santella?

Another unnerving cough blasted through the com, and we saw his thermal signal emerge from the woods about two hundred feet north of the small lake, which was more like a pond, shaped like a butterfly in the satellite view.

"Santella, move!" cried the Captain.

Splashing. More splashing. Perhaps they realized they wouldn't make it back to the Blockade. They dove in. Did they think they would be safer in the water? What were they doing? My thoughts were racing just as fast as the frantic footfalls of Santella, Ferro and Rutty were, all converging upon the pond.

But the enemy was racing too. They had appeared to rise above the tree line, desperate to avoid another torpedo shot by Rutty's launcher, and were now moving, speedily, in a direct line following Rutty and Sarah.

They reached the pond! Jentzen and Pettijohn could be heard waving them in. They could come back for their wet weapons later! One splash followed by another. Ferro and Rutty swam as quietly as possible toward their compatriots. Someone still had their headset on.

Santella's signal stopped at the water's edge, and he appeared to be thrashing with something. "Command, stripping off weapons. We're gonna need something to fire at them with if those guys' stuff gets waterlogged."

"Santella, hurry!" shouted the Captain.

"Take cover! They're on you!" Pete screamed.

Another splash as he stumbled forward into the water. And, unfortunately, another noticeable cough. We couldn't see him. Most of the others' headsets were soiled, but one, I couldn't tell whose, was still functional.

I looked over at the Captain, who had his hands over his face, breathing hard.

They were moving. Slowly moving, and utterly quiet, though their teeth were clacking together loudly from the terror of the cold, and the cold terror of the enemy.

"Guys, they're on you. Hold still," whispered Pete.

All noise died. Time seemed suspended as we watched their signals converge with ours. They were nearly overhead.

"Visual confirmed. Going under," said Santella, and then his signal disappeared.

Suddenly, things moved horrifyingly fast. The signals scattered, dodging this way and that. From one headset we heard a splash and a screech as something heavy emerged from the water with a roar.

Screams. Running. Teeth chattering from the frigid water of the pond. Someone panting in fear and scrambling to another side of the bank. Oh how I wished we had a camera in there! What was happening? Where was Rutty?

The sound of giant gulps of life-giving air before plunging below. And then, horror.

"No, no. No! Guys, where are you, go, aggghh! Get off me, you bastard gorg!" And then a cough, and more splashing.

From far away, we knew it was Santella's voice. He sounded as if he was locked in a deadly battle with the enemy who had settled upon him, and it sounded as if he were throwing fists at it bravely. His eyes had to be closed fast. We could hear deadly hisses around him, and swooping noises. The other one was still searching for the remainder of the team.

"They don't see you, they, gah, ow! They c-can't do it to you underwater, get *off* me!" yelled Santella. He was fighting with the enemy. There was a faint *sssss* sound like the bluish-green mist that they put out.

I could still hear scrambling. Someone was running. The sound of a merciless crack, followed by a high-pitched, rending shriek by Santella. "They can't s-" -here he clearly went underneath the water and came up with a choking gasp for air- "can't see you! It doesn't work underwater, get un- under wa-water! Hide! Guys! Where are-"

And then he looked. He *had* to have looked. Sarah Ferro cried out "No!" A macabre hiss followed that. His final cry was to warn his fellow soldiers before he was lost to the deadly stare of the enemy.

You just...don't...look.

A wheeze of air being expelled from a body.

Gunshots. Solid reports from someone's headset that they had kept above water, most likely to let Command know how they had met their demise.

The gunshots struck something, and there were two more heavy splashes into the pond.

I bowed my head as if I had been gut-punched. The air was sucked out of me.

One more heavy splash sounded. Santella. Whoever had been running obviously went back and retrieved Santella's weapons and headset and opened fire on the enemy, taking them out. Nonetheless, it was too late.

And now that those guns had sounded, it was inevitable that it would draw more of the enemy to them.

"Alex!" cried Rutty. "Santella!" he cried again. "Oh, no, no, no!" he cried a third time. "He's gone...he's *gone!*"

Santella was gone.

By that time, I realized that the remaining headset was Rutty's. He had held it in his hand as they swam, desperate to keep up communication, and perhaps to send a farewell to his brother. But he was alive, and Santella was dead.

"Leave him, we've gotta go back!" Pettijohn ordered.

"No!" Rutty protested.

"You know the rules, dammit, we'll never make it, and he's waterlogged and frozen. We've gotta get back, now *move! Move it*, Rutty! That's an order!"

Rutty began to weep.

Sarah was already weeping.

Rutty was mumbling something incoherent to himself. What was it?

They can't get you in the water…they can't get you in the water…they can't get you in the water…

Did that mean that their telepathy was rendered impotent underwater? It appeared to be that way. And then I remembered what Santella had said.

Going under.

He must have floated there, looking up. One of them saw him, dove in, and tried to paralyze him underwater. He must have opened his eyes to see where it was, and realized that it had no effect. He tried to save the rest of them by relaying valuable information. And then one of them got him. What a horrible, horrible end!

Poor Santella.

The rest were running, running with all their might, straight west now, pumping their cold blood through their legs, warmed by fear, pushed on by terror, desperate to get back to safety.

Santella was a valued human being. A friend. A soldier. He, like all of them, was our treasure.

It's not every day you lose a priceless treasure.

27 | SIXTEEN

| Rosie |

Thursday, June 12th, 2042, 1331 hours

It had now been sixteen long years.

We had another memorial, gathered around the edge of our little Pavilion, letting sixteen minutes go by, one for each traumatic year we have endured under the shadow of our enemy. That was six days ago, on June 6th.

Yet today, we were celebrating Rutty's nineteenth birthday, and there was joy in the Pavilion once more. Cameron was now twenty-two, twenty-three in October. They were both such fine soldiers! They still mourned the loss of Santella – we all did – and in those sixteen minutes of reflection, I said a prayer for him.

Following their February 8th mission, Sarah Ferro had resigned from service, returning to service in medical. The Captain graciously, but reluctantly, agreed. "I'm no warrior," she had said. "I thought I was, but I'm not. I may be ready again in time, you know, as needed, but not now." She was needed in medical. I was able to have a few solid conversations with her, encouraging her of the equal value of her service in nursing. She accepted it, but I could tell there was a yearning there; I just wasn't certain what it was for: Cameron, service, or perhaps her father, Ray.

Rutty had taken an interest in Shannon Hickey. She was born February 12th, 2015, which made her twenty-seven, eight years his senior, but who was I to judge? My Miguel was practically the same number of years my junior. Rutty and Shannon had been on a few missions together.

Shannon was a painter, and her paintings had graced the walls of the Pavilion with a growing number of portraits of people living and passed; of flowers and scenery, of random things that impressed upon her creative soul. Rutty loved to lose himself in a good book; Shannon loved to lose herself in a good work of art.

They were a good pair.

·   ·   ·   ·   ·

Friday, July 4th, 2042, 2012 hours

All we had were matches, but they were enough. Well, beside the baking soda bottles that a few of the kids in Mr. Arnold's class had made.

They filled a spray bottle with a solution of three-quarters vinegar and one-quarter water, dropping some baking soda onto coffee filters. Then, they dripped food coloring onto the coffee filters, spraying them with the vinegar solution. The baking soda reacted with the vinegar solution, and there would be a fizz. They threw in some food coloring for extra measure, and then you had color.

It was the best 4th of July celebration we could come up with. Two-hundred sixty-six years after the Declaration of Independence from England, we made our own Declaration down here.

We all signed it in an effort to boost morale. We declared eventual independence from the enemy, placing it on the far end of the Pavilion by the hydroponics farm, surrounded by pictures Hickey had painted of growing things. That way we could know that there was life growing around that edict…a promise of things to come.

That imparted a bit of hope.

A new team had arrived from Oklahoma City, led by a man named Matthew Candee. He was a new Beta Team leader, a Sergeant from the old Blockade there, sent to partner with us. I remember something sad happening at the Oklahoma City Blockade several years ago. 2027, I think. The enemy had gotten inside their Blockade, just as one had here, and killed off nearly everyone inside. Sergeant Candee must have survived somehow. Candee and his team made the long journey – seven hundred-fifty miles – to our doorstep. I was astonished to think that he had made such a long, difficult journey here over five years' time. But we would take anyone who was willing to serve. They arrived at the end of June.

They were killed yesterday.

I thought it so ironic, and so cruel.

They had been in deep conversations with the Captain that I wasn't privy to, although from scattered bits and pieces I heard from our existing patrols, they were going to attempt to cross the Cumberland into Clarksville proper itself. A few of our patrols had tried that, all with no success. There was always a mass of gorgons clustered around the Cumberland at the edge of C-Range, so it was an automatic no-go heading out that far.

But they headed out that far anyway, and the Captain allowed it to happen. I wasn't watching their patrol in Halcyon. I heard about it late last night when I went to say good night to Stone. All of them had been slaughtered by the enemy there at the trestle. That was a difficult pill to swallow, and I knew it was for the Captain as well; the only two ways east off of the spur of land we were located on were the Cunningham Bridge, and the trestle. The bridge had been tried a few times, but they could never get near due to a massing of the enemy there. The trestle apparently was more of the same.

A new directive had also been given. On recon patrols, all recon personnel were instructed to be on the lookout for small, circular, shiny objects. They were called 'amulets,' and they were somehow important in the coming war against the gorgons, though for some reason the Captain would never give the recon patrols a clear answer why. He had been simply instructed to gather as many as he could. To date, we hadn't found one.

There was a lot transpiring, with, undoubtedly, more to come. I just didn't like not knowing why. I knew that the other team members didn't like feeling kept in the dark either, particularly Sergeant Jet Shipley.

Something else was going on.

•　　　•　　　•　　　•　　　•

Sunday, July 6th, 2042, 1146 hours

"Thank you, Rosie, don't mind if I do," said Stoney. He had asked to see me after Sunday service, and now he was here in my office.

"Won't you sit down?" I asked him. "Water?"

"No thank you, Rosie, I'm good."

"What can I do for you, Captain?" I asked him, fetching my own water and sitting down across from him.

"Well, Señora Rosie, not much," he began. "I just wanted to talk to you first, being that you're the spiritual authority around here."

News to me, I thought. *That's the Father's role.*

"There's a lot going on down south of us. I don't know if you know but the President is in Nashville. She's been relocated from her original headquarters, but still in the city. There's this new technology that they're using that may provide a modicum of momentum against the gorgons. They're calling them DTF, or DTF emitters. Dissonant Tidal Flood."

"Oh? Intriguing. Tell me more," I said eagerly, feigning naivete. Of course, Miguel had already told me everything about them.

"Yeah. The President is issuing directives to the area Blockades, and she's wanting to coordinate some local operations using this new technology. We may have an opportunity here to really turn the tide. But," he paused, as if he was studying me, "I want you to withhold this information for the time being. Don't tell anyone about it."

"And why is that?"

"Well, because the time isn't right yet. The fact is, I miss Andrew Shipley. And I love these boys like my own sons. They call me 'Dad' for crying out loud. I love 'em,

Rosie. But I'm being asked to prepare for the coordination of some top-level ops, and I'm not sure that Sergeant Shipley, in particular, will be able to accept them. I'm sure you know that he and I have not exactly seen eye to eye on how to run ops out in the field. He can be a bit of a loose cannon."

"I've heard you use the term to describe him, yes."

"Right. He's a bit of a cynic. Got that from his dad. Some of this stuff coming down the pike is perhaps better suited for some alternates. So that's why I don't want you to tell any of this to Rutty either. You tell Rutty, Rutty tells Cameron, Cameron goes apeshit on me."

"Well, Captain Stone, with all due respect, you just told me now. This is the first I'm hearing of it," I said, lying through my teeth. I had to keep up the ruse, and I hated every dishonest minute of it.

"I know. Understood. But I'm coming to you not in a confessional. I'm coming to you as someone who loves his boys but feels he doesn't really know them or understand them as well as, say, someone like you. You've had a lot more intimate conversations with the Shipley boys. Now, I know Rutty'll fall in line. I have no doubts. Good kid. But *Cameron*, whew," he said, blowing hot air out and rolling his eyes like he had his work cut out for him. "We may be having an outside team come in to introduce some of this stuff, and Cameron – Jet – the Sergeant, whatever, dammit – oh, excuse me – he might not take that very well. He's kind of, shall we say, territorial. You remember how he kept Rutty from service."

"Hmm. I do, but I am fairly confident it wasn't to protect his territory. It was to protect Rutty."

"True, but this may be a little bit of both coming at him, from multiple sides. He didn't exactly take to Candee. And I don't think he shed a tear when Candee or his team died. He's gotten a bit colder after his breakup with Nurse Ferro, don't you think?"

I shrugged my shoulders. "In his defense, love makes one warm. Take away the love, we all get colder, right, Captain? I think all of them have gotten a bit colder since the invasion, since the attacks, since losing their parents, since the church, since Santella."

"I hear you," said the Captain, "I just. I-" He stopped again, studying me. "Maybe this was a bad idea. I just wanted to see what kind of read you had on him. They don't open up to me in the same way they open up to you. You have a gift. Or a skill. Or both. Something. I don't have it."

"You have command and leadership. And a great nickname. That's something."

"Thanks," he laughed. "I'll take what I can get." Stone paused. "How about this. Just, given what I've briefed you on, I'd like to ask that you report to me anything that you might notice from them – either of them – that might be out of character or suggestive of a break from form. Can you do that?"

"Can I break counselor-client privilege and report to you what they've relayed to me in a private setting? Is that what you mean, Captain Stone?" I put him on the spot now.

"Ha! You called me on it. I wouldn't put it exactly like that, Rosie. I'm asking you to see it a different way," he said, and then his tone changed, voice dropping in pitch and sincerity. "What I'm asking you, as your commanding officer, is to report to me any possible minor concerns before they become major. Does that make sense?"

I slowly nodded, wondering where all of this was coming from. Stone was hiding something, and he was hiding it from me and the Shipleys, and I didn't like it. As long as I didn't give him a verbal yes or sign anything, I would have something to fall back on, I figured.

"Good. I don't anticipate much to come of it, but, again, wheels are turning, and the higher-ups are in play. Orders and directives are coming down. If you saw the paperwork on my desk…"

"I've seen it. You are charged with many things."

"I am, Rosie, I truly am. You should try being a Captain sometime. Not easy. I've gotta oversee everything in here and out there. And the requisition orders!" He shook his head. "You should see the list that Harrison and Dupre just gave me. The things they say they need in there. And they're playing with those am-," he stopped himself, "-with things that they're not supposed to be playing with. Screwing around and wasting time. I have to play judge, Rosie. I have to grant and deny all kinds of crap all day long."

"I understand it must be difficult," I said, but I noticed his slip-up and subsequent correction. Stone was clearly hiding something. What were Harrison and Dupre playing with? Am- something?

He looked at me. Stone paused, looking me up and down, as if he sensed my sarcasm, then sighed. "Anyway, I appreciate it. You know I love those boys. I'm just needing to think about how to juggle all of this. We're potentially all on a precipice that can go one of two ways."

I nodded. "The way of transparency, or the way of secrets?"

Stone actually laughed. "Dammit. Whoops, forgive me again," he continued to laugh. "I knew you weren't going to be easy, Pastor Rosie. Shoot. Well, I tried," he said, and then he sat back and put his hands on his knees as if he sensed the conversation was over. "Thanks for hearing me. I trust we understand each other."

"As much as we can, given the limited information we've been able to share," I answered. "But I do know you love them. I love them too. Let's not let that love run cold."

Captain Stone locked eyes with me. I think he knew what I meant. I hope he did. From everything he had just relayed, something was coming. And with Cameron in particular, I didn't think he would like being kept in the dark. It was up to Stone to choose whether he would keep him there, or if he would keep his love warm.

Otherwise, it was going to be another sixteen long years.

28 | SORROW

| Trudy |

Friday, July 18th, 2042, 1306 hours

And just like that, everything changed.

We found a gorgon! It appeared to be hurt, but it wasn't dead. The gun towers had wounded it as it swooped in too close. Maybe it was young and didn't know the rules. We didn't care. This was our chance!

An emergency claxon sounded throughout the Blockade, and we suited up. Steph was ready to go. She was almost giddy. Joe gave her a playful headlock tussle, and she socked him in the arm. That was cute.

I was ready. I was a Lieutenant in the Science Department *and* on recon now. This was the mission I was born to do. We had a gorgon in our sights! Lying just over the brush line south of Vickery Creek, in the Chattahoochee River, on the edge. One of the tower gunners got it and confirmed the hit, but Lookout said that they were still confirming infrared movement from it. Gorgs eat other dead gorgs, but no other gorgs had converged on the area, so it was probably out there flailing right at the river's edge.

We got a *big* team together for this one, just like we planned. Six to wrangle the thing, including Robertson, who could most likely just lay on it and smother it to death, and six gunners to post up and stand guard. We were *going* to capture a gorgon, and we were all pretty amped to do it. Altogether, it was me, Joe, Steph, Robertson, Donner, and Raylin on wrangle crew. Additionally, as we would be out of range of our gun towers, we needed additional soldiers to post up as gunners. They included Gage, Shelly, Charlotte, Eric, Brant, and Mikkelson, the last of which joined us from the shadows of Alpharetta.

Donner and Steph headed up capture. The rest of the wrangle team followed behind. It was summer, which lessened the likelihood of more gorgons in the area. On the hotter days, gorgons congregated around rivers, submerging their heads underwater. To cool off? No one knew. We hoped we'd have answers to that once we captured one. But if that was the case, it stood to reason that we were heading directly for a mass of them. Yet Command reported only the one. We didn't need to explain the opportunity; we just needed to seize it.

Bayless had cleared all civilian personnel into the Rotunda and sealed it off. The post-capture plan was to move it into the infirmary as quickly as possible, strap it up, lock it down, do our thing. It wasn't going to be easy, but we were all jazzed to get a shot at this. To test a live gorg in captivity with my new mask prototypes? *Wow!* One for the history books, indeed.

Steph was joking with all the guys at the Launch, leaving them in stitches. Steph was great for that. There was palpable nervous energy all around us. We needed this to run smoothly and by the numbers. No room for a mistake of any kind. For that reason, we all donned our masks, and prepared to proceed forward, resolute.

We all catalogued with the lick n' prick and headed out in a big group. After all the planning, it was finally go time! The Chattahoochee was a fair distance south of us, and we would need to return before dark. Command was on the com with us from Lookout with Bayless, as usual. "Target still moving. Range one-hundred-fifty meters south-southwest," they said. Our recon teams had done a great job installing cameras along the telephone and utility poles running on virtually all the main thoroughfares. Command confirmed at intervals that they could see us.

"Roger that," echoed Joe, who was the ranking lead on this patrol. "Keep it tight, people. Due south."

Big Creek was passing us by on our right as we headed south. We were coming up on the convergence of South Atlanta Street and Indian Springs Drive to Riverside Road. From the last report, the gorg had plunged down off south of Riverside and was still there somewhere at that narrow inlet leading into Big Creek.

"Volume zero," said Joe. I looked over at him. He was so intriguing to watch. All business, stern face, tight grip on his M5. The man would be good in a battle, but I understood why Maureen was so nervous anytime he went out.

I could feel the sweat pooling around my back, under my knapsack, which had extra mags, some grenades, food, and whatever else we needed to carry out with us into this God-forsaken world.

The twelve of us made barely any sound as we continued south, passing the last house before Riverside Road. We thought we heard movement, like something heavy struggling along the ground.

"Alright, people," Steph whispered, "right here is why they pay us the big bucks. Any of you pussies can turn around and head back now."

I could see Joe smile while he told her to shush. I smiled as well. In all honesty, I missed being out on missions. Steph reminded me of the bond that happens between the soldiers out here, and I appreciated her spunk.

"Range ninety meters. Seventy-two. Sixty meters. You're almost there," said Command.

Indeed, up ahead we could see the trees thinning out, and Riverside Road looming up.

"Range thirty meters, southwest. Just below the bridge. Proceed with caution," Lookout instructed.

We would have to cross west over Riverside Road itself, and then head down the embankment into the river. It was reportedly right there.

Maybe it was fate, but I saw it first. *Oh man, that's it, that's it,* I said to myself, and pointed to Steph, who flanked me. "Target acquired, Command," I whispered. Steph nodded.

Just off Riverside Road, below the shadow of the bridge, something was moving. Slowly at first, but it was moving, nonetheless. Its grey, bumpy body looked like it had been thrown over the bridge only to land in the soft, muddy banks of Big Creek, just off the Chattahoochee. A slime trail could be seen behind it, slithering back up toward normal elevation. It had landed with a thud and wormed its way downward toward the water. Its head was submerged, so it couldn't see or hear us. I stared at it, transfixed by both awe and disgust.

We cut communication and resorted to our predetermined hand signals. Steph and Donner now took point according to the plan.

Raylin was carrying the gurney. She slowly unfolded it and laid it down as we reached the top of the bank, then turned and gave the gunners a thumbs up. The plan was to have the gunners establish a perimeter in case the gorg made too much noise and attracted other gorgs to us. The gunners all posted up, standing with their backs to each other in a circle along the bridge, and signaled to Donner that they were ready.

I looked at Joe, and he looked at me. I trusted that that wasn't fear in his eyes behind that mask; he breathed out hard for a moment, and his mask fogged. It was 'go time.'

Donner gave us the signal.

The six of us: me, Raylin, Steph, Joe, Robertson, and Donner on point.

Time to wrangle a gorgon.

Steph and Donner went first, down the bank. I couldn't believe we were doing this! My heart was in my throat! A gorgon was no more than twenty feet in front of us down the bank. It had its head down, and its slimy tentacles were extending back behind it. It must have been at least nine feet long. Pale and gyrating, the flaps on the side of its body pulsated and huffed. What was generating that activity we couldn't tell. It was quiet and seemed almost asleep.

It was so hot out.

Steph had her XM5 slung around her back. She brandished the tranquilizer dart gun and fired.

It flew into the back left of the gorg. The thing winced and jerked, but didn't move any further. Had that done it? Surely that wasn't enough. It was a reflex for it to spasm like that, but maybe it was so tired or spent from the struggle, and just needed water.

We proceeded off the bridge, slowly.

Steph was on its right. Donner was on its left. Step by step, they slowly inched down the bank. My mouth inadvertently formed an 'o,' my chin stiff and tense, as I carefully watched my own footfall behind them. Joe was on the other side across from me, and Robertson and Raylin were last. We were almost upon it.

Part of the plan was to inject it with the tranquilizer. We concocted what we could in the science lab back at DN282: benzodiazepines, gamma-hydroxybutyrate, opioids, and hell, even Ambien and Lunesta. The only problem was that we were uncertain of the dosage. Nashville had sent the dosage for what they had used to knock out their own gorg. If we got it wrong, there would surely be hell to pay. And what if we administered the wrong antagonist dose once we got it back to the Blockade? We would make it narcoleptic and hyper, tense and uncontrollable. There was a lot riding on this, not the least of which were our lives.

But the tranquilizer had been fired, and now came the real test. If that thing still had its strength and freaked out, it would be all over. But we could all see the large flesh wound in its right side where the gun tower had gotten it. It was shredded and bleeding dark ooze.

We continued to approach. Thankfully, there was some shelter from aerial view, given the trees all around us. Still, we had to be careful.

Raylin was right behind me as we descended. We were entirely noiseless – until the point where she stepped on a twig. The deafening crack sounded far too loud. The sound seemed to reverberate all around us. And then, in her haste to undo her action she stepped back and caught her foot against a stone, tripping and landing with a dull thud.

The vibration was felt. Dread gripped the entire team.

"Ray!" Joe hissed at her through his teeth in frustration and warning. But the damage had been done.

As if the very creaking of bones and flesh could take on a life of their own, the sound became movement, and the movement became a gorgon. It emerged from the water with a dark groan and a hiss, bubbling in its fury. The thing slowly pulled its head out of the water, droplets spattering down below it. We froze.

With horrifying speed it whipped around to face us, teeth exposed menacingly. And then it rose up and put its arms out and downward, bobbing its neck. It stared at Steph. She was the closest. Reflexively, she fired the second tranquilizer dart, striking it in the chest. The gorgon winced and cried. Its telepathy had been broken. Steph clutched at her chest for a moment, as if her injured lung lurched in pain. She wheezed. The mask had protected her, but not entirely. What was wrong?

Before I could finish my questioning, Robertson had sped past us and landed on it. All of us were trying to wrangle it as quietly as possible. I caught a quick sight of the gunners up above, looking down at us in raw fear, and flashing their eyes back up to the sky to ensure that we wouldn't be ambushed aerially.

The thing thrashed and whipped around like a crocodile desperate for a death roll. Robertson was thrown off. Donner was next, throwing his full weight upon it and waiting for the tranquilizers to kick in. Steph was loading a third tranquilizer in the chamber of her dart gun.

I moved toward her, but the bank was muddy, and I lost my footing. The gorgon identified her as the bearer of the weapon, and it turned toward her again. She got a shot off. A third dart penetrated the gorgon in its right abdomen, punching right through the injury site from the gun tower. That one went in further than the others. It was in!

But no sooner had she fired than the gorgon raised an arm and lashed out in fury, realizing that somehow its power was rendered impotent. The puny flesh creature had some kind of defense on it that prevented it from freezing her. They all did.

Its arm connected. Steph went flying back into the soft mud, her dart gun spinning off into the river. She landed on her butt and looked up.

The mist was everywhere, icing our flesh.

Her mask had flown off too.

She stared at the gorgon.

It moved in toward her.

Someone cried "Steph! No!" *Joe*. He threw himself on the gorgon, and it vomited. The tranquilizer was now coursing through its wretched bloodstream. Robertson got back up and hurled himself on it again. It spasmed and tried to heave them off, but it couldn't devote all its powers to either; it had to choose. Either the shooter would pay for it, or it would continue to throw the others off itself.

It chose Steph. She sat there, frozen in a contemptuous smile, locked in its connective stare, while the devilish mist framed the two of them in a pale light. Her skin went white and then drooped, but her spiteful smile remained: an eternal testament to her defiance of death. I watched in horror as Steph started to die right in front of us.

The gorgon, brazen and in utter contempt for human life, lunged out and bit off her leg at the knee, crunching and chewing violently. That sent the rest of us into a fury. Joe screamed, and then hammered away. Enraged, he pelted the monster repeatedly with his fists out of sheer recklessness.

The anger welled up inside me. But there was another feeling rising through my bloodstream stronger than anger. Stronger than hate. Stronger than fear.

Hope.

Her words ran back through my mind, surrounded in echoing reverberation, full of power and truth:

It's called 'hope for tomorrow,' Trudy. You might wanna embrace it, like, I dunno, before tomorrow.

In hope, I raised myself up, and then charged at the damned thing. Its long tentacles were whipping about, and it was rolling, rolling, putting up a damn good fight. The mist was everywhere, and it was deadly cold: colder than anything I'd ever experienced in my life. Colder than even the coldest hunt I'd been on with Nick, Badge and dad. *Cold.*

The gorgon had rolled over and taken Robertson with it. He was pinned underneath. Its soft underbelly was smeared with its own blood, fusing with the grass and mud from the riverbank. Before I knew it, right as I was upon it, I tried to roll it back over and free Robertson. It hissed and convulsed, and then flicked its arms out. My own mask was ripped from my face! I gasped in alarm and shut my eyes tightly. All I had left was sound.

The sound of grunts and wheezes.

The sound of humans desperate for a win.

The sound of the breath escaping Steph's lips. The sound of her leg pouring out blood.

The sound of Joe crying, torn between trying to do his job and wanting to cradle his sister in his arms.

Where was Raylin? I listened, but I couldn't hear her. A splash and a scream coming from my left. The gorgon lurched beneath me, and I heard the sound of something dull repeatedly striking the beast below us. Realizing it was about to lose this fight, it summoned up its whole fury and lashed out for one final stroke. I heard another scream, and then a horrible crunch, followed by a gasp and a gurgle.

Raylin.

I stayed at my post. I would not allow my masks to fail the rest of them. I reached out, feeling blindly with my hands to see where it was so I could smash its head with my rifle. I wanted to kill it, but the best I could do would be to knock it out cold and expedite the work of the tranquilizer.

Something sharp punched through the skin of my hand, right through the meat between the fingers. I dropped my rifle with a cry. The thing clamped down through my skin and I stifled a burning scream, not daring to open my eyes. My hand felt warm as the blood flowed down, dripping off my fingers. I swear the thing sneered at me.

My rifle had fallen to my feet. I knew where it was. I was tired. Tired of this bullshit. I wanted to give up the science and go for the kill.

That gorg was lucky that I grabbed the rifle and flipped it. With my mauled hand I slammed the butt of that rifle over and over into its horrid head.

The gorgon's movements slowed. Robertson piled his entire weight on top of it, as did Joe, weeping profusely.

•   •   •   •   •

Friday, July 18th, 2042, 1358 hours

Robertson handed me my mask quickly. The gunners were pleading for us to return. Command was warning us time was almost up, and that signals could be inbound at any moment.

By the time I opened my eyes once more, my mask was on, Steph was dead, Joe was a mess, and Raylin…poor Raylin had been bitten through the abdomen. They said that the gorgon reached out and grabbed her, pulling her close, and then it literally tried to stuff her into its mouth. She was a petite girl. A soldier, but a petite one.

Robertson shook Joe out of a trance as he held his dying sister. Faint wisps of breath could be heard. "She's still alive, she's still alive!" he moaned.

"Then let's get her and get the hell out. Move!" Robertson yelled at him. Joe reflexively shook his face to clear the air, and then picked up Steph, ghost-white, throwing her over his shoulder and struggling up the steep bank. The rest of us were left to move the gorgon onto the stretcher. Gage came down and carried Raylin up the bank, wrapping some gauze around her. She was bleeding profusely. Gage was a fairly lithe guy, but then, so was she. He manned up and lifted her up over his shoulder.

That left Robertson, me, and Donner. Brant came down and took up the last position on the gurney. We hoisted that thing onto it and heaved it up the bank. It was heavy, but somehow we managed it despite the stench.

•   •   •   •   •

Friday, July 18th, 2042, 1423 hours

We made it back to the Blockade. There was screaming and hysteria. Blood everywhere. They closed the doors. I must have been in shock. I didn't remember our journey back or the initial hours of our return. All that I recalled was just a massive ringing in my ears. I only knew a few things.

Raylin was dead. She never stood a chance.

Neither did Steph. We had lost two good soldiers on this mission, and I had no idea what would even come of it.

Joe was unresponsive, Maureen's arms wrapped around him in his bunk. He said nothing, and just buried his face in his hands, convulsing in tears.

The thing was in confinement in medical. I don't remember who did it. Everyone wanted to see it.

I hated this life, and I wanted out. I didn't see hope. Was there even any? Put aside the masks, those sound emitters, and the fact that we got one of them. But they got two of us. We seemed to be bound to always lose…

Just like that, everything had changed.

29 | VANCE

| Miguel |

Sunday, July 27th, 2042, 1612 hours

The message had been sent.

A Sergeant led me to the new offices they had made for all personnel, and I sat down at a terminal.

Now I was awaiting a reply from Captain Vance Cardona. He was made aware of the threats on the President's life, and his tone sounded jaded and sarcastic.

Probably not even very sobering for her. The woman has no shame. She thinks she's invincible and entitled to whatever she wants. I'm hearing rumors of an independent poll circulating amongst military and civilian folks. Don't know who started it. A poll about whether she stays or goes. That won't look good for her. Lowest approval rates ever. No one wants her here anymore; Earth wants a fresh start of course. She won't take that sitting down.

I pondered his words.

But if she succeeds, I wrote back, *it may garner support for her, as long as her nefarious motives aren't sniffed out. She may crush any opposition from those who know the truth. Including you. I fear for you.*

Fear for all of us, he wrote back. *Fear is a powerful motivator. Courage isn't the absence of fear, remember. It's the boldness to take action* despite *fear. And we're doing it. The Resistance was founded on courage, knowing full well what she can do to us. Those sweeps she's doing? Think about it. She can guide the gorgs anywhere she wants, my friend. I don't doubt she'll guide them to MC. We're preparing for such a contingency even now. Her little 'Operation Shake N' Bake' – silly name – is coming. She's deleterious now, my friend. Subtle. But she'll be outright savage later, and her true colors will be revealed for all the world to see.*

'MC,' Cardona had said. *Mammoth Cave.* If she wanted to wipe out Cardona and make it look like collateral damage, that the *gorgos* just 'happened' to go there, she could, and no one would question it. No one would be allowed to.

Stay well, my friend. Keep the faith. How are your new digs?

They're fine, I wrote back. *I miss the Embassy, but these will do. There's far more protection here, of course, and it's nice to see what's happening with the tech. These men and women are working* hard, *my friend. Churning out hundreds of emitters, large and small, every week. And now smaller projectiles able to be coupled with KEPs, APDSs and APFSDSs,* I said, noting the tank projectile types. *There has even been discussion about using them with USRs, uranium sabot rounds using depleted uranium. Scary stuff, but effective against the gorgs. They're all working in tandem with EMP technology though, so until all these vehicles get retrofitted with RF technology, they're going to be susceptible to the bursts. They've gotta launch and shut down.*

Patience, he wrote back. *We're working on that now on our own tanks. Way ahead of our little lady,* he said, meaning the President. *And speaking of little ladies, how is yours?*

I miss her, my friend. I miss her dearly. She is still in Clarksville, and she is safe, but the last time we saw each other was over Zoom several months ago, and I loathe the absences in between. Are you with your sweet bride?

No, he typed back. *She is at WP,* he said, indicating Wright-Patterson Air Force Base in Dayton OH. *I share your pain, amigo. One day we'll all be together again. One day.*

I longed for that day.

Suddenly, I was paged. "Lieutenant Monzon, Lieutenant Monzon to the PEOC please."

The new Presidential Emergency Operations Center at The Lab. What did she want?

I always hated these summons.

* * * * *

"Monzon, come on in. Thank you, Agent Grimstad."

The Agent moved past me once more and exited her office. She was sitting in a brightly-illuminated room full of papers and littered with trinkets. I daresay they were collectibles: things probably ransacked from other offices as creature comforts for her own little hideout here, to help her pass the time, no doubt. Odd to behold, but certainly something that we all resort to in times of questioning or uncertainty. It just didn't seem like she was questioning anything anymore. She definitely wasn't questioning her own ethics.

"Madame President." I saluted her. She had a faded sheet of notepaper on the desk in front of her.

She saluted me back, briskly. "Sit down, please," she said, motioning me to the chair seated across her desk. I obliged.

"I want to thank you. Operation Deep Breath was and continues to be a great success. That little tidbit of information you gave me almost three years ago has paid off." She looked down at the notepaper in front of her. "Growlers, EA-18Gs, EA-6Bs and EF-111A Ravens, oh my," she chuckled. "I was going to call the next phase 'Operation Plunge,' but I've got a better name. I'll unveil it when the time is right."

I already know what the silly name is, lady.

"Yes, Ma'am. I'm glad they worked. I've heard of what you've been planning, and it sounds like it's going to be a great success."

A slight expression of curiosity obscured her smile. "Oh, you've heard? What have you heard, exactly?" *Suspicious snake.* She was smiling in front of her forked tongue, and there was suspicion ringing out loud and clear behind her question.

"Just that you've been testing the jets conducting local sweeps, and the ability to herd the *gorgos* where you want them to go. Brilliant. Seems that alien technology works against them quite nicely."

I wanted to say, 'Relax lady, I know about your little nuclear strike plans, and it's cool' just to piss her off. Patience.

Something in her softened, as if she was feeling some form of relief that her little plan was still secret. "'Gorgos?' Is that what you call them in Spanish?"

I nodded.

Her eyebrows flicked up as she looked away momentarily. "Interesting. Well, anyway, yes, it has definitely worked. We're making progress. I wanted to thank you. We're finally going to be able to win this war and push them off the planet. And for that, I have some news for you. You're getting a promotion."

I didn't know what to say. My eyebrows rose in amazement, and I shifted uneasily in my seat.

"Wow, I- I don't know what to say, Madame President. Thank you."

"You're welcome, *Captain,*" she said, and she rose. I rose with her. "Congratulations," she said, and she extended her hand out to me.

A shiver ran through me. *Captain.* I had just been promoted because of information I had given her which she was using for good, yes, but she was also going to use as a masquerade for a truly sinister plot. Could I live with myself being promoted for such a thing? Could I live in integrity after she'd killed off the *gorgos, and* all of those struggling human survivors? I wanted to vomit, but I faked a smile instead, as I took her hand. Unsurprisingly, it was cold and tense. I expected no less.

"I'll have Cooper process everything for you and update everyone. You are appreciated, Captain Monzon," she said, as she gave me a smile that was half-endearing, half-patronizing. I know she was trying to be warm and fuzzy, but it came off as an act, and I saw right through her.

"Again, th-thank you. I don't know what to say."

She laughed. "No one knows what to say when they're given a gift. Accept it. Now, there are a few more things. I have two operations in the works that I'd like to discuss with you."

"Yes?"

"We'll be taking a Navy Corvette up the Cumberland sometime soon. There's a Blockade north of us that has need of testing some of the new technology. There's a mass of gorgs there that we need to disperse. I'm going to have a team dispatched there soon, using the new mask technology. I want to coordinate with that same team to be the ones that introduce the first handheld trigger tech to manually launch the new DTF bombs. I've had a few petitions from Captains in the area, but I like this one. Unpretentious. Wants the work. Captain Maurice Stone. Do you know him?"

I shook my head. I had never met him personally, but my heart suddenly pounded. Captain Stone oversaw DN436 at Clarksville! I was going to see my Rosie! I had to stifle my excitement.

"Well, we're at the drawing board, but it'll happen soon. I want you to come with me. We'll take a few others with us. There's a Lieutenant here that I'd like you to meet, and you'll have command over her and the others. Name is LaShawna Rawley. I'll let you know when we're ready to go."

"Which Blockade is it?" I asked her, feigning naïveté. My heart was already bursting with joy at the notion of seeing my Rosalita again.

"DN436. Clarksville."

I couldn't let the President know that my wife was there. *Come on, Monzon…keep your composure.* I would get to see *mi cariña*! Oh, what conflicting emotions now vied for mastery in me. I somehow managed to quell my enthusiasm and gave her a sustained nod, as if she had just doled out an insignificant detail, only minutiae.

"And the second operation?"

She smiled. "Oh yes! There's a particular pebble in our shoe who has been making waves. Back at the Embassy, they were investigating some of Colonel Cartwright's old footage around the time of the attack, and they came across a face of someone Cooper recognized."

My heart was in my throat. It had just burst with joy, and, now, turned to sadness and dread with this new revelation.

"Captain Vance Cardona. It turns out he came here and murdered Cartwright. Went after Cooper as well. Hell, he's probably angry that he got reassigned. He is considered armed and dangerous, and so we'll need a team to go up to Mammoth Cave. We'll get one from Clarksville since they're closer. He was supposed to be the acting Captain up there, but they say that he's been stirring things up and spreading propaganda. They say he's hard to find, and there's a risk that he'll be goin' Elvis soon, MIA. So we must act. Sadly, I've had to make the unfortunate decision to take him out. I'll need you on that team."

I knew she was lying, but that's not what concerned me. She now had the leader of the Resistance in her sights, and she was going to take him out.

I swallowed and nodded. "Wow. Uh, whatever you need, Madame President. Of course," I fumbled.

"Good." She rose. "Welcome aboard, Captain, and congrats again on your promotion. Couldn't happen to a nicer gentleman."

The woman smiled, and my stomach lurched. I wanted to punch her in the jaw and feed her to a *gorgo*.

The directive had been given.

She was on to Cardona.

The message had been received.

30 | TRUST

| Rosie |

Thursday, August 21st, 2042, 1612 hours

There wasn't any trust, and things were getting tense.

Harrison and Dupre were apparently working without the Captain's authorization on the alien technology. They were small, silver circlets with strange glyphs on them, and they were calling them 'amulets.' Apparently, they had been embedded in the necks of the enemy when they descended, shedding them off when they activated on September 3rd, 2026.

Stone presumably knew all about them, but his lips were sealed, and he wouldn't say much about what they were for. However, the word had been given for the recon teams to find as many of them as they could out on their missions. Apparently, they were becoming critical in the war effort. So, that was the new assignment: get them, and bring them back to Harrison and Dupre. These two men were working on new equipment in the science lab just off of the Captain's office, in order to experiment on them.

I only heard Stone mention briefly that he would announce their purpose in time, but I had not gotten a good look at one yet. I attempted to ask him some questions, but he was as tight-lipped as ever. He was becoming more and more that way, unfortunately, and that was not a good sign. It definitely would not go over well with Cameron, given my previous conversation with Stone. The Captain was hiding something.

As for Cameron and Rutty, they were doing well. All of the team members were; we had entered a state of relative collective calm.

I talked to Miguel yesterday. My dear husband couldn't share with me what had happened, but he was unnerved, and told me to be careful. He hinted that the President might be closing in on him. He was on edge and wanted to get out of there. And, apparently, his chance was coming. He would be coming up to Clarksville. My jaw dropped. I couldn't believe the news, and it made my heart so glad. My Miguel was coming! I could not wait to be swept up in his warm embrace, captive to his huge muscles. That would be a sweet, sweet day. It was all I could think about.

Apparently, Graham was dispatching teams in all directions with the new sound devices, including smaller ones that could be taken out into the field and activated by hand. The war had already been raging, but a *new* war was on its way: one in which we could actually fight and, possibly, win. These new devices all but assured us of that, and I couldn't wait to see what they could do. But, at the Captain's orders, I was not allowed to share this news with

Cameron, and that frustrated me. The teams were fanning out. The President had sent the Nashville team to the south. Miguel seemed to think she wanted a different team to head to Clarksville which would meet him and the President there, and that team would be the ones who developed this reported new mask technology. That was even *more* news that I was forbidden from sharing with Cameron.

More newsworthy, however, was that the President herself was coming to Clarksville! The chief architect of this insidious plot which Vance had uncovered, was coming here. All this time I had thought *gorgos* to be our real enemy. But, no: Graham herself posed the biggest threat to humanity. I wondered if I would be able to keep calm in her presence. I resigned myself to pray for her soul. That kept me in check. But I must admit it cast an instant pall over my excitement in seeing my *Miguelito*.

They were both on their way. My heart jumped at the thought of seeing one, and then sank at the notion of seeing the other. I just hoped I wouldn't see both Miguel and the President in the same place at the same time.

•   •   •   •   •

Friday, August 22nd, 2042, 0900 hours

"Roger that," said Jet. "Wish us luck."

We always did. We could see the Sentry on the inside camera closing the inner hatch, sealing Jet, Rutty, and Markus off from us. The heavy doors met slowly, silently in the middle, and then they were lost to sight. The next sight we would see was the visual from the gun towers.

Their destination was A-Range, and I knew that would be difficult. A-Range meant the Zinc Plant. And the Zinc Plant was where the boys lost their father, Lieutenant Andrew Shipley. Rutty wasn't on that mission, of course; he was too young. Thus, it didn't hold the same specter of fear for him. For Jet, however, the memory had seared itself into his psyche. He would never forget the final moments of his father's conscious life, before the enemy seized upon him. I will always remember when they brought his battered and lifeless body back to our Blockade.

The three of them slowly filtered out onto the grass once the outer hatch had closed, rounding the corner and heading due southwest toward the forest that lay just beyond the Blockade. Then the hill, the road, and the plant.

I clasped my hands and said a prayer that Jet would be strong in the face of such terrible memories.

•　　•　　•　　•　　•

Friday, August 22nd, 2042, 0937 hours

We were in Halcyon, watching them through the zinc plant's video cameras which they had tapped into all those years ago. The Captain was nervous. They were coming up on the main building in which the Lieutenant had been killed.

Rutty went first, crossing Zinc Plant Road, followed by Cameron, and then Markus taking up the rear. Jet and Rutty had their rifles and sidearms, and Markus had a sidearm and a flamethrower.

Halcyon reported no incoming. Good news so far. It was August, and that was no surprise; the enemy preferred to bury their heads in water during this time, tempering away the hot summer sun with the slow flow of the cooling liquid of the Cumberland.

I cherished these times where I was able to be with the Captain in Halcyon. He was most permissive in allowing me to be present; he knew I cared for all members of the teams, and especially for Jet and Rutty. I was present for every one of their recons; you would need to lock me in solitary to keep me away.

It was not going to be quite as hot today. The temperature readout on the wall read seventy-four degrees. Hot, but it had been hotter, and the enemy had definitely stayed around for even hotter temperatures before.

The team crossed the road, silently. The pitter-patter of their feet barely registered on whatever they called their master sound meter on Pete's monitor, which showed up as barely a fraction of a decibel.

They opened the door to the warehouse. They were in. Single file: Rutty, Jet, Markus. Pete flicked a switch and typed in some code. His camera switched to a different vantage point from inside the building.

"Lookin' good, Alpha, proceed west through the building. No signals inbound. Grab whatever you can."

Fanning out in all directions, they silently visited desks, cubicles and offices which they had not scoured before, attempting to find anything that would possibly be of use back here: sealed snacks, pens, paper, communication equipment, cables, reading glasses, file folders. Next they hit the break room, looking for anything even remotely still edible.

"Jet, you okay bro?" asked Rutty suddenly and silently. Jet didn't answer, but we could see him nodding. He was going about clandestine business, trying to just get it done and get out of there. It was obvious this building still haunted the recesses of his mind. No more than fifty feet away on that first floor, his father had died. There was a darkened spot where the Lieutenant gave his life. Jet didn't look over.

Yet, all around, the southwest corner of the first floor bore grim testimony to a battle that had taken place there not five years earlier. The ceiling had caved in. The walls were blackened and peeling. Remnants of office furniture and partitions rose up in clumsy, feeble mounds of dark grayish ash and slag. A flamethrower had set the corner of the warehouse ablaze in a desperate attempt to escape. Bullet holes lined the walls, and the glass had been shot out.

And there, in the quiet of that southwest corner, the dead, silent, partial skeleton of a gorgon lay.

Ten minutes later, they were done and exiting the building. It was over.

As the team left the building, one final interior camera caught Jet wiping his eye. Rutty was right behind him, hand on his older brother's shoulder.

•　　　•　　　•　　　•　　　•

They continued on. Passing out the western end of the building, they came across the old, scattered remains of human bones.

Christopher Jackson. Their old teacher. He was a fabulous teacher and a sad loss. He had pursued Jet and Rutty – just boys – into the zinc plant when they went out after some deer they had spotted. He paid for it with his life.

Many of his bones were all there, baking in the sun.

"Proceed south-southwest across the greensward," Pete said. "Next building up."

They proceeded, quieter than a mouse on Christmas eve. This next building held no such dreadful memories for Jet. Captain Stone had mentioned that Jentzen had previously scoped out the building. Jentzen led the way through the western entrance to the first floor. He opened the door.

Pete shot straight up out of his chair. "Whoa, whoa! *Hold, Alpha Team!*" he screamed, and I spasmed, my eyes going wide, trying to ascertain the source of his alarm.

Stone ran over to him. "What! What is it?"

Pete could not contain himself. "Hold! Signals, *four* of 'em, hot, you're right on 'em! Inside that building! Abort, abort!"

The monitors didn't lie. Suddenly, as if out of thin air, four infrared signals sprang to life within the building they had almost just entered. Whether there was some kind of shielding that prevented the satellites from clearly seeing down below, or the cameras were inoperative, the team was now dreadfully aware of the danger. They had nearly walked right into them.

The colorful infrared blobs slowly started to move. I reflexively sucked in air while my spine tingled nervously. My hands went to my mouth.

Our team froze. "Roger, confirmed. Saw 'em. Status, Command, we're out here in the open," breathed the Sergeant. "They're coming!"

Our three team members shoved themselves right up against the eastern end of the building just outside the door. Markus appeared to be blocking the door, with Jet and Rutty flanking him. If the enemy decided to ram the door, it would be all over.

"Haul ass, you know the drill," growled the Captain, composed but clearly strategizing. Pete was chewing his fingers and looking wildly back and forth between Stone and his monitor.

Markus held his ground. "Go!" we heard him whisper. "I can hold the door. The old foot wedge trick. The door won't open. Go!"

"No way, are you sure?"

"Guys, they're moving," said Pete. "You're out of time!" He had switched over to a camera inside the building belonging to the zinc plant, and there they were: four dark shapes moving in spastic zips around the room, but drawing ever nearer the door. They were hissing. I clicked my tongue in revulsion. *Abominations. Such evil creatures!*

"We can't all stay here," argued Markus through his teeth. "We gotta get some of us back at least. Captain's right, you know how this works, now go!"

I could hear Jet grunt in disapproval. We could see him looking around wildly for a way of escape. There might be more of them ready to appear out of thin air as these ones did. Maybe they were getting smarter and were lying in wait. Who knows? I hoped to God that they didn't have one of those berserkers with them.

Jet could be seen looking at Rutty, who didn't flinch, but had slid a rocket into his launcher, readying it. He was holding his sidearm.

Markus looked at both of them, pleading.

Jet inserted a magazine swiftly. "Rutty, come on. We'll draw them away from you, Markus. Hold that door. Gun?"

"Got it. Go!" he growled again.

Jet patted him on the shoulder. "Good luck, man." Markus nodded. Jet and Rutty sped off southward to run around the building out of sight. They would have been sighted had they sprinted across the greensward.

They were too late. The door to the building burst open and Markus was sent flying. He hit the ground and lay still, most likely pretending to be dead as they had been taught. One of his arms was underneath his abdomen.

The enemy was here! Four of them shot out of the building, and the door rocked clumsily on its hinges.

Jet and Rutty were around the corner. Rutty kept running. Jet, however, stopped to checked on Markus. He stood there and watched.

Two of the enemy were slowly approaching him, bobbing their heads and hissing. The blue-green ether flowed freely around them, enveloping their bodies and sending out cold, vaporous mist as a cloak. It floated over the figure of Markus Jentzen.

Suddenly, Jet took aim and fired. Rutty cried "What are you doing? Jet, go!" Jet fired again.

Instantly, Markus whirled onto his back and fired upward. Bullets punctured the air around his assailants, and they scattered. The tiny projectiles punched through their vapor as they sped off in all directions, hissing and shrieking. One of them was hit, and flailed midair, thudding to the ground clumsily. The rest fled.

Just then, I remembered something that Rutty had told me in a counseling session. They had been trained to look, and yet not look. It took much practice, but they were to understand mentally where their enemy was and look at least twenty degrees to the left or right of it while firing. That way, the enemy could not establish a direct telepathic connection with them. I assumed that's what Markus had just done. And it had worked!

Markus got up and sprinted off. I have never seen anyone run that fast. He zoomed toward the first building they had been in, firing aimlessly in the air all around him. He was whimpering. My heart went out to him.

Two of the remaining enemy descended on the corpse of the downed creature and began to feast on it. Utterly repulsive! They eat their own not *minutes* after death. The third hovered slightly above, looking this way and that, its arms outstretched with long snapping fingers.

But Jet and Rutty were still trapped at the zinc plant with three of the enemy! They ran westward, away from our Blockade, heading toward the Cumberland. I lost track of Markus, but Halcyon had him. Pete was relaying locations of the remaining enemy, and providing a safe course for him to evade collision.

Jet and Rutty were running. They must have been heard, because the enemy that was not feasting on their fallen mate had drifted south and hovered at the entrance to the alleyway the brothers had just run down. It hissed, fanned out its arms, and then launched at them.

They had shocking speed.

The thing sailed over them just as Jet yelled "duck!" and they both hit the ground roughly. Without wasting a minute, they split apart, I'm sure quite unintentionally. They were no longer together! Rutty took cover in the middle of the alleyway between some stacks of what looked like combustion equipment. We could see his thermal signature retreating inward behind them. The enemy had a refined sense of smell, it was said, and so I feared that would not be enough.

Pete radioed to him. "Sergeant Shipley, the Private is cut off mid-alleyway. Repeat, signals potentially preparing to converge. Jentzen is on his way back!"

Jet's thermal signal kept moving through the building and at breakneck speed. He crashed through a southern door and ran all the way around. *There he was!* He appeared on camera just south of the building, running up to the edge and stopping to peer around the corner. Pete was frantically trying to keep up, switching to new cameras of where he thought Jet might appear.

By that time, the enemy had gotten their fill of their fallen mate. They began to move. Slowly, they shifted their stance and drifted south toward the same alleyway Jet and Rutty had run down minutes earlier. A third enemy remained at the far end, and, evidently, was wondering what had happened.

Rutty's frail, solitary thermal figure could barely be seen, crouching there in the middle of the alley, just off to the side behind the structure.

The Captain strode suddenly toward Pete. "Give me that," he said, ripping the headset off Pete's head and placing his hands on the desk, nose to nose with the monitors.

"Shipley, it's Stoney. Rutty's pinned down. Mid alley. He can't move. Whatever you're gonna do, do it fast."

The figures began to move toward Rutty. All three, from both directions.

I looked at Jet. *No, Cameron, don't do it*, I thought. *You're not fast enough.*

"Jet. Move. Now!" whispered Stoney.

I watched him defy belief. He knew they were going for his brother. He knew where Rutty had ended up.

The three infrared signals were converging on a point in the middle of the alley. Soon, they would be on him, and it would be all over. Rutty would die today.

Jet ran. Rutty was always faster than him, even though he had the nickname he did. However you sliced it, the Shipley boys were *fast*. The enemy couldn't see Jet south of them; they were too deep into the alleyway.

Jet fled eastward. Pete was flashing between cameras to get the best angle.

There he was! Running now in full view of the enemy. He stomped heavily, shouting and firing his Beretta. The infrared signals turned and hissed, all pointing eastward. He was waving his arms wildly and shouting. "I'm here! I'm here! Come and get me, shitbags!" He was running full-tilt eastward, racing past the building where his father had been killed.

The three ghastly figures launched at him. Vapor spewed out of them, leaving a ghostly greenish wake. Jet was firing back over his shoulder behind him, blindly, rifle in one hand and Beretta in the other. In desperation and in pure foolishness, he fired. By the grace of God, he nailed one of them! It crashed to the ground and the others slowed.

My fists shot up in the air in triumph as I shrieked with joy. Tears were streaming from my eyes. The enemy did exactly what he thought they would do! The other two that had been pursuing him with their now-fallen mate began to descend upon the dead enemy. They sunk their long, bony fingernails into their own species, tearing at its flesh with their grisly teeth.

Jet ran like a jet.

A small thermal signal emerged from the alleyway. It crept quietly into the middle.

Jet ran, still firing.

The thermal signal knelt. It raised something over its shoulder.

Jet ran, like a bullet, straight toward the Blockade.

A yellowish-orange stream shot out from the small figure kneeling in the middle of the alleyway, straight for the remaining two of the enemy feasting on the carcass of their fallen comrade. A massive circle of yellowish-red ballooned around them, blowing their alien flesh into flying chunks.

Jet ran.

Pete cried out that more signals were inbound.

The small thermal signal also ran! He bolted into the building his brother had previously raced through, taking shelter in an office somewhere inside. A small object fell from him there in the alleyway, and we heard feedback and static.

"Shipley. Private Shipley. Report," Pete petitioned. "Shipley, do you read?"

Nothing.

Pete turned to us. "That was his headset. He's lost his com. We won't be able to communicate with him."

The thermal signal was lost to view because of interference from the structure. I shook my head. It was like a punch to the gut. We would have no way of knowing if he was alive visually or audibly.

Tearing through the sky, we saw a nightmarish trail of seven more infrared signals converge on the zinc plant from the north and west. They descended in a frenzy, presumably determined to find the assailant that had just annihilated two of their own.

Jet ran. His brother was trapped at the zinc plant. His ammo was spent. Jet ran. All he had was his wits and his speed. Jet ran.

The Launch doors opened, and he flew in as they closed. Stoney and I met him at the door. Markus was already there waiting for him.

Jet was frantic. "We need to assemble a team. Rutty's still out there! I know where he is, I can get him, Dad!"

"Son, there's no time. He's gotta ride this out."

"What? No! He's all alone out there! He'll never make it!"

"Sergeant, listen to me. He has trained for this very thing. Just like you. You know he can take care of himself."

I looked at Jet, and Jet looked at me. He turned around and put his hands over his head, tearing at his own follicles, a shower of sweat drenching him.

"Dad, *no*, there are more gorgs coming in, we've gotta go get him! Markus and I can go back with Pettijohn, Wilkes and Ferro! Hickey! Myrtle! Frye! All of us, we can *all* go, Dad. *We've gotta get Rutty!"* He hissed these last words through clenched teeth at Stone, mashing his fingers into bony fists readying for a stiff fight.

Stoney just looked at him solemnly. "No," he simply said, quietly. "Sergeant Shipley, I'm ordering you to stand down. We will not lose eight soldiers in exchange for one. Stand down now. Jentzen, escort him to his bunk please."

But Jet didn't stand down. He bore his teeth at Stone and looked as though he was going to charge at him.

"Stand down," Stone ordered him, and the Captain pulled out his Beretta. "You wanna sleep in your bunk, Jet? Or the Brig? Or worse? Shall we lose two Shipleys in one night? Stand…down."

"Jet! Stand down, man!" cried Markus.

Cameron tightened his fists and stared grimly at the Captain.

At that moment, I knew he had a choice to make – and it was going to be the wrong one.

"Cameron Alex Shipley!" I screamed at him, and it stopped him in his tracks. It stopped all of them. "Stop this *now*! Listen to the one whom you call *Dad!"* I yelled at him.

He released Stone from his gaze, and, thankfully, he softened. The sweat dripped from his forehead. He clenched his teeth and stared at me.

"I *was*," he said, angrily, and then flashed a saddened, sullen look at Captain Stone before stomping off to his bunk.

Captain Stone didn't waste any time. "Jentzen. Take your sidearm. Watch him. Make sure he doesn't go out through the back. For his own good."

Markus sped after him, gun drawn.

Stone breathed out hard and holstered his weapon. He looked at me.

"I'm sorry, Captain," I said. "He said he was listening to you."

Stone shook his head. "That's not who he meant. He was listening to his dad. He was listening to Andrew Shipley who would have wanted him to protect his brother. I'm not his dad, Rosie. I never will be." Stone gave me a weak smile of reluctant acceptance and walked slowly back to Halcyon to monitor Rutty's safety. If I knew the Captain, he wouldn't leave Halcyon tonight. He would watch and guide Rutty all the way through until he was back in our Blockade, safe and sound.

There wasn't any trust, and things were getting tense.

31 | DIEHARD

| Rosie |

Saturday, August 23rd, 2042, 0430 hours

His brother was dead?

Those are the words that just came out of his mouth, and we couldn't believe it. We had been up all night, the three of us, sitting there in Halcyon. We couldn't sleep, and we didn't want to. Pete stayed up with us, imbibing an unreasonable amount of caffeine.

I didn't want to believe it. I couldn't allow myself to. But how could Rutty survive such a large number of the enemy concentrated in one area, pinned down? We honestly didn't know if he was still alive; we had lost his signal.

The gun towers had sounded a few times through the night. The gunners had gotten a few of the enemy. At last report, five remained hovering around the plant, and they simply wouldn't leave. That was around 0100 hours: sixteen hours since Rutty lost communication with Halcyon. We hadn't seen any movement in or out of the building, and nothing came from his headset.

At noon yesterday, Jet broke down. He couldn't contain himself any longer, and made another impassioned plea to Captain Stone. Markus walked him back to Halcyon where the Sergeant was then glued to the monitors. At one point the enemy seemed to converge right where Rutty was hiding, and he couldn't take it.

His eyes were streaming and red. "Stoney, I'm begging you. *Please*. I just-" he broke off, raising his arms in helplessness. The Captain walked over to him. He didn't say a word, just looked at him and shook his head softly, heaving a labored sigh. I could tell Jet wanted to say something. Anything. But all he did was quiver his lip, clench his face, and collapse to the floor, his face in his hands. He lay there in a heap, and the Captain consoled him.

And now, that's all Jet said. "Rutty's dead. I can't believe he's dead."

I looked at the monitors. There was no movement or signal; we hadn't seen or heard anything. Pete turned and watched us surround Jet on the floor as he grieved. He walked over to embrace the Sergeant as well.

I had knelt by the despondent soldier. "Cameron, listen to me. Cameron, please," I said. His crying quieted. "We talked about this. You and I. Do you remember? Rutty is a soldier. I know that he is your brother, we all do. But Rutty is a fine soldier as well, kiddo. He will survive this. We must believe that he is fine, and we must trust. You already decided that he could make it when you left him."

Jet's breathing slowed, and the quaking of his body decreased. He was trying to compose himself. These were the only words of hope he had heard outside of his own self-recriminations for leaving him behind; his own depressing mind-tapes he was playing over and over. At length, he pushed himself up from kneeling, and sat. He wiped his face with his sleeve and turned toward me.

"I have to trust," he breathed, but his face was a pale and nondescript slate. "Rutty can do this," he murmured robotically, trying desperately to hold onto the truth of his own words.

I saw life return to his eyes for a brief moment. "Rutty *can* do this," I encouraged him. "That's why you drew them off, kiddo. You knew he could take care of himself. You knew that he *can* take care of himself."

I smiled endearingly at him. I told him how proud I was of him, as I rested my hands on his shoulders. He embraced my left arm with his right hand.

"Yes, he can," he breathed. "He can."

"He can," I echoed to him. "The walls are not caving in." His eyes showed a glimmer of recollection when I said that. "Let the air out, hmm?"

Jet slowly nodded, thinking back to our last session. He remembered. His body shook involuntarily from his tear-filled sobs, but he worked to clear it, exhaling a cleansing breath from his lungs. He nearly forced a smile, as he looked past me, briefly, at Pete. But then, suddenly, his expression changed to confusion. And then wonder. And then joy.

His eyes went wide. I could practically feel the tingles covering his skin. He breathed out one word.

Rutty.

We all turned. Pete whipped back around and stared at his monitor. There, for all our eyes to see, a thermal image was running. A small, yellow and orange blob was moving across the screen from the plant, heading straight for us. Not the enemy, and not someone from a previous recon patrol. This was not some unknown refugee or castaway.

This was Rutty.

One of the cameras caught him as he ran.

I thought *Jet* was fast. No. *Rutty* was *fast!*

He still had his grenade launcher collapsed down in his backpack and was carrying his sidearm as he ran.

Oh, boy, did he run.

And oh, boy, so did our tears. I lost it and bawled. The tears blurred my vision and five Ruttys careened toward us. My chest heaved and quaked. The Captain let out a moan of incredulity which turned to panting and exultant joy. Jet leapt to his feet. "It's Rutty!"

The Captain seized his headset and hailed the gunners. "Guns, guns, prepare to fire! Soldier inbound! Move!"

We could hear the guns rotating and facing west now, all of them, as the small figure crashed through the trees toward us. "Launch, Launch, prepare to receive soldier!"

"No inbound except him, he's gonna make it!" screamed Pete. Jet got up and dashed for the Launch. We raced after him.

There might still be some of the enemy out there.

And we were hot on Jet's trail in here.

But no one could outrun the Shipley boys.

The outer hatch opened. The Sentry held us back. The guns overhead fired, thundering loudly. I covered my ears. We raced up the gangway, and met Jet at the top, huffing and panting with joy.

The outer hatch closed. The inner hatch began to move, separating slowly in the middle, sliding up and down.

Rutty. There he was, panting and exhausted, shivering and cold from the night air and fear. But he had made it. He was dirty, and sweating, and his hair was plastered and matted to his soaking head, but it didn't matter.

Jet erupted into tears of joy and threw his arms around him. They both fell to their knees, as Jet sobbed. Rutty was still trying to catch his breath. His headset was gone, so we would never have heard him inform us of his timing or his plans. He used his gut, his intelligence, and his bravado, decided the time was ripe, and raced out of there.

He made it. Jet had trusted him, and he had made it. He was breathing so hard! The brothers locked foreheads and stared into each other's eyes. Apparently, the affection grew too much for them to bear, and they started giggling. Uncontrollable giggling which made them both sound like middle schoolers. The laughs came from deep within their souls, seemingly awkward at first until they surrendered their male pride and acknowledged openly how much they loved each other.

But then, I heard it differently. It was as though it came not from men. This was the sound of their boyhood. Boys who once played together, far away, long ago, amidst tickling and silly name-calling. Rolling around on the carpet of their home, perhaps: just being boys, wrestling and giggling together, striving for dominance and playing their own strength off of each other, testing each other's fortitude in complete innocence during a time when life was more carefree. The sound of their laughter together now was raining down in a cleansing sheet of warmth and joyful memory. And then Rutty broke it.

"Okay, can you get off me, bro? I need somethin' to eat, bad."

Jet broke into a wild guffaw and got up, wiping his eyes. "You can have whatever you want, man. Oh, Rutty," he breathed, and then he stood up, as his brother climbed to his feet, grabbing the railing. Headrush seized him, and he steadied himself.

"Whoa, buddy. Take a break first."

"Yeah," he said, and he just smiled at Jet.

A few of the other soldiers ran up, awakened by the tumult. Markus had run with us and witnessed Rutty's homecoming. Now, though, came Ferro, Myrtle, Pettijohn, Hickey, and Frye. Hickey ran to him and threw her arms around him.

"Hey, Shannon," he said. "Hey Cap. Hey Rosie."

I smiled at him through my tears, so proud of him. I couldn't help myself and stretched out my arms toward him. "Come here, kiddo."

He sheepishly strode over to me and stood before me.

"I can't tell you how gla-" I started, but then my throat caught, and I couldn't finish it, erupting in tears. I had almost lost this dear boy.

He smiled at me. Rutty slowly wrapped his arms around me and pulled me in for a hug. "I know, Rosie. It's all good. Me too. Love you," he said, and then he squeezed me tight until all my tears fell freely into his fatigues, cold from the night air.

My head was turned sideways into him. I could see Jet watching the two of us with a warm smile.

I smiled warmly back and winked at him. He winked back at me, and then raised his arms out, palms up, in token of receiving. His trust was rewarded.

His brother was alive.

32 | READYING

| Bassett |

Saturday, August 30th, 2042, 1411 hours

In my heart, I knew it. Steph's death would not be in vain.

Everything had changed that day, and frankly, I was still heartbroken. I had lost my kid sister to those damned things. And after all she'd been through! I shook my head.

"You hear me, hon?" Maureen asked, and she shifted my head right with her fingers, toward her eyes. Those sweet, beautiful eyes. "It won't be in vain. You got it. It's here. She enabled that, hon."

The gorg. We *had* gotten it here. She *had* enabled that. She'd been part of that damned mission, and we did it. I just couldn't believe she was gone. Nor Raylin. But one of those deaths cut so much deeper, of course. Grief is a palpable ache, and I missed my kid sis.

Trudy had her arm wrapped around me sitting to my left, leaning her head on my shoulder.

That damned gorg. The thing ate fish like crazy. The fish traps at the Chattahoochee were now feeding *it* more than they were feeding the rest of us. Recons would bring back what we caught, but so much of it was devoted to meals for the gorg, and that didn't give us any usable data other than it was a glutton and a slob. Last time I saw it they had it strapped to a near vertical gurney in solitary, behind Trudy's borosilicate glass protection. It had been blindfolded to boot.

Bayless sent the message up the chain to the President that we'd caught the gorg. She received a phone call nearly instantaneously. The President sent us her congratulations, as well as condolences for our lost soldiers. I appreciated it, but I still didn't like the hand we'd been dealt. Until this thing showed us some promise, it amounted to no more than my sister's cold-blooded killer.

•   •   •   •   •

Wednesday, September 3rd, 2042, 0918 hours

The flute sounded sixteen times. The flautist obviously had a lot of experience playing dirges. Hell, he had sixteen years of mourning the death of eighty five percent of the population. A growing number that now included Steph. Each note was breathy, somber, floating on a vibrato note, and then, fading into a wave of mournful silence. All sixteen of them, played on a single note.

We were all in the Rotunda as usual, gathered around the perimeter. It had now been forty-seven days since we lost Steph, and my heart still had a giant band-aid around it. Every breath was a labor, every picture a torture, every mention of her name a painful wince. This ache would never leave; it would make its presence known repeatedly until one day I was somehow able to mute it with the slow rolling-pin of time.

Bayless came up to me after the service. "In my office, please." I wondered what this was about. Casting one quizzical look at Maureen, I squeezed my wife's hand and followed Bayless back to her office.

"Sit down, please, Joe," she said, taking a seat herself. "I'll get right to the point, Staff Sergeant Bassett. The President is coming up from Nashville. On a Corvette. It's a small naval warship. Up the Cumberland to Clarksville."

That blew me away. "Why?"

"She's got the new mobile DTF tech; you've heard of it. Paired with triggers, ready for testing in the field. Along with that they've got them on missiles, torpedoes, and God knows what else. She's got her teams heading south and east, and they want someone here to head up to Clarksville and meet them for the handoff."

My eyes narrowed. "I-I don't understand. Do they want to test this in Clarksville? If so, why don't they just have one of the President's staff do it?"

"They want someone experienced. They also want the people who developed the mask tech onsite for when she gets there. That's Trudy. Beyond that, they want someone else in the field who caught a live gorg and has it in containment, for knowledge in the field. That's…you."

My heart raced. "Uh, wow, I-"

Bayless interrupted me. "I know. You're honored and flattered."

I raised a hand. "No, that's-that's not what I meant," I said, and forced a sigh. "Major, I just lost my sister to one of those damned things." She nodded. Of course, she already knew, and wasn't going to send any patronizing condolences. "I don't know why they'd want me?"

She leaned forward on her elbows. "Joe, listen to me very carefully. Something very big is about to go down. We've never been this close, and a battle is brewing. Now, we can all sit back and reflect and say, 'well, it happened sixteen years ago today,' but they'd be incorrect. Our *annihilation* started sixteen years ago today. The battle, however, starts now.

"We now have technological weapons as well as defenses, manpower, and of course classical weapons to fight them off. Our time is now. The simple fact is that the President has actually conscripted Trudy. She has no choice. She developed these masks. She'll be going."

"What? How can she do that?" I leaned forward, my face becoming hot.

"I believe it's because she's the President, Joe."

"That's horseshit. Trudy's a scientist."

"Allow me to correct you," she said, as she put up a hand. "Trudy is a *warrior* who just happens to specialize in science. She'll be going. And there's no one that she trusts more than you. Now, you've also been requested for that reason. You can volunteer, which would make it much easier on all of us, or you can be *voluntold*. I do not like to have to hamstring you like this, but my hands are tied, Joe."

I looked at her, long and hard. I knew Major Bayless. She was a good woman. There's no way there was any personal ambition or deceit in her.

The poor woman was simply passing down the edict.

I blew out hot air. "Does Trudy know?"

"Yes. I just told her."

"What's her response?"

"She's elated."

"What? Really?"

Bayless nodded. "She wants to get out and make her mark. She's stuck in here, she's got gumption, skill, she's a great shot who was skilled at hunting, and she wants to see this through. The mask technology is going far and wide, Joe. And," she said, pausing, her eyes twinkling at me, "she actually requested you."

That hit me like a ton of bricks. Allison requested that I accompany her. I couldn't even begin to fathom such a journey. I waited, calculating our odds and thinking about the feasibility of this crazy assignment.

"How far away is Clarksville?"

"Two hundred eighty-eight miles. Four days. You'd be using as many tunnels as you can, between the cities, bored out by the drills. Pinballing. Come up when you need to for air, food, transmitting sit reps, all of it. You'll have help along the way."

"I don't get it. This is crazy. Why me? Why us here at this Blockade, aside from the masks Trudy made?"

"Fine. Plain and simple? Ego. A lot of soldiers now know about this tech. There have been rumors stirring. The infantry is waking up all over the world, roused by this new stirring of hope."

Hope. Yet again, I thought of Steph.

"Several Commands are petitioning the President, even now, to be the one who gets to pull the trigger. She wants someone who isn't trigger-happy. Someone not eager to make such a name for themselves and jump the gun. That's why you'll be getting the first – and *only* one issued – manual DTF trigger. You'll rendezvous with the Nashville team, get it from them, and bring it with you." Her words held promise and fear. What we would be receiving from them was something that could change our fortunes in this war. "They want someone humble. Trudy and I could think of no one better."

I studied her suspiciously, yet with horrendous optimism, lost in thought.

"Staff Sergeant Bassett, what is your answer?"

I sighed. "Sounds like I don't have a choice anyway, right? I either volunteer willingly, or the government of the United States thanks me for my 'faithful service' to them."

"Something like that," Bayless said. "But I think, personally, for you, it would be one helluva way to avenge Steph. One helluva way to make your mark. I think we're almost free of this scourge, Joe. The President won't forget those who helped wrest control of our planet away from these damned things."

She was right, and I hated it.

Worse, Maureen was going to hate it too.

•   •   •   •   •

Wednesday, September 3rd, 2042, 1059 hours

Trudy was summoned to Bayless' office with me, and we sat down to talk this through. Trudy came in and looked straight at me. There was no apology for recruitment, no plea for understanding. We just knew this was what we both needed to do.

The plan was to rendezvous with the Nashville team on the way up to Clarksville, receive the firing trigger and the

DTF bomb, and bring it with us to test in the field. We
would bring up a few masks with us. The Nashville team
would come down in a tank with these pulse emitters: ones
that would send out a DTF pulse at intervals, meet us, and
then we'd drive back halfway. Then, it would be on foot to
test the mobile ones that we carried and see how they worked
in the field. The tank would shadow us on the way up. Made
sense. For me, I would have liked to stay in the tank the
whole time, but I understood the necessity of testing these
mobile emitters.

The journey would take us four days normally, as
Bayless had mentioned, but we allowed two weeks for the
pinballing through the tunnels while the tank shadowed us
above. Two weeks would allow us to flex for any other
contingencies that may arise.

The Major mentioned that there was a large mass of
gorgons clustered around the Cumberland between Blockade
DN436 and the city of Clarksville itself. That would be
where we would test the DTF. She was in touch with the
Captain there, Maurice Stone. He had the manpower and the
guns to accompany us.

The President, she said, was preparing for a trip up
north to meet us. She would be riding up the Cumberland in
a Navy Corvette: her own small, personal warship.

The mission was not to be spoken of to anyone lest
we, to use a phrase I would understand, 'revealed our hand.'
Such a false start would prompt someone else eager to make
a name for themselves to jump the gun. For some reason, the
President was especially resistant to that. Our trigger needed
to be the first. The President was overseeing the operation
herself, and she was adamant about that. *No one* else would
be allowed to have or fire a trigger: the purview, and the
privilege, would be ours alone.

●   ●   ●   ●   ●

Sunday, September 14th, 2042, 1201 hours

So there we were, Bayless and I, one mid-September day on a video call with Captain Maurice Stone of DN436.

"Captain Stone? Major Bayless. Pleased to meet you," the Major greeted him.

"The pleasure is all mine, Major," Stone replied. "How is our little operation coming?"

"We're getting closer. The President has not given us a green-light yet, but we're close. Can you tell me how you're doing on the collection of the amulets?"

Stone looked behind him and then moved over to obscure more of his camera, as if there were someone nearby that he didn't want to hear anything we discussed. "Fine, fine. Per the President's orders I've only got one primary team searching. When she opens up the floodgates, we'll bring them all into the fold and expand the search."

"Good," Bayless replied. "She's calling this *Operation Shake N' Bake* for now."

Stone chuckled. "So I heard. Fitting."

"Do you have your men picked out for this one?"

"I do. Two, in particular, just to keep the info stream contained. With your two, that should make for our usual recon patrol config. We had another team here temporarily that came from Oklahoma, but we lost them. I'll tell my guys that your guys are here to replace them as a new Beta-team. That should make sense and not arouse suspicions."

"Alright. Keep me in the loop please. When the President gives the all-clear, we'll get these guys off to you and send word."

"Copy that," he said, saluting, smiling, and signing off. Seemed like a nice chap, but I didn't like that his men were being kept in the dark on so many levels. Why the secrecy? That part of it bugged me. I don't think even Trudy knew the whole picture.

When all was said and done, Trudy and I had 'volunteered,' and were set to leave for Clarksville sometime in November. It was coming up fast.

•   •   •   •   •

Monday, September 22nd, 2042, 0548 hours

"I still don't understand why you have to go," Maureen complained.

"I'm not allowed to say, hon. It's *that* mum," I replied. "I know it's a long journey, but it's gonna be four of us on our way up there. They're providing extra men, extra mags, and some portable 'DTF emitters,' they're calling them. These guys can carry them, and then, when we get to Clarksville, they'll keep 'em and stay there at the Cumberland close to that Blockade. They're starting a new base there with ships from a local navy base somewhere, I don't know. And lots of tanks. The President's committed a lot to this, hon. Plus, we'll be using the tunnels below ground. The gorgs don't like it underground, or, at least that's what we've always seen."

That didn't seem to satisfy her. "I hear what you're saying. I don't like it, hon."

I stared into her ravishing eyes and smoothed back her hair. "I know, darlin.' I know. I don't have a choice. But even if I did, I need to do this. Bayless is right: we've never been this close. There's a battle coming, and one that we just might win."

Maureen stared at me.

There we were, standing in the hallway down the corridor from the Launch. I could feel the Sentry's eyes on us from up above, cold and piercing. I had her in my embrace, and I could smell her beautiful hair. But, no matter what I said, she pulled apart and was now cautiously staring at me.

"Joe, I don't want you to go. That's that. Please."

"Sweetheart," I said, shaking my head. "I don't have a choice. It's either volunteer or be volunteered. Trudy has already voluntarily committed. Someone needs to go with her. She asked for me specifically. Don't blame her or hold any ill will, hon, it's just the way it needs to be for this one. I *promise* you, I'll take care of her."

She scoffed. "Joe, give me a break. I know you will. It's *you* I want to be taken care of. I'm married to *you*, not Allison."

She ripped herself out of my embrace. I called for her, but she sped off down the hall. I was watching her go, all alone with nothing but the Sentry above in silent witness as she fled.

The air escaped from my lungs at the exact opposite speed that she had torn herself from me and fled to weep.

•　　•　　•　　•　　•

Sunday, September 28th, 2042, 0512 hours

"Any change with Maureen?" Trudy asked. She was sitting to my right at breakfast in the mess hall.

I shook my head. "Nothing more than 'good morning' and 'good night, hon,'" I complained. "But she'll come around. I know it."

Trudy watched me closely. It was time for a conversation that we've needed to have for a while now.

"Joe," she said, scooting over to me. "I want you to know I'm sorry. They said you'd be conscripted anyway, even if I didn't choose you. Even if I had chosen Gage, they wanted someone with experience, with leadership. My hands were tied."

I turned to her, smiling. "I appreciate it. Don't worry about it, woman. We'll be just fine. I'm actually looking forward to the trip and getting to use this new stuff. I get to be the first triggerman in history to take out more of those bastards at once than anybody ever has. That's an honor, Trudy. A real one. Maureen'll come around. We'll be just fine. Besides," I added with a wink and a smile, "I think she knows that someone has to come along and keep you in line."

"Yeah, I'm a handful," she said, bumping shoulders with me. "I need a big, gruff soldier to keep me in line. Know anybody?"

"A few names come to mind. Very short list of who could actually keep you in line, Trudy. I'm at the top."

"You *are* at the top," she smiled at me.

We looked at each other, and I remembered the little girl again, so filthy and shaking when she first arrived. Now, here she was: a Lieutenant, inventor of masks, wrangler of gorgons, world-traveler.

I was honestly looking forward to keeping her in line.

"Gonna be a long journey, Trudy. Three hundred miles. Nashville's gonna meet us here, and we'll split it between the tank. It's gonna be a cold, dark, scary road heading up there. Let's watch each other's backs."

Trudy said nothing, but that smile she gave me told me that she was excited, ready to trust me with her life, and grateful for my companionship. She put out a fist, and I bumped it, then squeezed her close to me.

"Love ya, young lady."

"Love ya, old man."

•　　•　　•　　•　　•

Saturday, October 11th, 2042, 1522 hours

I stared at it. *Subject Zero.* Disgusting creature. The room stank, and we had to run the blowers on it constantly with that thing in the room. That friggin' mist they put out. No one knew exactly where or how they produced that stuff. Each time we poked and prodded the captive, it would flail, emit their frigid, horrid fog, and force our science team to evacuate the room. No one could stand to be around it for long. You almost needed a thermal suit to safeguard against frostbite and hypothermia.

Gage had the skin sample from our captive, and he studied it intensely under the microscope. We already knew they were cold-blooded. The thermal scan showed nothing in that room, while the infrared registered electromagnetic pulses throughout its body. I was watching that too. On that spectrum, wave after wave coursed through it, darting to and fro: some kind of radiation. In particular, where you could see what might be called its abdomen, it had something going on in there that undoubtedly generated the power of flight. But the way it was strapped in that gurney, it was hard to see anything through its tentacles, up in its crotch. We had to repeatedly tranquilize it before any such exams could be done. It defied belief that there was no consistency to how long the sedation would keep the thing asleep. Despite using a uniform dosage each time, duration of sleep state was anything but uniform.

What I was most curious about were the flaps on its side, close to the head. Were those ears? We already knew they were sensitive to sound, and it was pretty much established that they couldn't see stationary objects clearly. As long as we didn't move a muscle, we could be relatively undetected. The flaps undoubtedly helped air to flow through it and keep it aerial. However, unless we could kill it and perform an autopsy, we would never know. We hadn't received any such authorization yet, because, as far as we knew, it was now the only one in captivity.

Of major concern up and down the chain was its telepathic paralytic: how that functioned, and where it came from. I studied one of them up close without its blindfold. I had the improved mask on, and it looked right at me. Its pupils have a tendency to dilate and glow somewhat greenish when it zeroes you. There is some kind of chemical force behind those eyes: an aerial or projected vaporous neurotoxin, perhaps, that I believed minimized over distance. It was invisible to the naked eye, but it was there.

My muscles tensed every time I went near it. In the throes of that wicked stare, I felt numb and nauseous. And when it did its thing – which was fairly immediate once it zeroed me – I became even more tense.

The masks aren't full proof, as Trudy had said. They're more of, say, a 'graduated resistance.' In time, they would be perfected, and she'd be the catalyst for that, I had no doubt. I would move to the side, and its head would stay locked onto mine, rotating in perfect step with me. It became almost calm, but humming, pulsating, and its chest cavity would breathe in and out, relaxed, while it attempted to paralyze me.

I could withstand looking at those glowing eyes through my mask for only a few minutes before my body succumbed to exhaustion and nausea. Gage and I took turns studying it up close, day after day, curious, engrossed and disgusted. These things had to go.

I couldn't wait to blast the crap out of a ton of them out in the field. We were getting close. We were going to find out all about these things. We were going to knock them off the Earth and live again.

Trudy and I would make it. We'd be safe enough with those devices and with the armed escort of the tank. We'd be part of this final revolt, even if it killed us. We were going to win. Finally. Maureen would see. They would all see, every last one of 'em.

It was gametime, and we were about to go.

In my heart, I knew it. Steph's death was not in vain.

33 | TRAVELS

| Miguel |

Sunday, November 9th, 2042, 1041 hours

The time had almost come.

We were arriving at Wright-Patterson Air Force Base in Dayton, Ohio, after a journey of three hundred twenty-six miles. It had taken us a little over six hours with our fleet, all sounding DTF emitters loud and proud. The enemy fled before us.

The President was in a different tank ahead of us.

She had a fleet with her, and there were five tanks in it, all outfitted with these new pulse emitters that would regularly sound blips to protect the fleet. We met no opposition. She was to meet with a Colonel Keegan to verify that all tanks and fighters were in a state of readiness up at Wright-Patterson.

This change of plans of hers caught us all off guard. The President told us that she wanted to be mobile again. The threats on her life had begun to see her moved around which gave her a taste of life outside the Embassy. She was constantly relocating. The current plan was to drop in on Wright-Patterson, return to Nashville, and then make our way up the Cumberland to the Clarksville Blockade.

I, however, suspected something grimmer and more nefarious given what I knew about her, and what Cardona had told us before he left.

The tank I was traveling in included Lieutenant Rawley, and I enjoyed some good banter with her and a few others.

We arrived at Wright-Patterson without incident, thankfully. As with BNA, there was a force of jets here, C-17s, even an F-35 and an F-22. I beheld them in their glory and looked upon them with lust.

Oh, how I would have loved to hop in the cockpit of one of those beauties.

Upon disembarking, I spotted Andi Cardona, Vance's wife, briefly. We did not speak of course. She appeared in a group of soldiers congregating around the President, feigning deep respect for Graham's rousing speech. I saw the look of cold distrust on her face. She nodded, subtly, in my direction. I returned the coded sentiment. Clearly, the Resistance was alive and well, and right under the President's nose.

Graham chummed around with various folks, surveying the operations. We stayed overnight before it was time to head back the next day. Progress was now happening all over the world, and it was remarkable to behold all the activity under this new environment of optimism.

Something the President oversaw filled me with alarm, however. On all the jets at Wright-Pat, she was having trackers installed by men loyal to her. Neither the pilots nor the commanders knew about the lojacks. Even now, she was protecting herself, suspicious, and ensuring her own survival as opposed to the game-face she put on with the troops. She wasn't there to rally them to survival. She was there to ensure her own, and to thwart any attempt to her power, and her coming operation.

•   •   •   •   •

Sunday, November 10th, 2042, 1826 hours

It was approaching nightfall when we returned to Nashville. We would be boarding a Corvette the very next day, sailing up the Cumberland for Clarksville. I was tired of all the travel in the tank, and my head hurt. I longed for the embrace of my sweet Rosalita. I couldn't wait to see her.

I quickly fired off an encrypted update to Vance and my Rosie, and bedded down for the night. Vance wrote back, and I received the message the following morning.

I don't envy you being in such close quarters with her. Watch your back, friend. We need to all watch our backs. Operation Shake N' Bake is coming. See you soon, on your way up to kill me by order of the President. :)

The mission to assassinate him. I shook my head.

•   •   •   •   •

Monday, November 11th, 2042, 0827 hours

The following morning, we loaded on the Corvette, one of the smallest in the Navy fleet. It would hold enough of us. As with the other ships, it was outfitted with several DTF emitters.

It would be a slow-going, zig-zagging journey up the Cumberland to Clarksville. The Cumberland had varying depths, and they had to take soundings frequently.

An LST, one of those tank landing ships, had gone ahead of us, already unloading tank after tank. Another one was behind it. Other tanks were rolling on the ground, already massing south of Clarksville and prepping for a major assault. The Captain up there had helped to coordinate everything. Things were really rolling.

The President had her nice cushy quarters where the Captain usually bunked, if you could call it 'cushy.'

This would be my home for the next few weeks. The President had varying locations to visit on the way up the Cumberland for the journey to Clarksville, and outposts were alerted to her presence and destinations, cleared by the Secret Service. There was a fleet of other Corvettes accompanying us, and a PG Gunboat, the largest vessel in our entourage. Why she didn't take that lofty perch surprised me, but whatever. She had her reasons. Perhaps any attackers would target the biggest boat, and she would then be safe in one of the more inconspicuous, smaller ones.

We were underway when the President summoned me, once more, to her.

"Captain Monzon! How are you liking all this traveling?" she asked, getting up from her desk and greeting me with a handshake.

I saluted, and approached her, putting on my best happy face. "Oh, fine, Ma'am. Nice to see a bit of the world again."

"That's right. Listen, I have Captain Stone on the line here from DN436 in Clarksville. Captain Stone, can you hear us?"

"Yes, Ma'am," he said. I could see his face on her computer screen, which she tilted toward me.

"Monzon, I was just talking with Stone here. I've another idea, which I think is critical for this new phase we're in." She was almost giddy with delight. It was disgusting. "You know that our own team was able to do this, and now a team in Alpharetta has done it as well. I think our troops need to be prepared to incorporate this tactic into their own protocols should we need to take more stringent measures against the gorgs."

"What tactic is that, Madame President?" I asked.

"Sorry! I got ahead of myself," she said, and then giggled with pretentious bliss. "I want the Clarksville team to lojack a gorgon. Not right away. We have another team heading up to meet them from Alpharetta. I'm issuing the same command to as many Blockades as I can. With Clarksville, in particular, there is a mass of gorgons on the east side of the Cumberland spur outside Clarksville, underneath a train trestle there north of the Cunningham bridge. That's going to inhibit passage by water or train, once we get the trains running again. We have nearly six hundred Blockades still active around the world, but this is a particularly valuable one given its geographic positioning close to the Cumberland.

"What I'm mostly concerned about, however, is their nesting behavior, and where they go when they disappear during the heat of summer. If there are, in fact, giant nests and places of retreat for them, we need to be able to locate those.

"Therefore, I've issued a directive to Stone," -here she turned to me - "to have a few of his finest on that mission with the Alpharetta team when they arrive. I don't want you on that mission. You have your own, of course."

Right. The mission to kill my contact and friend, Vance Cardona, you deranged, psychopathic witch.

"I've also issued orders to continue searching for more of these so-called amulets, so that we can continue to generate as many DTF emitters and bombs as we can. Stone here will be part of that as well."

"Well, that's great, Madame President. Wonderful, Captain Stone. Thank you for all you're doing for the cause," I said to him.

The President smiled at me, playfully. She was eating all of this up, trying to look every bit the savior.

"Right," said Graham. "So, after your team has done that, we should be arriving soon, and then you can coordinate with Captain Monzon here for the mission up to Mammoth Cave to visit our little friend up there."

Stone simply nodded. By his lack of questioning, I assumed he knew about my assignment to take out Cardona. And, by his silence, I guessed that he approved.

Graham smiled at me again. I felt sick to my stomach, and it wasn't because of the rocking of the boat. Graham herself was rocking a much bigger boat.

I prayed, right there with the two of them, that it would not be Cardona's end, but hers.

I couldn't wait to see my Rosalita.

And as for Graham? The Resistance against her was rising.

Her time would come.

34 | THE PLANT

| Rutty |

Saturday, November 15th, 2042, 0900 hours

"Bring them out, repeat, bring them out," said Stone into the com.

There we all were, standing inside the Launch, the inner hatch closing. Myself, my big brother Jet, Will Pettijohn, and Celeste Frye, ready to go.

Markus Jentzen, Evy Myrtle, Tommy Wilkes and Shannon Hickey were on a separate mission, and they would leave in an hour. I hoped Shannon would make it back okay. I was scared for her every time she headed out. Their mission was to find as many amulets as they could, and bring them back. Additionally, we still had the usual mission: bring back any supplies, ammo, or usable food we could find.

I briefly thought it odd that, this time, we were not assigned the same mission, but whatever.

I checked my pack. Got it. *Alien: Out of the Shadows* by Tim Lebbon. What the heck, figured a little fiction might be cool this time around, and these things seemed a little less scary than gorgons. At least, in print. It was lying at the bottom of my pack next to a can of WD-40, because, ya never know.

Jet was now twenty-three, and we had celebrated my big brother's birthday in the Pavilion per usual. I remembered, so many years before, when he outran that adult. They nicknamed him 'Jet' because of that. I was faster, really, but who's keeping score?

My torpedo shooter was strapped to my pack, and I patted it for good luck.

Stoney was at the bottom of the launch when we left, but he was acting a bit strange, like he had a lot on his mind, or was spinning a lot of plates. He was a bit scatterbrained. Maybe it was just me, but it seemed like he was becoming more inaccessible lately, locking himself in his office, and having a guard posted up outside.

But there he was now at the bottom, telling us to 'enjoy the hawk,' meaning the cold weather. I smiled, but also wondered what exactly was going on. I was thankful that Rosie was still allowed to watch us during recons. I knew she was praying for us.

The inner hatch closed. The outer hatch opened. I felt Rosie's prayers going with us. I told myself this would just be another simple recon and we'd be back in no time.

•   •   •   •   •

Saturday, November 15th, 2042, 1119 hours

We were in A-Range again, once more fated to hit the zinc plant. Couldn't believe I made it back from that last one. That was so close. When I got back, I told the Captain what I found in the building to the south of the alleyway. Lots more stuff to ransack. Desks plum full of supplies for us to take home.

Jet was in the lead. Since that last mission, our protocols had changed. We were to wait a full minute and duck down if there was even a hint of any sign of gorgs nearby. Especially since that cluster of them were right there in the zinc plant, unnoticed, additional cautions were critical.

We proceeded west, slowly, silently. The recent snow had melted which meant no snow crunching underfoot to worry about. About twenty-five minutes into the patrol, the rain came down, washing away any snow melt still clinging to winter's chill.

We advanced.

Destination: 'Rutty's Hideout.' That's what they were all calling it. The building I hid in for all those hours. There was a lower antechamber, a basement off the main floor, through a back room and then a floor hatch, and some stairs. Lots of filing cabinets and discarded old equipment down there. That's where we'd go. If we happened to come under attack, it would be the safest place.

Time to move.

•   •   •   •   •

Saturday, November 15th, 2042, 1201 hours

We made it to the building without incident.

Command reported that Markus' mission was going well and that everyone was accounted for on his team. They were in B-Range. I can't remember the last time I was out there.

"Fan out, guys," said Jet. "You know the drill."

"Roger that," I said. I stowed my RPG launcher on my back, holstered my Glock 19, and looked around. Plenty of stuff to grab, and then we'd have lunch.

So far, so good.

•   •   •   •   •

Well, we never saw them coming. Neither did Halcyon. First, there was the screech outside the northwest corner of the building. Almost got Pettijohn! He cursed and fled back toward us.

"Come on, come on, this way! Jet, hurry!"

All of them converged on my position, and we retreated into the bowels of the building.

They came out of nowhere, punching through what sounded like *all* the windows. One of them whooshed in, right past Celeste, and she fired reflexively toward it. The thing screeched away. Pettijohn ran toward it, spraying his flamethrower. More of them zipped out of view.

Jet reached me, flying through the narrow space into the back room, and then down the stairs through the hatch.

I could see Pettijohn and Frye racing toward us, but then the glass exploded, and they changed course. A fireball erupted past them, sending gorgons flying off in all directions. And then the wall collapsed around them, cutting them off!

"Rutty, close it, you've gotta close it," Jet said, tugging at me. "Come on, bro!"

Man, I didn't want to. If there was even a chance they could get through, we had to leave it open.

The sound of gunfire. The sound of flames. The sound of screaming. If they were screaming, they were still alive.

Command broke through our headsets. "Shipleys, get undercover, they're okay for now. Move!"

That was all I needed. I pulled the hatch closed, quietly. The last thing I saw above us was a dark shape flashing into the room with a hiss and greenish vapor encircling it.

It was looking for us.

•   •   •   •   •

Saturday, November 15th, 2042, 1315 hours

"Is it gone?" Jet asked.

I shook my head. "I don't know. I don't hear anything."

Both of us were still perched on the ladder down at the bottom, both guns aiming upward, flanking each other. He was right behind me. If we had to shoot, his gun would thunder right in my ear.

There was, unfortunately, no lock on the hatch, and we were pinned down. Our muscles ached, holding steady for so long right there at the bottom of the stairs. My body was still, but my mind was racing, plotting my next course should we have to bolt out of there.

Muted sounds came from afar here and there, but nothing distinct. There was some garbled chatter over the headsets between Command, Will and Tommy. And something from Markus confirming with Command that Jet and I were most likely okay. After that, nothing. They were probably ordered to maintain radio silence since we were jammed in.

"Rutty," Jet whispered.

"Yeah."

"You got any pizza?"

"You're a dork," I whispered back.

•　　•　　•　　•　　•

Saturday, November 15th, 2042, 1327 hours

There were no more sounds. We stealthily descended the rest of the ladder: every step was a muscle tester and an incredible balancing act. Jet reached the floor first, set down his XM5, and then served as a counterweight, holding me up by my sides as I slowly lowered myself down over the last rung to the floor. All the while, we kept our guns trained on the hatch above.

We sat there for some minutes, in the quiet. We had flicked the lights on when we went into the building; they activated down here as well, so at least we didn't have to sit in the dark.

I started to say something, but he motioned for us to stop. He pressed his com button. "Command, Shipley," he whispered, ever so softly. "We're pinned down in the basement of the big building south of the alleyway in the plant. What's the status of Pettijohn and Frye?" His voice barely registered over a whisper.

"Back in pocket, over. Safe at home. You guys okay?" I recognized the voice as that of Pete Beckinsale. I had met him with Rosie once upon a time.

"Roger that. We're holed up here. What's the sit rep? Any infrareds?"

"Stand by." There was a pause. "Four signals, three more inbound. Something must have attracted them to the plant, and they're not leaving for now," he said.

"Confirmed. Standing by."

Jet looked at me, and sighed, quietly. "I guess we wait," he said.

•   •   •   •   •

Friday, November 21st, 2042, 0716 hours

Something startled me out of sleep. I was supposed to be on watch, and I drifted off. *Dangit!* I thought. Jet was snoring quietly beside me.

Almost a week since we've been in here. They wouldn't risk sending another team out. Last night, the gorgs were still up above in high numbers. Here is where we would stay. We didn't talk much, because we just weren't sure if they were directly above us, waiting to ambush us. They had done that before. Maybe they were getting smarter.

I couldn't even read my book. Jet had seen it earlier and nearly slapped it out of my hand. "Put that away, dude. You brought a book on freakin' *aliens*?" I put my hands up as if to exclaim *What?* But he just sneered at me and shook his head.

And now, lying there this morning, we were so hungry. Our iron rations were running low, and MREs just don't satisfy your innards the way they should. We were almost black on them. It had been six days. We got to pee at least. In the far corner there was a waste basket with a thin garbage liner. Anytime one of us had to pee, the other took all the guns and laid them beside themselves on the floor at the bottom of the ladder, pointing right up at the hatch. Miserable. The room was starting to reek of urine. Thank God that was *all* we had to go.

He had woken up and relieved me so I could relieve myself. I finished up and sat back down next to him, sighing quietly. It was cold down here, but not too bad. They hadn't run heat into this part of the building, but that didn't matter: our warmth came from primal instinct, fear, and readiness.

Nonetheless, he put his arm around me.

"Dude, I don't even know if you knew, but we were trapped by gorgs in our house before we even came here, and the only thing that separated us from them was a hatch."

"What?" I asked him, incredulous. I had no memory of that.

He nodded. "The night before we left home. You were sound asleep. I think mom gave you Benadryl, dude. We were all in the attic. Hatch was closed. I had Jack and was holding him. Dad and some guy – dude actually rescued all of us from the attack during that race – were pulling up on the attic ladder from inside, while a gorg was trying to pull it open from below. They were both sweating.

"Anyway, I let go of Jack and dropped a full can of Coke through the trash chute to distract 'em. Then all of 'em flipped out and took off after it. I think you stirred but went right back to sleep. That scared 'em all off, and it was Sergeant Jet Shipley for the win."

I truly had no memory of that, laughing quietly through my nose. "Here we are again, nothing but a hatch to separate us from them. Too bad we don't have a Coke."

Jet turned to me, smiling. "Like we could even open it, ya moron."

"You're the moron," I teased back.

He smiled and looked slowly away, back up at the hatch. My bro let out a long-winded sigh yet again, staring up at the ceiling. "Man, this is the most we've had to wait in a long time. I'm glad you're with me, buddy."

"Same," I said, and I meant it. I hated staying down here by myself that last time, and that was only for a few hours. "Love ya, bro."

"Love ya too, Rut. Just two regular grunts waitin' for fate," he said.

"Well, we wait too long, you're gonna be the long pig, not me. I'll outrun you." Stone once told me that 'long pig' meant when a human is used as a source of food in desperate situations.

"Don't even think about it," he said, quietly, and he yawned.

That made me smile. He rarely said that he loved me, so it was nice when he did. I felt safe with Jet. He'd always protected me, even when I didn't want him to.

I glanced over at him again while he stared upwards, and his eyes were slowly closing. It was still early, and I was, technically, still on watch. He needed sleep, so I just let him drift off.

Here before me was a good man, and a fine soldier. I wondered what Mom would say to him if she could see him now? Or what Dad would say? He was a bit closed off, and never really took faith seriously. It was always kind of a laughingstock to him. In that way he was so like Dad: ever the cynic. Mom was so much more the believer. But I knew both would be proud of him. Rosie too.

Man, I missed Rosie. I knew she was praying for us, so that was some comfort.

I missed Shannon as well, and hoped she was okay.

Looking back once more at Jet, I got all kinds of melancholy for things I don't even remember. Our home, our attic, our trash chute. No recollection of those things. They came from a bygone era never to be revisited, and even Jet barely remembered them anymore. It was another world, another time. *Man,* I missed Mom. Missed Sissy. Missed Dad. Missed all of them so much.

This was not the place to cry. I didn't like to, anyway. I much preferred being joyful. I guess maybe that's why I liked books so much: they were an escape…a journey…a real odyssey into something with no gorgons. Granted, this latest one was about aliens, so, sure, Jet maybe had a right to get upset. But that's why I loved them: they were anything other than here and now, and they provided a brief escape from the harsh realities of Earth in 2042.

A sigh made its way out of me as I stared longingly up at the ceiling. Jet began to snore.

A guy can do a lot of thinking in a place like this.

I fished out my green laser pointer and ran it around the room, watching the light play. I was bored out of my mind, hungry, stressed, and just wanted to get back.

Funny how a laser pointer can pass the time.

•   •   •   •   •

Wednesday, November 26th, 2042, 1931 hours

The gorgons just didn't leave. But, finally, one day, we caught a break. "Shipley, Shipley, come in, over. Inbound, repeat, inbound." Jet shot up and grabbed his headset, looking confused.

I could hear the transmission come through even where I was, it had gotten so quiet in here. 'Inbound?' What did that mean? The gorgs were already here, so how could they be inbound? Were there more?

We had plugged the headsets in over by the wall, as they were digging into our craniums. Jet threw his on as I rubbed my eyes. He had been the one on watch, and I was allowed a little rest. My jaw stretched in a massive yawn. This concrete floor was getting irritating, and it was a little stuffy in here. Jet kept listening to Command.

"Roger that," he said. "Rutty, get up."

"Wha-?"

"Get up. Markus is here. Grab your bang-bang."

It was coming up on two weeks since we had set foot on the muddy snow-melted grass out just beyond the Launch. We had been utterly trapped in here, and this was the longest stint ever. Unbelievable.

And Markus was coming? Could this be the rescue we've been waiting for?

I stood up and stretched as the blood flowed through me, tensing my muscles for a most-welcome stretch. I snatched my Glock from the ground and pointed it upward.

"Uh, okay, roger," said Jet, and then he turned to me. "What the hell?" he asked. "We're supposed to stay down here!"

"What? Why?"

"Hang on."

In a few minutes, there came a soft rap on the hatch, followed by Markus' whisper. Jet climbed up the ladder and opened the hatch slightly. There was Markus, lying on the ground with his head just outside the hatch. I could see past him. There was Shannon! And Evy and Tommy just behind them! What was going on? They were holding position and taking aim beyond the corridor.

"Take this," Jentzen said. "Don't ask questions. Just take it." He handed Jet a small pouch. Something clinked inside it. "Give half to Rutty, in case you guys get separated. Do it. Do it now. There are too many of them out there." Jet opened the pouch and retrieved half of whatever it was, handing it to me. I looked it over, but didn't know what it was. It was hot; there was definitely some heat emanating from it. I looked back up at them.

"I don't unders-" Jet started to say.

"Come *on*, Markus!" Evy pleaded behind him.

"No questions, bro. We can't all move together or we'll all be dead. We have one of these too. You're on our way back. We've been out here all this time as well. We're gonna draw their fire. Just hold on."

He reached through and extended a hand to Jet, and Jet took it. "I don't understand, bro – *what?* We have the manpower and the guns to send out a halo of protection, and we sprint back."

"No time!" he hissed. "Just stay here." Markus was agitated. Tommy cursed behind him; he was watching through the windows higher up. Markus looked back, flashing an angry look at Tommy.

Command must have heard what Jet had suggested, and they burst through on his com. "Negative, Shipley, sit tight, repeat, sit tight. Can't lose all of you in one go, and we would prefer not to lose *any*. Wait for the order."

"Affirmative," Jet said through a huff. In frustration he ripped off his com. "Shit! Really?"

"No time, bro, we gotta go. Wish us luck. Just hang on to that. Good luck."

I looked through the ladder and there was Shannon Hickey. She had never looked more beautiful. I tried smiling at her, but she was too nervous, flashing me back a half-hearted attempt. Her eyes were ringed with fear.

Jet started to say something, but Markus closed the hatch, and then the hurried but muffled sound of boots on wood took over. They were all scrambling out of there.

Then gunfire erupted. A *lot* of gunfire. I thought I heard Shannon scream, and nearly scurried up the ladder after her. Jet held me back, holding a finger in my face. Something glinted in his hand.

There we were, and there we had to still stay.

•　　•　　•　　•　　•

Tuesday, December 2nd, 2042, 1857 hours

It had been seventeen long days, longer than any other mission we'd ever been on, by far. But now, at long last, we were *finally* given the order to prep for evac. Jet was on the com with Command. The gorgs had thinned out, but they were still roaming around. They were in much smaller numbers, to be sure, but still a terrifying and disquieting presence. We were to make our way as quickly as possible, and Command would guide us in using the existing infrareds. We confirmed we still had our weapons, *and* the special pieces that Markus had delivered. We had no idea what they were. They were two halves of a perfect circle, but something not quite from around here. We were clueless. Jet placed his in his pocket; mine went in my pack with everything else.

Stoney had come on at one point, but he was somewhat evasive, and it was clear his only desire was for us to just get home. He informed us, sadly, that Markus' team was not all accounted for yet. Evy Myrtle and Tommy Wilkes had returned. Markus Jentzen and Shannon Hickey were MIA. That absolutely filled us with dread, and for a while, there were no words spoken. We could only hope. Stoney encouraged us. "Just keep your wits about you. You can do this. We're not going to lose you too. *I'm* not going to lose you too. Just keep safe, race home, and whatever you do, do *not* expose those things Markus gave you. Keep them safe. That's alien technology, boys, and we need it. We don't want to attract the gorgs to you in any way, so don't show them anything they'll recognize. Copy?"

"Yessir," we echoed. "OK. Thanks, dad."

"Wait for the go signal. Good luck, guys. Doors close at 2000 hours for good for the night. Get home," he said, softly, and switched off.

I was ready to pull off my headset again, and was so surprised to then hear the sweet voice of Rosie come over the com.

"Pastor Rosie!" I squealed with delight, and Jet shushed me.

"Boys. I'm praying for you. You can do this. I believe in you."

"Thanks Pastor Rosie," I said.

"Thanks, Rosie," Jet echoed.

"You've been out there long enough. This is your chance. Don't waste it. You are needed. The tide is turning."

For a split-second, I thought that perhaps she was talking about something else, but I couldn't get it, because Command broke in. "Shipley, Shipley, confirmed go. Proceed with caution, over?"

"Roger," said Jet, and he looked at me. "They're still out there. You ready?"

"Born that way."

He smiled at me and laughed through his nose. "I'll miss this place, being stuck here in Rutty's Hideout."

"No you won't," I corrected him.

He thought to himself for a second. "Yeah, you're right. No I won't. Wanna get home to some crappy coffee and imitation eggs?"

"Let's do it."

•   •   •   •   •

Tuesday, December 2nd, 2042, 1912 hours

Go time. Command relayed the gorgs' latest coordinates and wished us luck. As far as they could tell, no gorgs were in the plant building with us as they were all concentrated in the north half of the plant.

Halcyon confirmed that there was still no contact with Markus or Shannon. That truly worried and bothered me. I said a quick prayer for Shannon, and then, realizing that we were about to head out to gorgon central ourselves, said a quick prayer for Jet and me.

I had my launcher strapped to my back and loaded up. Firm grip on my Glock, I tailed right behind him up the ladder. He pushed it slowly open. The warehouse was empty and quiet. Soft moonlight streamed down through the window cracks, glinting off broken glass shards from the blown-out windows.

Jet was carrying his XM5, and I had my Glock. Our plan was to head straight down the same alley I had previously been pinned down in, dart across the greensward, cut diagonally across the parking lot, and right into the forest. If we're chased, we'll at least have some tree cover. We knew the drill; we'd been out here plenty of times before.

We passed beyond the inner room that had concealed us for so long and held steady behind a desk adjoining a large load-bearing wall. On top of that desk was a little glass bowl, and in that bowl was a single little candy bar, still encased in a crinkly red wrapper. I was squinting through the dim light, but I could dimly make out "100 Grand" in bold white letters with a yellow outline. I'd have to try it later. Perhaps the desk once belonged to some receptionist or something, handing out candy to visitors. As hungry as I was, I grabbed it and put it in my pack. We'd eaten almost all of our food rations. Now I had one candy bar for later. And one torpedo to protect us on our journey home.

We crept along inside the warehouse. I followed my brother, five paces ahead of me, along the inner north wall of the building. He was a pro at this. The consummate soldier, with excellent posture and battle-hardened will. Loved being on his patrol. Maybe someday I'd make Corporal and inch closer to him.

He posted up at the corner and held up a fist. I stopped. Jet peeked around the corner. Command came through and chirped instructions through our headsets.

His fist relaxed and waved me forward. We were just turning out into the alley, when the unthinkable happened. His Beretta must have loosened in its holster on his way up the ladder, because it now fell clumsily out and ricocheted along the ground behind us as we moved. It rattled away across the floor. The sound was deafening! In a reflex, we scrambled for cover. Going for his Beretta would be pure foolishness, and anyway, he had his M5. The little cove I had taken shelter in before wasn't big enough for the two of us. Jet hid in there behind the dumpster. I raced further east and took cover under a tarped off area at the edge of the next building over.

"Rutty, Rutty, come in," I heard him whisper.

"Yeah, bro, you good?"

He laughed nervously. "Yeah. No. I guess. Hold tight and- oh shit! Oh *shit!*" he hissed.

"What, what?" I asked him. "Jet?"

"My rifle. It's out of ammo. I didn't check it. And my Beretta's back where we were! I can see it."

"Jet, don't go for it, bro."

"Rutty, it's right across the alley, I can get there and back. Hold on."

"Jet, no! Don't!"

Command broke through, saving the day. "Contact, contact, range thirty meters, bearing two-seven-two west. Stay put!"

Jet stopped talking. So did I. We listened.

We could hear them, sure enough. Here they came, down the alley near Jet. He was trapped!

"Jet, just hang on," I breathed over the com. "Hang on, Jet!" I thought I saw another one coming down out of the sky.

Time to pray. My mouth started moving soundlessly.

I couldn't see my brother.

I prayed. That's all I could do was pray.

That, and ready my rocket launcher. I took aim, and inhaled deeply, staring down the alley. I couldn't see Jet.

I prayed.

I fumbled for my laser pointer to signal that I was still here. But the laser pointer was no good at decimating gorgons. For that, I'd need a torpedo. I pulled my last one out and loaded it up.

I held out my arms palms up to receive whatever came our way. All I could do now was pray.

"Bring us out, bring us out," I breathed into the night.

TO BE CONTINUED...

The Resistance is rising.

Read all the books in the series, in chronological order:

Dissonance Volume Zero: Revelation
Dissonance Volume Up: Rising
Dissonance Volume I: Reality
Dissonance Volume II: Reckoning
Dissonance Volume III: Renegade
Dissonance Volume IV: Relentless

| AFTERWORD

I was wrong.

(Here is where my wife grabs a tape recorder and asks me to repeat that.)

I thought I was done with the world of *Dissonance*. I tried to put a bow on it with Dissonance Volume Zero: Revelation, but there was still so much material to explore, and too much emotion to not mine. With the five-year gap between Andrew Shipley's death and Jet and Rutty fleeing back to the Blockade in December 2042, I saw an opportunity. I just had to dive back in. One of the greatest delights I had in fleshing out this novel's predecessor, *Dissonance Volume Zero: Revelation*, was hunting through all the backstory mentioned in the original trilogy volumes, finding chronological events that were addressed, and fleshing out narratives for how those events precisely unfolded, then, including them all in that installment, writing out those sections and expanding on all of them. With this new prequel, I've had the opportunity to relive that process, and it's been utterly enjoyable! Dovetailing new narratives into previously-referenced narratives takes hard work, ensuring that details remain correct and that you don't 'break' the storyline. It's been a painstaking but enjoyable process.

And now, as I plunge headlong into this not-too-distant future to world-build once again, I'm also seeing possibilities for a continuation of the series following *Dissonance Volume III: Renegade*, which was the original trilogy finale. If you've already read through that particular installment, you'll know that there is potential for a continuation of the saga despite the numerous elements of closure. Time will tell, but the future of *Dissonance* is bright.

I want to thank screenwriter Alan Roth of *Act II Media* with all my heart for injecting me with a bounty of hope by creating a compelling screenplay for *Dissonance Volume I: Reality* beginning in April 2024. That has filled me with an unquenchable hope and expectation, and has driven me to create more good works subsequent to that. Thank you from the bottom of my heart for lighting a fire under my butt, good sir!

Many thanks to my faithful audiobook listener Vance Pease, and once again to Walker Armstrong for your help with titling, ideas, and reviewing everything. You guys rock. I'm immeasurably grateful for the unending and faithful support and affirmation you've given me as I've continued on this authoring path and built this world. Thank you for being the very best readers and listeners I could hope for.

Thank you to Janine Graves and Denouement Editing for your incredible attention to detail, your interest in reading my novels, and for your delight in them. Additionally, thank you so much for your incredible wisdom in helping me better flesh out narratives and create more compelling stories. I am so grateful for your wisdom and expertise!

Thank you so much to Roland and Rachel Kouhsen, for your friendship, encouragement, affirmation, and your immeasurable support in coming to all my events and cheering me on. I LOVE YOU. You are fantastic friends and compatriots, and I couldn't imagine life without you and your family.

Finally, thank you to all my readers, beyond words. My favorite review I've ever received is where an individual called one of my books "unputdownable." I think this word should be coined, and I love that it was attributed to something I've written. That was an incredibly flattering review. Thank you to ALL of you who have left me a review. I'm immeasurably grateful for the time you've taken to do so. THANK YOU for partaking of the *Dissonance* universe, and for telling others about it.

With love,

Aaron Ryan

I ABOUT THE AUTHOR

Aaron Ryan lives in Washington with his wife and two sons, along with Macy the dog, Winston the cat, and Merry & Pippin, the finches.

He is the author of the bestselling & award-winning *Dissonance* sci-fi alien invasion saga, the Christian post-apocalyptic trilogy, *The End*, the sci-fi thriller *Forecast*, the business reference books *How to Successfully Self-Publish & Promote Your Self-Published Book* and *The Superhero Anomaly*, the *Christian Kids Values, Identity & Affirmation* picture book series, and nearly 30 other books.

When he was in second grade, he was tasked with writing a creative assignment: a fictional book. And thus, "The Electric Boy" was born: a simple novella full of intrigue, fantasy, and 7-year-old wits that electrified Aaron's desire to write. From that point forward, Aaron evolved into a creative soul that desired to create.

He enjoys the arts, media, music, performing, poetry, and being a daddy. In his lifetime he has been an author, voiceover artist, wedding videographer, stage performer, musician, producer, rock/pop artist, executive assistant, service manager, paperboy, CSR, poet, tech support, worship leader, and more. The diversity of his life experiences gives him a unique approach to business, life, ministry, faith, and entertainment.

Aaron's favorite author by far is J.R.R. Tolkien, but he also enjoys Suzanne Collins, James S.A. Corey, Marie Lu, Madeleine L'Engle, C.S. Lewis, and Stephen King.

Aaron has always had a passion for storytelling.

For the rest of the books in this saga, including the odyssey of Andrew & Melissa's sons Jet and Rutty, visit dissonancetheseries.com or authoraaronryan.com.

If you liked my book or the "Dissonance" saga, please visit the Amazon and Goodreads pages for this book and leave a positive review. Once it shows up, please email the screenshot of it to me@authoraaronryan.com for a discount on your next book purchase! Thank you from my heart…reviews really do help so very much!

Visit my website and sign up at the Blog:

Subscribe to Author Aaron Ryan

Follow me and connect on Social Media: